SOURCE FIRE

ARCTURUS ACADEMY, BOOK 5

A.L. KNORR

Edited by
NICOLA AQUINO

Edited by
VICTORIA KNORR

PROLOGUE

Targa's glossy black hair streamed out behind her as she sprinted for the ocean. She wasn't running for the pure joy of it, that was painfully apparent, she was running to get away from something. Her bare soles flashed white in the dim luster of a stormy but moonlit sky. I floated along behind her, bodiless, a distant observer.

The girl could run.

No...siren. The siren could run.

She was alone, but the feeling of some sinister presence was not far behind her. Her breathing was fast but steady, her gait smooth and confident. There was something in one of her fists, but the way her arms pumped made it difficult to see. Whatever it was, she held it so tightly her knuckles were white.

She leapt tussocks, dodged saplings and tangled shrubs, even launched over a fence, clearing it as easily as a trained showjumper would.

The sea was not far; I could hear it now. I could hear it the way Targa could hear it, like a million voices singing her home. The sighing of the surf was angel's music to our ears.

She would make it to the safety of the ocean, that was clear. She was unbeatable; a storm wrapped in pearlescent skin, with jeweled eyes and liquid grace. She was magnificent.

As she approached the chalk cliff, she glanced behind her—eyes wide and skimming the landscape. She faced the sea. It was a long drop to the ocean, even for a siren, but it was less dangerous than the threat behind her. She faced the water, her perfect forehead marred with worry lines, and leapt, fist tightly curled.

A bright red lance of fire appeared like a gash along her arm, then another on the back of her leg. She screamed in agony, spasming in mid-air. It looked like she were made of cinders, burning through her skin from the inside out. As she arched toward the waves, another bright fissure of light appeared, this one across her back. It burned away her clothing like the fabric was made of dry, woven grass.

With a hiss and a sizzle, her entire body was consumed, breaking apart into ashes to be whisked away on the wind. The dust of my friend lifted and swirled, gently flying, before congealing into the shape of a bird. A dove, made of embers and smoke.

It flapped toward the moon.

A STRANGLED CRY reached my ears. My eyes were open but unseeing, my neck and forehead lined with a slick layer of sweat. Panic sank its claws into my heart. I lurched from my bed, groping for my phone. My heart refused to slow. All I could see was the shape of that dove, trailing ash dust and sparks as it flapped into the sky.

Hands quaking, I found my phone in the front pocket of my bag and fumbled for Targa's number. I didn't check the time, it didn't matter. I had to hear her voice, know she was alright. The dream was too vivid to bear.

Putting the phone on speaker, I set it down as it rang; too jittery and sweaty to hold it. I was too wrung out and freaked to even get back in bed, so I paced back and forth on my area rug, mentally begging Targa to answer.

"Saxony?" She answered with the voice of someone who'd recently been deeply asleep.

The sound of her siren tone released a thousand white birds from the brittle cupboard of my heart, setting it to pounding with relief and joy.

"Targa." I smiled and brushed away the tears leaking from my eyes. "You're okay."

She gave a tired huff. "I'm fine, or I was. It's too early for me to be up. What time is it?" There were noises on the other end of the phone, the rustling of fabric, possibly the sound of slippers sliding over a floor.

"I have no idea." I grinned through the moisture rimming my eyes. "I'm so sorry to wake you, but I had to."

"I think the question is, are *you* okay? Good grief, Saxony. It's five-thirty. That makes it four-thirty there. What are you doing up?" She sounded fully awake now, though she might have stubbed her toe on something; there was a thump and a muttered curse.

"I had a nightmare, you were in it. I thought maybe... I thought maybe you were in trouble." I was beginning to feel idiotic now I knew she was fine, and that I'd woken her for nothing more than a dream.

"I hate those." She kept her voice low, and seemed unbothered now that she was awake. "Give me a second. I don't want to wake Antoni. He slept through the buzzing, thankfully. But I think he could sleep through a stampede of buffalo coming right through our room."

I laughed, picturing her slinking from their suite in the Novak manor, probably barefoot and possibly naked. There was some rustling and the click of a door before she came back on the line, yawning.

"That sounds like a stress dream," she said, making more noise in the background. "I'm just putting the kettle on; I'm starting my mornings with herbal tea these days. Do you want to tell me about the dream?"

I blinked. Targa started her mornings with herbal tea? She'd always been a java girl. "What kind of tea?"

"Um, hang on, I'll read the box. Antoni picked it up for me, I don't even know what it's called." A few seconds passed, then she burst out laughing.

"What?" I was already smiling, though I didn't know the joke.

"Well, if I read you the label, the cat will be out of the bag, and it's a bit early for that."

My spine went flagpole straight, my eyes stretched wide. "Targa—"

"Yeah. It's early," she said, sounding like she was still smiling, which was great for my nerves (a whole new batch of them that had nothing to do with the dream had just sprung up and swallowed me). "I'm pregnant. We were going to wait until the end of the first trimester to tell anyone, you know, the way humans do, just in case anything goes wrong. But I don't think these babies are about to close up shop and call it quits on us, they feel strong."

"They?" I felt dazed.

"Yeah, twins, just like mom had. Isn't that crazy? And she's right, sirens can feel it the moment it happens. Not the fertilization, but the implantation. Antoni and I were out for dinner at this little place we like in old-town, and"—she made a popping sound with her lips—"there they were, making themselves nice and cozy in the wall of my uterus. To be fair, I didn't know it was twins at first, that came a month later."

I half-sat, half-fell onto my bed, landing hard enough that the frame creaked.

Targa was my age, not even out of her teens yet. For most human girls, this was too early to be having babies, but not for a siren.

"Congratulations," I managed to say, after I wrapped my mind around the fact that my friend was going to be a mother. "That's... I'm... so happy for you."

The kettle whistled and a moment later I heard water being poured as she replied. "Antoni is still in shock, but he's happy. Mom and Jozef are over the moon, of course. Mornings have been a bit rough for me. Mom had no sickness at all, so I'm hoping it passes quickly. It's not nice."

I didn't know much about pregnancy, but I thought morning sickness began around the six-week mark. "Wait, how far along are you?"

"Six and a half weeks. I'm so excited, it's the perfect excuse to spend less time at the office and more time at home, or in the sea."

Targa and I chatted until the sun made hints that it was coming. I yawned. Targa was fine, the dream seemed like a distant memory, and my eyes were burning. It was still early, I could catch another few hours of sleep. Ms. Shepherd and Mehmet wouldn't arrive until after nine.

When she heard me yawn, Targa yawned too. "I could easily go back to bed."

"Same."

"We never talked about your dream," she said. "Do you want to tell me about it?"

"No. It doesn't matter. I can hardly remember it anymore." I lay against my pillows.

"If you're sure—"

"I'm sure. Hey, does Georjie know?"

"No, we haven't told anyone, other than Mom and Jozef. I was planning to conference you and Georjie and tell you at the same time. Don't say anything; I'll call her myself. She'll be so excited. These babies will have the world's most incredible aunts."

I laughed. "You can say that again."

We said goodbye, I slid my phone onto the night table near my bed and was unconscious in seconds.

PART I

TUNDRA

1

——

IDLE TALK

No one was smiling.

Wind lashed rain at Chaplin Manor, making the chimney whistle, and the fire swell and crackle.

Ryan, leaning against the radiator under one of the lobby's huge diamond-pane windows, glowered at the floor, his face pinched and pale. Tomio sat on the front edge of an overstuffed chair, his elbows on his knees as he looked into the fire with a frozen, sightless stare. Basil paced in front of the fireplace with his hands behind his back, adjusting his glasses every few minutes when they slid down the bridge of his nose. Mehmet—who was short and broad in the flesh, with lively eyes—sat on a couch with his laptop open on his knees, utterly absorbed by the screen. Ms. Shepherd stood behind Mehmet, worrying her bottom lip with her teeth. She had developed a rash on the side of her neck, but I knew it was from her nervous tic.

Now that I'd met the woman in person, she was much less intimidating. Over our video conferences she'd seemed stoic and in control. In person, she seemed nervous and uncertain. Or maybe that was because the situation had deteriorated since Naples. Another fire had gone out. Tomio and I had assumed she was a mage, but we were mistaken about that as well. Ms. Shepherd wasn't even supernatural; she was ex-military with competencies in logistics and operations.

"So, the new data point proves it, the question is, what can we do about it?" Basil sent a piercing look toward Ryan and the rest of us followed his gaze. Ryan had more first-hand knowledge of Nero's shenanigans than anyone else, yet he'd been cryptic and evasive about what he knew.

The collective of agencies had added a new metric to their data gathering after Ryan suggested they track the colors of the snuffed mages' idle fires. The agency had resisted. Idle fire was a thing of childhood, they claimed, something whimsical and cute—certainly nothing to consider in this matter—just a passing phase in the youth of all magi, like losing baby teeth. The collective (under Ms. Shepherd's leadership) argued that with the limited resources they had, they'd be better off adding more relevant data points, like ethnicity, since there was a correlation, even if it wasn't consistent.

But Ryan insisted, and when Ryan was proven right, Ms. Shepherd had looked appropriately sheepish and the agency had gone quiet. Idles came in seven colors, like a rainbow. Five had now been snuffed out: orange had been first, last December; yellow in March; red and pink in early July—although we didn't understand how Nero had managed that only three days apart; and now a fifth one, only two weeks later.

No one openly discussed the fact that Ryan's father had been a member of the pink group, and was even now speechless in his grief. The pink group had also included my friend Jade, the Academy's professor of Fire Science, Tyson Hupelo, the beloved Dr. Price and her daughter Cecily, not to mention many others.

Ryan rubbed his eyes with his thumb and forefinger. "The quenching that happened yesterday," he blinked at Mehmet through a bloodshot gaze, "Do we know which color that was?"

Mehmet looked up, eyes as red as Ryan's, but from straining at his computer screen. "Yes, it was indigo."

Silence coalesced again over the lobby.

In the heavy pause, Tomio moved from the chair to sit beside me on the couch. He took my hand and tucked it inside his own with a squeeze. His thigh pressed alongside mine, solid, reassuring.

There hadn't been time for Tomio and me to think, let alone talk, about our blossoming feelings, or the passionate kiss we'd shared outside the Mount Vesuvius observatory. My throat went dry with desire every time I relived that moment: his lips against mine, urgent, with an edge of desperation. We'd been painfully aware that there was a chance Tomio and Ryan might run into Nero in the subterranean lair. There had been more raw honesty and vulnerability in that kiss than in any other kiss, conversation or glance I'd ever shared with anyone before it. He'd laid it all bare, saying everything without saying a word, his body calling to mine with all the bright clarity of a ship's bell. There was nothing I wanted more than to be alone with Tomio, listen to him, touch him, kiss him, pretend this whole ghastly nightmare wasn't happening.

But the threat Nero posed to the remaining magi loomed like a hurricane gathering on the horizon. Janet was missing, and Gage lay in a hospital bed in the quiet wing of a Neapolitan hospital. Comatose.

Angelica had promised she'd call the moment anything changed, but so far, all we'd received were texts with Gage's vitals and the haunting words: no change yet. There was always a tiny bit of good news (I suspected Angelica made extra effort to wheedle some small bit of encouragement from Dr. Burr or one of the medical staff); if there was no improved measurement to share then Angelica would add something subjective, like: I think his breathing seems deeper today, more robust.

I appreciated her effort to keep our spirits up but every time my phone lit with a notification that Angelica had texted, my heart picked up speed. I longed for the call or text containing only two simple words: *He's awake*.

Instead, the same message came on repeat.

We'd arrived at the academy three days ago, on July 21st. England rarely got summer thunderstorms like the one we had right now, but this was Dover. It was unpredictable, temperamental, and also somehow remarkably in tune with how everyone under the academy's roof was feeling right now.

With all the intel we had, there was one piece of vital information that we desperately needed in order to mobilize: where Nero was going to strike next.

We also didn't know exactly what he was doing to snuff the fires, but the actual mechanics of it seemed less important than stopping him.

"Think back."

Ms. Shepherd's voice broke through the fragile webbing of my thoughts. For a second, I thought she'd been addressing me, but she was looking at Ryan.

"There must be something you noticed, something you remember from your interactions with Nero that will give us a clue as to where he'll go next." She fiddled with the teal scarf at her neck and did the hard rub underneath it. The woman needed restraints.

Ryan's jaw flexed with impatience. He looked harassed. "Nero acts immediately on new information, he doesn't store it for later or sit on it. If he hasn't revealed the next location for himself then how can *I* know it? And if he's only figured it out now, then you'd have better luck scanning your network for flight bookings under one of his aliases, or combing security footage. Just because I've spent time with him doesn't mean—" Ryan's expression snagged like a fish caught on a hook. He took on the faraway look of someone deeply lost in a revelatory new thought.

The rest of us exchanged nervous glances and waited.

"What? What is it?" Basil asked.

Ryan looked like a newly enlightened sage. "Just, let me think for a second."

Tomio and I, holding our collective breath on the couch, let out long simultaneous groans as Ryan moved away from the window and headed for the stairs leading to Basil's office. He settled into pacing in front of the antique telephone booth.

"I think we've lost him," Mehmet muttered matter-of-factly, sounding unbothered as he went back to his laptop.

"I need a drink." Basil moved away from the fireplace. "Anyone want anything?"

Mehmet's head snapped up. "I would murder for an old fashioned."

The headmaster raised his brows.

"Right. Magi. There'll be no alcohol under this roof." Mehmet gave Basil a bright, comically exaggerated smile. "I'll have water."

"Me too," Ms. Shepherd said.

"I'll bring enough for everyone." Basil left the lobby for the nearest lounge.

Tomio spoke so low so that only I could hear him. "Funny how Mehmet acts like he was never one of us to begin with, now that he's lost his fire. It's incredible how well he's coping."

I nodded but my mind was on something else. I sank deeper into the furniture and let my head rest on the poufy back as I studied Tomio. "You've had fire for a lot longer than me. You were—what, did you say—nine when you were endowed?"

Tomio nodded as he sank into the couch alongside me and let his head tilt back.

"Did you ever see your idle fire?" I asked.

He shook his head. "I must have been too old. Basil did say the idles don't often show themselves after the age of six or seven. You're lucky you got to see Ryan's. It's super rare for an adult to be carefree enough for it to come out."

After the snuffings by idle fire color had been confirmed, I'd told Tomio in detail about finding Ryan on the beach, throwing green flames into the wind and watching them twist and spiral into the sky. It had been spectacular, beautiful, and savage in the way only nature could be.

"But we know that I'm green, because Basil and Ryan are green, as was Gage, and I have bonds with them. Had, in the case of Gage." My voice hitched and I took a hard swallow. "That would logically make you—"

"Violet, since my fire didn't go out with this last group."

We stared at one another, thoughts and fears spilling out through our eyes. Tomio touched my cheek and traced my bottom lip with his thumb. "Try not to think about it."

"That's impossible," I whispered.

Whatever Nero was doing and wherever he was headed

next, it would most certainly mean that one of us would lose our fire if we didn't figure out a way to stop him. How would Tomio react if it was him? How would I react if it was me? Would one of us go on fighting to protect the last idle while the other fell apart?

The reason we were having these meetings at the academy was because the agency's offices in London were being used as a convalescent home, since they had medical facilities and staff. Felix, Harriet and Brooke, our friends from the Fire Games, were all sequestered there, being cared for and therapized. I wanted to visit them but I had to prioritize protecting the remaining idles. Basil had convinced me that visiting the bereft magi, as nice a gesture as it would be, would only serve to traumatize and distract us, and possibly make the patients worse as they were reminded, in the flesh, of what they had lost.

"Where are you, Green?" Tomio asked, touching a fingertip to the end of my nose.

"Just thinking about what it must be like at the agency's headquarters."

His brow creased. I could almost see the gears turning, his imagination firing up. Suddenly, I felt bad for reminding him that most of our friends were among the snuffed.

"Sorry, Violet," I whispered. "Let's think about the artifacts we saw in Nero's bunker instead, maybe we'll remember something helpful, a clue or something."

His expression lifted almost imperceptibly. "We're going to stop him, Saxony. We will figure this out. We have to."

"For the greens and violets."

Basil returned to the lobby carrying a tray stacked with glasses and a large carafe of water. He set them on the ottoman in front of us. "Where did Ryan go?"

We sat up and looked behind our couch. Ryan was indeed no longer pacing the lobby.

"Didn't see him leave." Tomio turned the glasses upright as Basil filled them.

I handed Ms. Shepherd and Mehmet each a full glass. "I hope he's remembering something good, because it feels like we're coasting on fumes, here."

Mehmet barked a single, "Ha!" Then: "Fumes would imply that there was gas in the tank to begin with. We've been four steps behind Nero this whole time."

Ms. Shepherd bristled, holding her glass of water close to her narrow chest. "Easy now. We know more now than we ever did."

Mehmet slouched and kept his eyes on his laptop as he tapped away at the keys. "Yeah, thanks to a bunch of teenagers."

Ms. Shepherd raised her eyes heavenward in an expression like a prayer, then took a drink. Basil winked at me as he picked up a glass and turned his back to Ms. Shepherd so she wouldn't see his thinly veiled amusement.

It was the first time I'd seen something of Basil's old self since we'd arrived from Naples, and it lifted my heart.

The sound of thumping on the stairs made everyone turn, glasses poised in the air.

Ryan crossed to the seating area, eyes fever-bright. He had his cell phone in his hand, lit and open to some webpage that was all text. His hair stood up in tufts and spikes, like he'd been yanking at it compulsively.

"Good heavens, man." Basil said at his harassed appearance.

Just for good measure and thoroughness, Ryan raked his other hand through his already-tousled mane. He looked from Basil to Ms. Shepherd. "By some wild and unlikely chance, do you have any radiation physicists on staff?"

Ms. Shepherd and Basil shared a confused look.

Mehmet did a double take. "A radiation physicist? Like, a human one?"

Ryan waved a hand. "Human, supernatural, doesn't matter. Someone who knows about radioactivity."

Ms. Shepherd straightened with bewildered curiosity. As she pondered Ryan's question, her expression crept to the threshold of understanding but didn't quite cross over. "Because Nero is radioactive? You think we might be able to track him that way?"

Gage's twin began to pace, looking more like his brother than ever as he exuded the excitement of his eureka moment. "Thinking about airport security got me wondering how he is managing all this flying around the world. Even if you take a private plane, if you were actually as radioactive as Janet and Nero both seem to think he is, then security would be the least of his problems."

"Actually, I don't think metal detectors are built to detect radioactivity," Mehmet murmured. "But maybe the planes themselves have alarms."

Basil's brow furrowed, his gaze fastened on Ryan. "Go on."

"Now, I don't know anything about radioactivity, but a quick search"—he held up his phone and shook it, looking a little like he was on the edge of madness as he did so—"tells me that radiation breaks apart chemical bonds, including the ones inside our bodies. Enough decay and you'll die. But Nero isn't anywhere near dying; in fact, he's only getting stronger, which goes against the laws of physics. Am I wrong?"

The room was quiet.

"Go on," Tomio said, shifting to more easily view Ryan's fascinating presentation.

I turned on the couch too and propped myself on a hip. "Janet thought she was suffering from radiation poisoning whenever she spent too much time with Nero. *Something* was making Janet feel sick, but are you saying Nero *isn't* radioactive?"

Ryan pointed at me and paced in the other direction, his head swiveling on his neck like an owl's. "Yes. What I'm thinking is that he's not actually radioactive, but that he's expelling some kind of... supernatural effluent... that a nearby human reacts to with symptoms that look like radiation sickness."

He paused and a shadow of something ugly crossed his features. It was there and gone so quickly that I had no time to identify it. Maybe he was recalling what Nero had done to Gage.

He went on, "Whatever he's doing when he travels to these places is increasing that supernatural effluent, which is why Janet felt progressively sicker whenever he came back from another journey."

"And you think this supernatural effluent might register as radioactivity on human-made devices?" Ms. Shepherd had a look that was positively hungry. "But how would we get close enough to Nero to detect him if we have no idea where he is? We have no evidence of him leaving Italy by plane, and no visuals of him crossing any official borders."

"There's been no sign of Janet anywhere either," I muttered, my stomach cramping with worry. The last words I said to her rang accusingly in my memory: *We'll be back for you.*

But Ryan was shaking his head. "We're focusing on the wrong thing. We've been so busy watching for clues about where Nero is *going* that we haven't paid enough attention to where he's *been*."

Ryan held up his phone so we could see what he'd been reading.

Tomio and I crawled onto the back of the couch together to get closer to the screen. Ms. Shepherd and Basil came around either side of the sofa to peer at the information on Ryan's phone. The four of us crowded so close together that I could smell coffee on Ms. Shepherd's breath and Basil's aftershave.

My pulse sped up as I took in what he was showing us. Ms. Shepherd's hand flew to her mouth in shock.

Basil muttered, "Well, I'll be damned."

"Would someone please read that out loud?" Mehmet said from the couch, his laptop chirping and buzzing with the sound of processing. "I can't abandon my post here."

"Areas of naturally high background radiation are known as HBNRAs," I husked, reading from the screen until a dry spot in my throat make me choke and cough. I took another drink.

Tomio patted me on the back as he resumed reading. But soon his hand stilled and lay warm between my shoulder blades.

"These areas include Yangjiang, China. Guarapari, Brazil. Ramsar, Iran, and Karunagappalli in India."

Goosebumps rippled across my arms. "Ryan"—I looked up—"these are words I never thought would fall from my lips, but you're a genius."

Ryan gave a grin so wide that he looked certifiably insane, especially with the hedgehog hairdo. "What's that saying about skinning cats?"

"Is Australia on that list as well?" Ms. Shepherd asked.

"Not on this site, but yes. Arkaroola, Australia is also an HBNRA," said Ryan, lowering his phone.

Ms. Shepherd turned away. "I need to make a phone call. We have to get someone on this immediately." She began rooting through the red satchel she'd set on the floor, unearthing one of her many mobiles. She left the lobby for the nearest lounge, presumably to call the agency.

"Are those places ranked in order starting from the highest?" I climbed over the back of the couch to peer at Ryan's phone.

"Not at this website, but Wiki says Ramsar is the number one spot in the world."

"Where Nero sent you," Tomio said.

"Yes."

"What were you doing there?" I looked up into Ryan's face, studying his micro-expressions.

His eyes shifted and he stepped away, like he felt crowded. "He said there was an orb there. He told me to fetch it and bring it back for him."

"And did you?" Basil took a cloth from his jacket pocket and cleaned his spectacles.

Ryan's energy changed, the same way that look had come and gone from his face earlier. His gaze flicked to a nearby window, then to the fire, then to Basil where it steadied. "Yes. And speaking of the orbs, you'll be wanting to fetch those from the agency."

The headmaster tucked his kerchief and fixed his glasses into place. "Why?"

"Because even though the HBNRAs are a clue, we're still going to need those orbs to confirm Nero's targets."

"And, you know how to do that, I presume? Because I have handled those orbs extensively and I can assure you that they are as inanimate as garden gnomes." Basil crossed his arms, expression doubtful.

"I might." Ryan stared at Basil, unflinching.

Basil blew out a breath. "Right, well. I don't have to go to the agency to fetch them, they're here, at the academy."

Ryan appearing unsurprised to hear this, held out a hand and flicked his fingers twice in a hand-them-over gesture.

Four sets of eyes settled on Basil. The headmaster looked like he wanted to protest.

"Why are you hesitating?" I asked, assuming that Basil didn't trust Ryan, and completely understanding if that was the case. "Ryan is on our side now. If you'd seen him inside Vesuvius, you wouldn't doubt him."

"Thank you, Saxony," Ryan replied, not taking his eyes from Basil. "If you'll recall, my twin is still in a coma thanks to Nero. I want to stop him more than anyone."

Truthfully, I did trust Ryan now, but that didn't mean he wouldn't keep things from us to protect himself. I already suspected he was keeping something private about what he'd been up to in Ramsar, but the important thing was to rescue Janet and save the magi, and if Ryan said he knew how to demystify the orbs we had in our possession, then that's what we needed to do.

"It's not that." Basil tugged at his lower lip with his teeth. "It's just that they are priceless, and no one has handled them except for me. If anything were to happen to them..." He trailed off, perhaps realizing that it sounded as if he was prioritizing a couple of artifacts over the well-being of the remaining magi and a certain ancient language expert. "Right"—he tugged on his jacket—"I'll fetch them, shall I?"

Ryan put down his waiting hand, jacking his eyebrows with an impatient: "That would be great."

Basil headed for the stairs.

Ms. Shepherd reappeared from the lounge. "Ok, we have someone looking into the radiation theory. Good work, Ryan. It's not a pin-drop, but it's a start. Where's Basil?"

"He went to get the orbs," Mehmet said, eyes skimming his laptop screen.

"Excellent, that is the next item on the agenda. If we can figure out how Nero unlocked them, then we should be able to formulate some kind of plan, rather than sitting around with our thumbs up our butts, feeling helpless."

I shot her a look of surprise. I'd never heard Ms. Shepherd express personal feelings about any situation before and wondered if she'd been feeling closer to the end of a rope than she'd let on.

Basil came down the stairs, cradling a shiny black box against his chest. He crossed to Ryan and stopped, hesitating a moment before handing the box over.

All the air seemed to vacuum from the room as Ryan took it and moved to a table. Tomio and I crowded in on either side of him for front-row seats. Ms. Shepherd came to stand behind me, and even Mehmet finally put his laptop aside to view the moment from behind Tomio.

My mouth felt dry and my heart thrummed with anticipation, even my hands felt shaky as Ryan unclasped the golden latch holding the lid down. He opened the box and let the lid settle back on the table, exposing a bright silver orb nestled in a red velvet cushion, like a Fabergé egg.

My breath caught, and Ms. Shepherd let out a gasp of admiration.

It was beautiful; perfectly round and made of a metal too bright to be silver but not reflective enough to be mercury glass. It had been laced with a raised, organic line, like the stitches on a baseball, but meandering in an aimless way. The line stood proud of the orb's surface without crackles, fractures, or tell-tale welding lines. It was as if some elegant, celestial worm had crawled beneath its surface, leaving a trail raised in the glimmering metal behind it.

Ryan seemed unimpressed as he looked up at Basil, but then again, he had handled one of these orbs before. "You said you had two."

"And so I do," Basil replied, defensive yet resolved. "If you can get information out of this one, then you'll have earned the right to the second one. Prove I can trust you and we're in business."

Ryan let out a breath and closed the lid. "Fine. I can live with that."

A mild disappointment settled over me now that the orb was out of view. I wanted to hold it, examine it, but didn't have the courage to ask, at least not in this moment when Basil was looking so tense and paranoid.

"But, mark my words"—Basil raised a warning finger—"if you do anything to damage it, you'll be very, very sorry."

2

CRASH COURSE

"What do you suppose he's doing?" Tomio asked, leaning back in his chair and resting a hand on his full belly. "Did you see the look on Basil's face when Ryan didn't show up for pizza?"

We sat in the cafeteria, empty pizza boxes on the table between us. Basil had eaten and gone into London to see how things were at the agency. Ms. Shepherd and Mehmet had wolfed their food and enclosed themselves in the headmaster's office where they were in ongoing talks with Ms. Shepherd's team about the radioactivity lead.

Ryan had taken the orb and left without waiting for pizza or telling anyone where he was going.

"Yeah, he looked like someone kidnapped his child." I closed up the boxes and took them to the nearest bin. There were no cleaning staff and it was my turn to take the bag to the dumpster on the street for the town to pick up. No one would be by until morning, so I could at least procrastinate until then. Returning to the table, I slid a leg over Tomio and settled on his lap.

"Oh, hello." He put his hands on my hips and looked up into my face with hooded eyes.

"I'm not sure I care much where Ryan slipped off to if it gives us time for... other things." I curled my fingers through the hair at the back of his head and enjoyed the way his eyes rolled back in his head in an exaggerated fashion.

"Sorry, did you say something?" Tomio slurred as though drunk.

I lowered my lips to his, pulse jumping, stomach warming.

"Plenty of time for that later, kids," Ryan said from the doorway.

I jerked upright and got off Tomio's lap, face heating with embarrassment. He shot me a weird look, appearing completely relaxed and unbothered by being walked in on. He was so much cooler than me, I had to admit. Maybe it was all the MMA—conceal your thoughts, or some other martial wisdom.

"Relax, Saxony," Ryan said, looking bored. "I don't give a crap who you snog." He clutched a full brown paper grocery bag in one arm.

"What's in the bag?" Tomio got to his feet.

Ryan's expression grew sly. "Just a few household chemicals. Come with me, Cagney. We've got work to do. Get your gear on."

"What work?" I followed, albeit slowly. Work didn't sound near as nice as kissing.

"Between the radioactivity and the orbs, we're going to figure out where Nero is headed next very soon, and when we do there'll be no time for coaching, let alone access to the forge. Now, move it."

"You want her to coach you?" Tomio sounded intrigued.

Ryan's laugh was dry and sarcastic. "No. I'm going to

coach her." His gaze cut to me and he crooked a finger. "Time to learn some alchemy."

I exchanged a wide-eyed look with Tomio, but before I could react further Ryan had vacated the cafeteria. I went after him.

"Can I come?" Tomio called.

When Ryan didn't answer, Tomio added a short conversation with himself: "Why am I asking him? I don't care what he thinks, I'm not missing this."

We fetched fireproof clothing, put it on, and met Ryan outside the CTH.

The stale smell of neoprene in a room that hadn't been aired in a while was strong in my nose. Evening light filtered in through the skylights, casting angular shadows on the mats. My mind cast briefly back to the mind-bending, surprise kiss Tomio and I had shared on these very mats not so long ago. I stole a glance at him. He appeared oblivious to my thoughts.

When we crossed into the forge, I flicked the ventilation on and Tomio got the lights. The quiet but powerful industrial fans began to circulate the air and the stale smell dissipated.

Ryan carried his bag over to one of the hafnium sinks and set it down. He began to remove items and line them up along the counter. "The way Arcturus teaches alchemy is slow and relatively safe, we don't have time for that."

"That sounds ominous." Tomio picked up a red bottle that looked like engine oil. "Redheat." He shot Ryan a look of mild concern. "Diesel additive?"

When he was finished setting out the items, Ryan disappeared inside the metals closet. Drawers opened and closed, then he emerged holding a jar containing a soft, silvery-white metal, a bowl with dull gray metallic chips in it (which I knew was boron), and a bottle containing a lump of bright blue copper chloride. I'd seen it among the academy's stores but had never worked with it before. He set these items on the table along with the rest.

"Vodka, potassium chloride, boron, calcium chloride," Ryan listed off.

I ran my eye over the items. "These are all dangerous. If they're not downright explosive, then they're caustic or unstable."

Ryan grinned. "Yes, and if Basil knew what I was about to show you, he'd have kittens, so this stays between us, at least until you've recovered."

Tomio's head snapped up. "Until she, pardon?"

Ryan leveled Tomio with a look and jacked a thumb at the door. "If I'm going to have trouble with you, lover-boy, then leave. Aside from Nero, Saxony is the most resilient Burned mage we know. She'll be fine. She's going to need alchemy in the near future, trust me."

Cockroaches of anxiety scuttled along my spine, but there was a hot thrum of excitement as well. "I'm ready."

Ryan sent Tomio a questioning look.

Tomio put up both hands. "It's fine, I'm just here to observe. I won't interfere."

"This is what Nero taught you after you delivered the orb, isn't it?" I could still see the way Nero and Ryan had exchanged colored fire across the lava of Vesuvius. It was a sight I'd never forget.

"Yes. He couldn't teach me everything because I'm not as strong as he is, but he gave me the principles and how to accelerate them, though you won't have time to master it fully. That takes years. The faster you learn alchemy, the more danger there is. To you, I mean. You won't feel great when you go to bed tonight, but you'll recover. Can you trust me on that?"

"I guess." I understood that when I saw the assortment of compounds he'd assembled. If this was easy, everyone would do it, and I'd already seen something of what alchemy in rookie hands could do.

"Good. Very quickly, it's important for you to recognize the difference between alchemy and idle fire, since both come in rainbow hues."

"Adults don't produce idles..." I paused, remembering the gorgeous deep-emerald flames Ryan had produced down at the beach, "...at least, not very often. And children certainly can't do alchemy."

"Yes, but more than that, you can tell an idle from alchemy by its hue. They each come in orange, yellow, green, blue, violet, red and indigo, but alchemy is brighter."

"More artificial looking," I guessed. "Almost neon?"

"Yes, how did you know that? From Vesuvius?"

"Before that. The intruder I chased before our first year started produced bright, sapphire flames I'd never seen before. It reeked of chemicals and ignited things superfast."

Ryan nodded. "Which brings me to the next difference: most alchemy has a smell, though not always, since there are other factors at play, such as environment. Also, an experienced mage can minimize the stench they give off." He picked up the redheat diesel additive. "Let's start here. Each of the alchemical colors will enhance your abilities in a different way. This additive contains nitromethane, which will increase your combustive abilities. I couldn't find pure nitromethane, so you'll have to absorb the blend and burn off what you don't need."

My throat closed up and it took me a second to process what he was saying. "You want me to *ingest* that?"

Tomio made a suppressed gargle in the back of his throat then fisted a hand into his teeth.

Ryan ignored him. "Yes, but not through your mouth, through your skin. I'll pour some into your palm. Hold it and raise your body temperature steadily until you've absorbed it all. The nitromethane has to penetrate to the core of you, where all that volcanic lining is hidden. When that lining cools, the additive will be part of you."

"Permanently?"

Ryan nodded. "Permanently. This is what you'll never learn here at the academy. They teach Unburned mages with a tiny drop of substance at a time. It's less dangerous for the student, but the effects are weak and temporary. Only Burned magi are strong enough to do what you're about to do."

"Have you done this for all the colors?"

Ryan unscrewed the cap. "This isn't about me, and you're stalling. Hold out your hand."

I made a shallow cup with my palm and Ryan poured the oily substance. He set the bottle down and put his hands on my shoulders. Frog-marching me to a clear space in the forge directly beneath the ventilation, he said, "Don't allow yourself to combust. Think about pulling in, not pushing out. And don't raise your temperature too fast."

"That's a lot to think about," I muttered, stoking my fire to life and letting it wash around my body beneath my skin.

But already I could feel what he meant. By channeling the energy of my fire into slow-moving turbines churning from my skin into my center, I could feel the chemicals sinking into my hand. A sizzling feeling began in my palm and crawled up my arm as I raised my temperature. A moment later, a whooshing sound filled my ears.

"That's it." Ryan's voice sounded like it was coming from the speakers of an old-fashioned radio.

When the sizzle reached my shoulder, it rushed forward, filling my torso with a churning, acidic burn. It scorched its way up my throat. My mouth and esophagus felt swollen and it became hard to concentrate on keeping my temperature steady, as my breathing became labored.

"Ryan—" I gasped, as his face blurred and refocused, blurred and refocused, like a vintage movie reel.

"Don't stop now." His words buzzed in my ears like static.

Nausea clenched at my stomach as the chemical poisoned me, soaking its way through my stony guts. My head began to pound and my muscles felt lethargic. I wanted to sit down. No, I wanted to lie down. Right now. I desperately needed to be horizontal.

"Keep it up." Ryan's voice drifted into my ears. He sounded like a tiny wasp perched at the threshold of my ear canal.

Tomio said something but I couldn't understand him. Either he was too far away, or he was speaking Japanese, perhaps to himself.

There came a change in my fire and flesh, a subtle shift of flexing coolness. The nausea began to ease. My vision slowly cleared and the thick feeling inside my mouth diminished. My heat faltered as my heart jumped. Was I finished?

"Don't stop now," Ryan said, sounding clearer. "You're almost done."

I increased the temperature of my body further and felt the quickening of something deep within. Something foreign but tolerable, the way bone heals around the screw for a dental implant. "Ryan," I gasped, this time in a dizzy wonder.

His voice was muzzy. "Did you feel it?"

I nodded. Well, I'd felt something.

"Feel what?" Tomio's voice came from somewhere far away, rasping with exasperation and strain.

"You can come down now. You're past the point of no return," Ryan murmured. "And I'm right here."

I let my temperature fall and my fire slow its circular, curling flow, wondering why Ryan thought I was worried that he was going to leave or be too far away.

Then my knees buckled.

Ryan caught me and lowered me to the neoprene mat. The world spun around the central axis of his face as a strong malaise rushed over me with a vengeance. Tomio's concerned face appeared over Ryan's shoulder, his eyes huge. I gagged and twisted against Ryan's grip, turning over to vomit my pizza onto the forge's floor.

"WHAT HAVE YOU DONE TO HER?" Tomio hissed as I hung my head between my knees. He rubbed lazy circles on my lower back and held a glass of water where I could reach it.

I was still too dizzy to open my eyes, but I found enough voice to croak, "I'm okay."

"See?" Ryan replied, who sounded like he was pacing impatiently back and forth in the middle of the forge. "And I'm doing her a huge favor. You have no idea what we're up against."

"I was in the volcano, too, remember?" Tomio snapped, sounding more irritated than I'd ever heard him.

I pawed the air, looking for his knee. When I found it, I squeezed gently, trying to let him know that I really was okay. I wasn't feeling nearly as ill as I had. By the time

Tomio and Ryan had the vomit cleaned up and the smell ventilated out of the forge, my stomach had settled.

Ryan blew a sarcastic breath. "That was nothing. He was toying with me. Don't you realize that? Mages are dropping like flies. Of the Burned on the agency roster, only me, Saxony and Basil remain. And even working together the three of us might not be able to take Nero down."

Tomio stiffened and I thought I could imagine something of what he was feeling. He was a champion fighter. He wasn't Burned, but he probably thought his martial arts abilities made up for that. To be so easily discounted had likely lifted his hackles, maybe even sparked doubts in his own abilities. I expected Tomio to protest, but he didn't say anything about Ryan's obvious dismissal. Instead he addressed me in a soft tone.

"Think you can sit up yet?"

I wasn't quite ready, but for Tomio's sake I nodded. Leaning back, I opened an eye and took a few deep breaths as the room spun. When it slowed, I opened my other eye and aimed a smile at him.

He smiled back and held up the glass of water.

I took it and drank. It did help.

"I wouldn't bother waiting for the sickness to pass," Ryan said, still pacing. "In fact, I found that I felt better right after I used it."

I rubbed my eyes and blinked at him, blearily. "You're saying I should use the redheat now?"

"Yes. As soon as possible."

"Why as soon as possible?"

"First, because it's the final step in solidifying the alchemy in your tissues. And second, because this is going to take all night if you don't move through the colors faster, and I'm exhausted. I'd really like to get some sleep before the sun comes up."

"Charming," Tomio said, rolling his eyes.

I got to my feet, swaying unsteadily. Making sure I was beneath the ventilation, I lifted a hand and sent a blast of fire shooting from my palm. The light from my flame reflected on Ryan's face and in his eyes as he stepped back.

"Doesn't look much different, to be honest." Tomio's voice came from directly behind me.

I lifted my left hand. "That's because I wanted to set a benchmark."

Expressing will to use my newly acquired alchemy, I threw another jet.

A neon yellow pillar of spitting, hissing fire—as fat as a bike tire and so dense and bright that stars popped in my vision—exploded from my palm with a sound like a dragon's roar.

Tomio yelled in surprise. Ryan blinked at the glare, shielding his eyes with a hand. He smiled in a self-satisfied way.

I stopped the jet and relaxed, realizing that Ryan had been right. All of the dizziness and nausea was completely gone. I felt fine.

There was a moment of silence, and then Tomio uttered a rare curse word, impressed.

"Was it easy?" Ryan asked.

"So easy," I breathed. "All it took was a thought. It was effortless."

"Welcome to the world of alchemy." Ryan strode toward the counter loaded with toxins. "Let's do lithium next."

"What color is that?" Tomio almost ran over to the assortment of bottles, eyes wide and curious, all irritation with Ryan had vanished.

"Red." Ryan picked up the lithium and beckoned.

"What does the red one do?" I asked, not moving from my spot.

Ryan gave me a withering glance. "What do you think? It's *lithium*. The same stuff used in batteries."

"Stamina?"

"Exactly."

I crossed to the boys, a small amount of dread kindling in my stomach. Extra stamina would be nice. I could easily recall how I felt after carrying Ryan's dead-weight through miles of abandoned mine. Still, I'd only just started feeling better and wished I had more time before tackling the next one. "Will it feel as bad as the redheat?"

Ryan answered cheerily. "Worse, I'm afraid. You'll feel this one more in your head. Wait till you do copper chloride. That's the green one. What a trip." He paused when he saw the look on my face. "You'll be fine. Pain is beauty. Right? Isn't that what girls always say? Or is it 'beauty is pain'? I forget. Anyway, hop to Cagney."

3

WITH ORB IN HAND

Tomio was too much of a gentleman to be tapping on my door at two o'clock in the morning.

Or was he?

Throwing the sheet off, I got out of bed and padded to the door, bare soles cool on the hardwood as the tapping came again. Whoever it was, it wasn't urgent. The knocking was half-hearted at best, almost like they weren't sure they wanted to wake me. Maybe that's because I'd only had a day and half of rest after all the crazy chemicals I'd taken in, and I still hardly felt like myself. But even I had to admit, though the process had been miserable, I felt like a loaded weapon in a way I never had before. The dread I used to feel when the team finally pinpointed Nero's next target had somehow morphed into impatience. I hoped the chemicals weren't making me over-confident. If they were, Ryan would never admit it out loud. Doubting ourselves was the kiss of death.

I pulled the door open to see Ryan standing in the hall, one hand behind his back. He gestured that I should come with him.

"Where to?" I whispered, but he walked down the hall

without waiting for a response, pulling his hidden hand in front of his torso.

I made an educated guess about what he was holding, and withheld further questions as curiosity got the best of me. Grabbing the fireproof shirt and shorts I'd thrown on my chair, I changed out of my pajamas and slid my feet into a pair of flip-flops. I scampered after Ryan as I pulled my shirt into place. Dover was hot tonight, in spite of being close to the Channel.

I caught up to him and fell in step with him as we crossed over a landing, heading for the CTH. As suspected, Ryan had the black box containing the orb cradled against his stomach. He put a finger over his lips and didn't speak until after he'd closed the CTH doors.

"Are you going to tell me why we're doing whatever it is we're doing in the middle of the night?" I asked, shadowing him over to the forge. This place was quickly becoming associated with some wild memories. Why did I get the feeling I was about to make one more?

"Because if the others knew we were doing this now, they'd want to be here. The fewer people around, the better it is for you."

"For me?"

"Yep." Ryan set the box on the edge of a hafnium crucible, then crossed to the wall and switched on the ventilation. He returned and flipped the lid open, exposing the silver orb.

My gaze was drawn to its smooth, curved surface.

Ryan plucked the orb from its nest. "It needs to be someone other than me."

"Why?" I asked, having somehow lost the ability to look away from the relic.

"So there's more than one witness." Ryan took my elbow

and steered me to an open place on the forge floor, directly beneath a fan and not far from where I'd tossed my pizza.

He placed the orb in my hand and stepped back. "Heat it up."

The ball felt cool and hard, totally inanimate, but heavier than a rock of the same size. I rubbed a thumb over the raised line, feeling its smooth coolness.

"How high?"

"As high as you can."

I shot Ryan a look of concern. "You mean, melt it?" I didn't know what the metal was, it wasn't like anything I'd handled before, or memorized for my classes.

"It won't melt." Ryan leaned against the edge of a sink, crossing his arms.

"You sure? I don't feel like getting on Basil's bad side." I could produce somewhere in excess of eight-thousand Fahrenheit, maybe more. I'd never pushed myself to the limit before. Whatever this little orb was made of, it wouldn't survive the kind of heat I could produce. There wasn't any material that could except hafnium.

Ryan rolled his eyes. "Just do it, Cagney. You are such a freaking Mary. Do you want to get to the next location before Nero, or not?"

I blew out a breath and looked down at the artifact, rolling it in my palm and admiring its glistening surface. My fire burst into life, more eager than I was, it seemed, to see what would happen. Pushing aside the thought that every time Ryan told me to do something lately, I either ended up vomiting or face down on the floor, or both, I pitched up the temperature.

Ryan nodded, a slow smile crossing his face. "Atta girl."

"Does it matter how fast I do this?" My eyes hardened and lit up like kerosene lamps.

"The faster the better, we don't have all night."

"Okay, then." Like yanking the ripcord of a parachute—half because I was afraid that if I hesitated, I'd come up with a reason to calve out—my fire spiked into the thousands of degrees.

The orb did not change, in fact, it didn't even get hot. The metal remained cool against my blazing palm. I sent Ryan an amazed glance. The air baked with waves as the ventilation system sucked the heat up and spewed it into the night air over the coast.

Passing four-thousand degrees, then five thousand, I stopped counting and jacked it further. Still the orb remained cool and intact. Somewhere around the eight-thousand-degree mark, I heard a sound like wind, then waves crashing against something solid.

"Can you hear that?" My voice echoed eerily within my skull, halting in my mouth. I coughed at the strange feeling, and the cough flared my heat further as I realized some black shadow was crawling over Ryan's face. Fingers of darkness crept over his skin like special effects for a ghost movie. He didn't appear to notice. He was saying something, calmly, like there was nothing unusual going on, only I couldn't hear him. I felt an urgent need to warn him about the shadow, which had darkened further, but then it swallowed him completely.

Then it swallowed everything else, too.

Even the forge was gone. I looked into my hand, but I had no hand. There was no longer an orb, and I was bodiless, without form or skin sensation. I was weightless, yet somehow dropping. Falling. Thoughts dissolved like butter in a warm skillet.

A canopy of stars dipped and swayed on all sides, then I was falling through them, passing lasers of white light, tracers left behind by celestial bodies whizzing by at terrifying speed. Then I was swallowed by sudden darkness and became aware of a dramatic, bone-chilling cold; aware of it, but not suffering from it.

A new visual emerged.

Frost cracked the edges of my vision. Beyond and far below swirled a black sea full of ice. Water churned over the icebergs, frothing and crashing with unending, impotent rage. The sea came up to swallow me, but water became blasting snow as a hurricane of maniacal flakes battered around and through me, ripping my non-existent breath from my non-existent mouth.

A huge white bear with snarling jaws and flashing yellow teeth loomed against the snowy backdrop. It was there and then gone, replaced by the sight of a woman's face peeking from a ring of fur. Her dark eyes glittered with intelligence. Then she blew apart, her cheeks and lips turning into snowflakes. The snowflakes diminished, spiraling away, sparkling in the darkness like glitter.

Fat, silver fish burst from the black velvet backdrop, flying horizontally across my field of vision, writhing and curling and vital with health and life. A silver spearhead so big it blocked out everything slashed from horizon to horizon, trailing streamers of bright red blood behind it like Maypole ribbons.

Voices sang and chanted, emerging and receding against the background audio of an angry sea and the soft sound of snow swirling. A barrage of firelit faces, old and young, craggy and smooth, like paintings on canvas, brought to life by magic, took shape then swept by like the scenery outside a fast-moving train. Their eyes were bright with life and hope. One set of eyes flared with the orange light of a mage;

I tried to call to them, but I was voiceless and they vanished along with the rest.

A river emerged below the faces, it broke into many rivers. Many rivers became soggy tundra, what seemed like hundreds of thousands of miles of it, flying by. A fat rabbit with snow-white fur burst past on my right, running in a wild zigzag pattern, evading some unseen predator. The rabbit's footfalls left ripples of ice-blue light hanging in the air. A growl loomed on my left, a snap of shining canines and the rabbit vanished in a plume of smoke. The smoke thickened and pulsed like a living heart, sending fat bursts of iron-gray plumes into a starry night sky, like signals.

A raspy voice spoke slowly and eloquently behind the sound of a crackling fire; a storyteller, both old and wise. Life lessons, given in a language I didn't recognize, poured into young imaginations. Juvenile intellect matured there, under those stories, grew wise and passed on that wisdom in a never-ending, generational chain that remained unbroken for thousands of years. I understood all of this in moments with inherent comprehension.

And there was fire.

At times, only flashes of it, in astounding hues of purple, pink and green. It raged past me in a line so straight it looked laid against a ruler, spewing orange and red sparks. It hissed and cast embers which burned wounds through my vision the way a cigarette leaves holes in cotton. Through those wounds lay a whole other vision layered beneath this one. I was drowned by a sense of awe as I understood that these layers of history were without end.

Other times, fire appeared in my periphery, only to disappear when the spectacle swayed in response to my desire to see the fire better. Each time it evaded me, like a star you see only when you focus on the blackness beside it. To look meant to lose it entirely.

There were many faces, so many, from all angles. There were animals, and wilderness, and northern lights in spectacular displays of emerald and violet.

There came a man's face, as clear as spring water.

High cheekbones, a long and angular skull with fierce beauty. Deep, black eyes with coals at their centers. Thick, beautiful lips that curved with an alluring smile and snarled with a dangerous cruelty. This face came with the sound of a deep and powerful heartbeat, and crackles of fire. He was somehow more than the others, more of everything. More substantive, brutally strong, breathtakingly arrogant, and yet tender-hearted.

If I could have sensed breath in me, he would have taken it away.

Instead, he opened his mouth stretched in a smile that seemed like it would never stop. Then that grinning mouth opened wide. Looking straight through me, he swallowed me whole.

"How is she?"

Whispered words punched through the darkness like a wrecking ball through wooden paneling. Who was speaking, and why couldn't I open my eyes? The sensation of fabric against my cheek emerged next. I was lying down, but not on neoprene mats, on a proper mattress.

"I think she's coming to."

My heart quickened at the sound of Tomio's voice, the hope in it, the worry. It felt like drugged blood was sludging through my veins. I sucked in a deep breath and some of the lethargy lifted. I became aware of a warm patch across my torso. Lifting my eyelids with monumental effort, Tomio's face swam into view.

"Hey." He smiled and shifted closer, his features zooming toward me in 3D. I clenched my eyes shut against a woozy feeling.

"Hey," I croaked, lifting a hand to touch my face. Was I corporeal again? Well, yes. I knew I had a body again because my arm weighed at least four thousand pounds.

"Thank God. I'll get Basil."

I recognized the other speaker now, it was Mehmet.

The sound of a door creaking open made me want to open my eyes. A shudder took my body as Tomio reappeared. Ryan stood behind him, studying my face with the detached interest of a scientist.

"Can you sit up? I've got water." Tomio moved off screen for a moment, then returned. Cold glass pressed against my fingers.

"Why do I feel like I was run over by an elephant?" I fumbled for the glass, my fingers slow to respond to mental commands. "Make that, a herd of elephants. Pissed-off ones."

"It'll pass," Ryan said, helpfully.

"I'm never doing anything you tell me to do again, Ryan," I said, lifting the water to my lips with Tomio's help. After getting the water down, I pulled myself up into sitting and saw the reason for the warm patch on my torso. A beam of sunlight lay across my bed, but I didn't recognize the bedroom. "Where am I?"

"We brought you to the closest room to the CTH," Tomio explained, then added with apparent annoyance, "Well, Ryan did. The rest of us were sleeping."

"How long have I been out?" The room seemed to tilt behind the men's faces, but it settled as I drank more water. I looked down at myself and saw that my fireproof clothing looked like something unearthed from the tomb of an ancient king: ragged and fragile. Still, I was impressed it had survived at all. I tugged at the hem of my shorts and the material stretched like spider web, then broke apart. Best not to touch it, then.

"Eleven hours or so—a good night's sleep." Ryan's words were infused with forced cheer.

Tomio shot him a warning look that made me wonder what words they might have exchanged while I was unconscious. He turned to me. "What do you remember?"

I put the heel of my hand to my temple where a dull throb had surfaced. It felt like some tiny creature had taken up residence in my head and was mining for something… with a pick-ax. "A lot of crazy visions. Faces, voices, animals, fire." I looked up at Ryan. "What was I seeing?"

Ryan paused, then cocked an eyebrow. "What makes you think I would know?"

I made an incredulous *duh* face at him. "The whole thing was your idea! Ow." I covered my eyes; raising my voice was a bad idea.

"Yeah, but this is Basil's orb. I've never used it before," Ryan said.

"So, they all give a different experience, is that what you're saying?" I went to drink more water and found my glass empty.

"I've only… traveled through one, but I think so, yes."

"Traveled." I thought about this. "Yeah, that's a good word for it."

Tomio poured more water into my cup.

"Thanks." I downed it, and the sharpness of my

headache subsided a little. I held my glass out for more. I was going to spend a lot of time in the bathroom today.

The hinges of the bedroom door squeaked again and I looked up to see Basil enter holding a black box, his face flushed and eyes bright. He handed it to Ryan before addressing me. "Mehmet said you were up. How are you feeling?"

"Like I partied all night, with alcohol... and drugs that don't mix well with alcohol." Handing Tomio the glass, I turned and put my feet on the floor.

"Do we have anything yet?" Ryan asked Basil.

Basil shook his head. "Not yet, but soon."

Feeling my soles flat on the floor did a lot to steady me. I looked up at the headmaster. "What are you talking about?"

"The words you gave us."

"Words?"

Basil looked from Tomio to Ryan and back again. "You haven't told her?"

"She just woke up, give her a second," Tomio replied, exasperated.

"I don't need any more seconds. Tell me what's happened?"

Ryan took his phone out of his pocket and woke up the screen. Flicking through his device, he turned the screen toward me.

Taking the phone, I studied the image. Amazement slowly dawned. I looked up at Ryan, "*I* did this?"

"All you, baby."

On Ryan's phone was a photograph of a piece of paper with the kind of scribbles on it that we'd seen in Nero's underground hideaway. These were clearly a completely different language, but the outcome was basically the same —a mess of nonsense scattered across the page.

"The original is being analyzed by someone Ms. Shepherd knows in London," Basil explained, speaking quickly. "He's not as talented as Janet, but he thinks he can give us an origin within a few days, maybe as soon as 24 hours. That, combined with the information her physicist comes up with should give us enough to mobilize." His expression wilted. "Exactly *how* we mobilize is a little less clear."

I handed Ryan his phone, stunned speechless at what I'd produced and wracking my brains to try and remember it. "How did the pencil and paper not burn up?"

"All the heat gets sucked into the orb, that's when the visions start. That's when I moved you to a counter and put a pencil and paper in front of you," Ryan said.

Basil headed for the door. "I'd better go. Your color is looking good, I daresay you'll be on your feet in no time." He gave the men a final directive. "Take care of her. We still have one orb to go."

I watched Basil disappear and then stared at the empty doorway. "We have one orb to go—" I parroted, marveling at how much Basil had changed his tune. He'd been so terrified Ryan would damage the orb that he hadn't wanted to trust him with both. I couldn't remember much about the visions I had, and nothing about the scribbling, but based on Basil's reaction, the orb had survived the encounter just fine.

Ryan lifted the black box with a smile. "Let me know when you feel up for round two?"

A snake of dread curled around my stomach and settled there like it planned to move in permanently. Ryan put the box in my hands. Even opening the lid and seeing the beautiful orb within didn't lift the unpleasant feeling.

This one was a shining green metal, with a depressed pattern rather than a raised one. It was pretty, but knowing how badly it could knock a mage on their ass tempered the charm of it somewhat.

I closed the box and held it back out to Ryan. "Can't *you* do it this time?"

It's not like heating up the orb had endowed me with superpowers. I could now admit that I had half hoped it would. All I'd gotten out of the experience was an excessively trippy high, followed up by a hangover.

Ryan's face fell as he took the box but he didn't seem surprised by my request. "I suppose. It isn't very fun, is it?"

I rolled my head to work out some of the kinks. "It's the opposite of fun. How did you even know what to do with it?"

Tomio moved to sit beside me on the bed. To my utter delight, he began to give me a massage, his fingers working into the tight muscles at the base of my neck.

Ryan took Tomio's chair, balancing the box on his thigh. "When I found the one in Iran, I was supposed to bring it straight back to Nero without touching it. I've never been one for following orders—"

Tomio and I shared a simultaneous snort.

Ryan smiled. "I figured that an orb made by a fire mage should logically reveal its secrets when exposed to high temperatures. It would be the perfect obstacle; setting the orb to awaken at eight-some-thousand degrees would ensure that only the most powerful of Burned mages could access its hidden information."

Tomio's hand paused. "You can conjure eight-thousand degrees?"

Ryan nodded. "Fahrenheit, of course."

Tomio tugged on my neck and looked into my face. "Can *you* do that, too?"

I nodded without bothering to tease him that if I hadn't

been able to, the orb wouldn't have given me anything. I gestured for him to continue his massage.

He resumed rubbing and muttered, "No wonder I'm just the masseur."

"So, you heated it up, and voila?" I closed my eyes as Tomio's fingers found a sore spot.

"Yes."

"Weren't you worried about damaging it? Basil thought they were super fragile."

"Basil is clearly not an authority, as much as he thinks he is. If he'd been more willing to take risks he might have found an actual orb instead of faffing about in his basement making plaster replicas."

Ryan's contempt for the headmaster brought out feelings of protectiveness, I glared at him. "Give him a break. He approaches things like a scholar, unlike you."

Ryan approached things like a court jester—in my opinion—leaping before he looked. But in this case, it had worked out.

"Plaster replicas?" Tomio dug into my shoulders, making me groan.

Ryan slouched, ignoring Tomio's prompt for more information. "But no, I didn't worry about damaging it. If by some chance I had, then I would have told Nero that I'd simply failed to find it."

"Why doesn't that surprise me." I winced and let out a moan of pleasure-pain. "But there's something else I don't get. If the orb doesn't give you any enhanced ability, as I had thought it might after seeing the way you fought with him inside Vesuvius, then how did your skills accelerate so quickly?"

Ryan paused long enough for me to open my eyes and look at him. He looked... caged.

"Nero taught me," he finally replied.

"After you got back from Ramsar?" I gave Tomio's hand a grateful squeeze and rolled my shoulders. He stopped massaging my neck to listen.

"That's right," Ryan said.

"So, you didn't acquire those abilities in Ramsar, so as far as you know, he never suspected you'd used the orb?"

"No."

"And where are the scribbles you produced?"

Ryan's cross-armed pose tightened as he straightened from his slouch. "If I did any scribbling, I don't remember it."

"Huh. So, you returned from Ramsar, no different than when you'd left, handed the orb over to Nero, and then he taught you how to accelerate the learning of alchemy?"

He nodded. "Exactly. And shortly after that, I got Tomio's message and realized you hadn't been lying about Gage, and called you. Fast forward a few hours and we were slinking through a volcano."

"So, you learned all that fancy alchemy in... what? A matter of days?"

Ryan's eyes cast to the floor, then to the window.

Ms. Shepherd poked her head in. "Ryan?"

He perked up. "Yes?"

"We need you on a call in fifteen minutes, can you come to lecture hall C?"

Ryan stood. "Yes, I'll go with you now."

She stepped back to let Ryan pass. He disappeared into the hallway. She glanced at me. "How are you feeling?"

"Better, thanks. How's the stuff with the physicists coming?"

She dropped an excited wink. "We're closing in." Then she too, was gone.

Tomio and I looked at one another, frowning.

"Does something seem off about Ryan's story, or is it just me?" I asked.

He tucked a curl behind my ear, expression contemplative. "It's not just you."

4

TRAVELING

The decision was made for Ryan to travel with the final orb in the fire-gym, rather than the CTH, so that Mehmet and Ms. Shepherd could safely observe from a pod. Tomio and I sat along the wall near to where Ryan would do the work. Our job was to position him in front of a mobile fireproof desk we'd pulled from storage, so that he had a solid surface to write on. Basil waited at a distance with pencil and paper tucked into a heat-safe neoprene envelope, ready to be whipped out the moment Ryan stopped producing heat.

"He doesn't look nervous." Tomio threw an arm over the back of my chair as we watched Ryan pluck Basil's orb from its velvet bed.

"Why would he? He's done this before." Settling back against Tomio's arm, I glanced at the camera we'd set up in one of the pods to film the event, making sure the recording light was on. Heat rose from Ryan's body in visible waves already, drifting toward the ceiling and speeding up as the fans sucked them outside. His eyes became coals and his gaze turned flat and unfocused. Throughout it all, the orb did not change. The temperature in the gym climbed as Ryan's internal furnace spewed out degrees. It baked off our faces and moved my hair with its currents. Tomio moved his arm away from me so our bodies didn't gather further heat.

Basil hovered nearby. The headmaster seemed barely able to breathe and his eyes were bright in anticipation of something one might only see once in a lifetime.

When the change came, it was sudden and drastic. The heat baking from Ryan ceased abruptly, though his eyes continued to glow. He did not blink, but switched the orb from his right hand to his left in a sharp, artificial-looking motion. Like he was a robot operating by pistons beneath synthetic flesh and skin instead of organic muscle, blood and bone. His right hand began to move in a series of sharp gestures.

The headmaster rushed forward as Tomio and I leapt from our seats.

"I waited too long," Basil cried with an unmistakable giddiness. "I expected there would be a window after the heat stopped."

Ryan's hand jerked around wildly, beneath wide and sightless eyes. It was downright spooky.

Tomio steadied Ryan's body as I caught and stilled Ryan's hand so that Basil could insert the pencil between his fingers. Ryan's arm continued to jerk around, fighting for the freedom to move. When his fingers touched the pencil, they grasped it the way a hungry dog snaps at meat.

Basil slid the paper beneath Ryan's writing utensil and we stepped back and watched, a bit winded.

Ryan took to the task with vigor. His illuminated eyes never once dropped to the page, never once blinked, yet the pencil scrawled without running off the edge or going over any of the white space twice.

Tomio twined his fingers through mine as we watched the display, fascinated and a touch horrified. A peek at the words and shapes spewing from the end of Ryan's pencil gave me no understanding or revelation at all; they were as foreign as cuneiform. The only observation I could make was that the shapes were tighter and more elegant than the ones I had produced.

Tomio released my hand, and he and the headmaster closed in, preparing to catch Ryan when he collapsed. As the last of the white space was used up, Ryan's eyes went dark. They rolled up in his head and his body went limp. Tomio caught him as he crumpled, sweeping him up the way men lift fainting women in old movies.

We left the page of scribbles for Ms. Shepherd to collect.

Basil and I held the fire-gym's doors open as Tomio carried Ryan up the winding steps to the archway, then down the hall to the nearby bedroom we'd made up for the purpose. Ms. Shepherd and Mehmet followed at a distance. Lying on his back on the bed, his head cradled by a pillow, Ryan looked to be in a deep and dreamless sleep.

We stood around looking at him for several moments, making sure his breathing was steady. My life was rife with weird supernatural elements now, but I still felt a bit winded by the whole experience. To give myself something to do, I grabbed the empty carafe from the bedside table and went into the bathroom to fill it.

When I returned, Basil was mopping his brow with his handkerchief. "That was remarkable."

"Should we stay with him?" I set the glass where Ryan would see it when he woke.

"If he's anything like you, he'll be out for hours," Tomio said, studying Ryan's sleeping face.

"If he's anything like me, he'll wake with one hell of a

hangover," I murmured, grateful that Ryan had agreed to spare me the experience a second time.

The traveling part hadn't been too bad, mostly just disorienting, but the aftermath had been brutal. I wondered if Ryan saw a face at the end of his travels, or maybe even the same face. I made a mental note to ask him as we left him to his rest.

As the clock journeyed toward the end of another day, Tomio and I sat curled up on the couch in the first-years' lounge, tummies full of takeout. Empty sushi trays and crumpled napkins lay across the coffee table. The lounge had the faint aroma of soy sauce and vinegared rice.

Technically, we were second-years now, but the first-years' lounge was where we felt most at home, even if it made me a little sad. The vast majority of our friends would not be returning to Arcturus. The unanswered question hung in the air of every room: would Arcturus Academy even have a school year in September?

Basil had said nothing about the impact the snuffings would have on how he would proceed as headmaster, and I didn't have the courage to bring it up. If I were him, I wouldn't know what to do either, and if we weren't able to prevent Nero from snuffing the remaining fires... well, the thought was too horrible to contemplate. Life would look different for all of us come fall.

Tomio lay against the opposite armrest with my foot in his lap, giving me a half-hearted rub. His eyelids looked about to close up shop for the night. The pad of his thumb pressed into a sore spot in the arch of my foot. Somehow, he was able to find all the achy bits. He'd missed a calling as a therapist.

"Shall we check on Ryan before we go to bed?" he asked.

We'd looked in on Ryan once every hour since he'd gone limp this morning but there'd been no change. His breathing was deep and even, his slumber appeared peaceful. It struck me that both the Wendig twins could be considered comatose at the moment. Thoughts of Gage made me even more morose than wondering about the future of Arcturus.

My phone buzzed from the coffee table and I peered at the screen. "Speak of the devil." Angelica Wendig's name flashed on the screen.

Tomio's jaw cracked with a yawn. "Who is it?"

"Gage's mom." Reluctantly, I pulled my foot from Tomio's lap and straightened.

Normally she texted, but this time she was requesting a video call. Heart jumping with hope, I hit the answer button. Angelica's face appeared against a backdrop of pastel green paint. Something had changed. Her expression was bright and excited. Her blond hair was piled on top of her head in wild curls and tied with a red kerchief. Fat gold hoops swayed at her jawline and she wore bright red lipstick. She looked like a movie star from the forties.

"Saxony. Hi!"

"Hey. You look great. What's happened?"

Tomio scrambled to my end of the couch and put his forehead to mine to peer at the phone. "Hi, Angelica. Wow, you do look good."

Angelica smiled, tears shining in the corner of her eyes. "Tomio, hey. I'm glad you guys are together. There's someone who wants to say hi to you."

Tomio and I mashed our cheeks together further, as

Angelica turned the phone toward Gage's hospital bed. My heart began to sprint and my breathing felt shallow.

The head of his bed was lifted at an angle, and he lay propped against a couple of pillows. His eyes were half-open as he watched his mom. His gaze shifted to the screen as she turned it toward him. Emotion clutched at my throat. Gage looked tired, thin and pale, but he was awake. Though he wasn't smiling, his gaze was clear. He was all there behind those blue eyes.

"Hi, Gage." My voice came out wispy. "How are you? How do you feel?"

Tomio lifted a hand in greeting. "Hi, Gage. Amazing to see you awake. You gave us a real scare."

"He sure did." Angelica's hand appeared, brushing the hair at Gage's forehead back. "But he's going to be okay. Doc says he's out of the woods. If his vitals continue to improve at this rate, I'll be able to take him home in a couple of weeks. Maybe even less."

"Hi, guys." Gage's voice was a croak.

"I'm so sorry we aren't there," I told him, the guilt now slipping between my ribs in repeated thrusts, like someone was stabbing me with wire.

"Mom explained everything." Gage spoke slowly, and couldn't seem to enunciate the way he usually did. "I owe you both a debt I can never repay. She told me what happened inside the volcano." He gave a long slow blink and took a breath. "So, thank you."

"I'm only sorry we didn't make it sooner," I said, my words heavy with implication. I didn't have to point out to anyone present what it might have meant for Gage if we had found him before he'd lost his fire. This led to another thought that briefly took my breath away. He would have woken to the rude realization that he no longer had fire.

How was he handling it? It was impossible to tell from his sleepy face and slow drone of words. This Gage seemed a little drugged.

His eyelids lifted a fraction further. "I'm just happy to be alive, Saxony."

My sinuses stung with unshed tears. There was a lot of the old Gage in that answer. He was always so positive, so upbeat in the face of difficulty. It was one of the reasons I loved him.

"I'll figure out the rest later," he continued. "I want to get strong enough to go home and see my dad."

We nodded.

"How is Mr. Wendig?" I asked.

Angelica chimed in from the side, keeping the camera on Gage. "No news there, I'm afraid. His mom is still looking after him. He's... not fantastic."

Chad was worse than not fantastic, he was in pieces. If nothing had changed, it meant that he still wasn't speaking. Grandma Wendig was probably struggling to get him to eat. But I guessed that Angelica didn't want to hit Gage with the full and harsh reality of the state of his dad until he was stronger, so she downplayed it.

"Is Ryan there?" Gage asked.

Tomio and I exchanged a look. Tomio's raised brows meant he'd leave the answering of this question up to me.

"Ryan is asleep right now. We'll be heading to bed ourselves, shortly." The words had only just left my lips and I wanted to smack myself in the forehead. Tomio and me heading to bed wasn't a visual I wanted to leave Gage with, but now if I added that we were going to our own rooms to sleep, it would only be more awkward. I battled through the embarrassment. "There's other developments to catch you up on, but we don't want to overwhelm you."

"Thanks, Saxony," Angelica replied. "Gage does need a lot of rest. I only meant to let you see each other for a moment. I don't want to tire him out."

"Of course."

"Why don't you catch me up, and when Gage is stronger, I'll pass along the details?" Angelica turned the phone toward Gage again without waiting for an answer. "Say goodbye, honey."

Gage's lids were drooping again. "Bye, Saxony. Bye, Tomio. Take care of..."

My heart twisted as he paused. For a horrible moment, I felt sure he was going to say, my girl.

But he finished with, "...each other."

Tomio let out a sigh and relaxed, and I wondered if he'd thought the same thing.

We waited while Angelica kissed Gage and closed the door to the hospital room. She sat on the same couch I'd been near when I'd first seen her come strolling into the wing.

We relayed as much as we could, which wasn't much because we'd been forbidden to discuss certain details over a cellular line by Ms. Shepherd. But Angelica was more interested in Ryan's state anyway, and asked us to alert her when he awoke. The twins would benefit from seeing one another as soon as possible.

We agreed and said good night.

Tomio leaned back against the couch and threw both arms across its back. I felt his gaze on me and turned to look at him.

"You okay?" he asked.

I blew a stray curl away from my cheek. "Well, my ex-boyfriend has lost his fire because he came to Naples to help me when he didn't need to. I can't help but feel... Oh, I don't know, crippling guilt? On top of that I've fallen for his best friend."

"Ex best friend."

I put my face in my hands and let out a long sigh. "It's awful, but I also feel like I'm not entitled to feel any selfish emotions until after we stop Nero."

He lay a warm hand on my lower back. "You're entitled to feel everything you're feeling, Saxony. The situation is complicated and confusing. Whatever your fears are, Gage will be okay. Body and heart. Can you believe that?"

I looked over my shoulder. "I want to. He says he's just happy to be alive, but he only just woke up. He probably doesn't know *how* he feels yet."

"No, you're right. He needs time." Tomio leaned forward, his face coming close, his gaze penetrating.

He brushed a long curl back over my shoulder. His fingertips grazed my neck, lifting the little hairs along my arms in a pleasant way. He leaned forward, his lips hovering mere inches from mine, but he went no further. An invitation, but not for anything more than a kiss. I understood that. I pressed my lips to his, softly and slowly. My eyes drifted closed, every sense homing in on the sensations of kissing him. It had thus far never failed to surprise me—how it felt to kiss without any fiery reaction leaping up between us. A warmth and longing expanded within my belly. My arousal was strong and pleasant, but came with a heavy-handed serving of chilly guilt.

I hesitated and Tomio felt it, pulling back.

"He isn't the only one who needs more time," he said.

"My body doesn't want more time," I whispered, "but I think my mind needs it."

We drew apart at the sound of someone approaching.

Mehmet appeared in the doorway, his expression lifting when he saw us.

"I thought you'd gone to bed but nobody answered when I knocked on your doors. Ms. Shepherd and Basil need to see you in Basil's office, right away."

Without waiting, Mehmet vanished from the door. We scrambled from the couch to follow.

We found Basil seated behind his desk and Ms. Shepherd pacing behind the largest sofa. Mehmet's computer sat open on the coffee table. Voices could be heard buzzing through his headset. He sat in front of the laptop and jammed the headset over his ears, pulling the computer onto his lap as he sat back in the sofa.

Tomio and I took the two chairs in front of Basil's desk.

"Thank you, Mehmet," Basil said, though Mehmet clearly couldn't hear him.

"With the information Ryan gave us about background radiation, and the results of the scribbles you produced"—Ms. Shepherd eyed me—"we've narrowed one of Nero's two possible next locations to a remote region of the Arctic."

That it was an Arctic region did not surprise me, given that I'd been the one to travel with the orb, but Tomio visibly reacted.

"The Arctic? Really?"

Ms. Shepherd nodded. "The language Saxony produced is, of course, unknown and uncategorized, but our language expert was able to loosely connect it to a Northern Athabaskan Indigenous group in the Arctic who speak a dialect of Dené-Diné."

"If it's a loose connection then how do you know it's the best one to pursue?" Basil asked, leaning his elbows on his desk in an uncharacteristic slouch.

"We don't. Not for sure. But our physicists have at the

same time found an area of high background radiation a region where this language is still spoken today, by a very small group of people. That makes it a target."

My heart had begun to trot. We were closing in on Nero, but making a mistake here would be devastating. "How do we know Nero will head to this location instead of to the other one?"

"We know because a contact in Bolzano has linked Nero —by an alias he used to use years ago but hasn't used in recent years—to a private flight booked with an airline we know he has a contact at. The airline flies privately to Yellowknife from Verona every Sunday. We believe Nero is presently in Verona and will be on that flight."

"And Janet? Any news of her?" I asked.

Ms. Shepherd frowned. "She is still MIA, I'm afraid. We don't know if he has her with him, or if he's keeping her somewhere, or if he's... done away with her for her betrayal."

I swallowed hard. "I refuse to believe she's dead."

"Either way, our best chance to recover her is to find Nero." Basil tented his fingers and stood. "We have three days to get to that site before Nero does. I'll speak to our London Airport contact and arrange a flight as soon as possible. We'll have to strategize on the way."

"What about Ryan? We can't leave without him and he's not yet woken up."

"He will. And if he's still woozy by the time we leave, well..." Ms. Shepherd paused, pulling her cell phone out of her pocket. "We'll make sure the seats recline. Mehmet?"

He cocked one side of his headset off his ear. "I'm on it. There's a landing strip on Mahoney Lake. It's probably not in prime shape, since its only used by bush-planes, but it's thirty-seven kilometers from the epicenter of the radiation, which, given the pure vastness of the tundra, is pretty damn fortuitous."

She checked her watch. "Perfect, I'll get Joanie on the line to make provisions. It's only three in Yellowknife, so she'll be available."

"What should we do?" Tomio asked as we got to our feet.

Ms. Shepherd left the room, already speaking to someone, presumably Joanie. Mehmet tapped away furiously on his laptop.

Basil turned to us, mobile glued to his ear. "Check on Ryan, see if he's lucid enough to understand that we have to leave in a hurry."

"And if he's not?" I asked.

My mind went in several directions at once. Should I let my family know what was happening? What did one take to the Arctic? And once we were there, what exactly were we planning to do about stopping this super-powered madman?

"How about you pack?" He waved his fingers in a shooing motion. "With any luck, we'll be on a plane by this time tomorrow."

5

TOMIO'S REQUEST

"What supplies does one pack for this kind of expedition?" I stood at the end of my bed in front of an empty duffle bag, wondering aloud as I sorted through my things and made a mental list. It was past midnight, but I was too excited to sleep. My desk was covered in toiletries, everything I owned in terms of clothing and shoes, fireproof and not, was either laying across furniture where I could see it, or sitting in piles on the floor.

"Soap and layers?" Tomio looked like a sleep deprived hedgehog, his hair standing up in spikes and his eyes glazed, but he insisted that he was also too over-stimulated to sleep. He hadn't stopped pacing around the piles of my stuff since we'd spoken to Ryan, who had been awake when we entered his bedroom—and annoyingly perky. Tomio was silent as I'd caught Ryan up, and now seemed uncharacteristically mopey. I only now clocked how little he had looked me in the eye since he'd come into my room.

I threw the bunch of socks I'd been holding into the duffle bag. "Is something bothering you?"

He stopped pacing and looked up, eyes wide, thumbnail between his teeth. "No. Why do you ask?"

"No reason. Only, you're chewing your thumb down to a bloody stub."

He dropped his hand. "Nothing's wrong... exactly."

I crossed the room to stand in front of him, my gut twanging. I thought I knew what might be on Tomio's mind. "Is it Ryan? It really annoys me, the way he discounts you sometimes."

Tomio blew out a big breath and his shoulders dropped. He took my face in his hands. "No, it's not Ryan, you beautiful idiot. It's you. I keep hoping you'll realize on your own, but you haven't yet, and now we're leaving tomorrow. So, you've given me no choice but to do something I promised myself I'd never do."

"What?" My stomach gave a new and unpleasant twist. The only other time Tomio had been upset with me was after I'd gone after Dante in Naples without telling him where I was going, and *that* had upset him so much it had made him throw up.

His hold was gentle on the sides of my face. His thumb brushed across my bottom lip, his voice almost a whisper. "Ask you to take me through a Burning."

I backed out of his reach, horrified, shaking my head and hoping I'd misheard him. I repeated in a different tone, a harder one: "What?"

He sighed again, letting his hands drop. "I was afraid you'd react like this."

"How else am I supposed to react when my boyfriend asks me to watch him die?"

Gruesome visions of Tomio's insides turning to ash, the heart in his chest stilling forever, and those beautiful dark eyes going dull and cloudy made my mouth go dry and my throat close up. I grabbed the glass of water sitting on the corner of my desk and downed it.

Tomio rubbed his face and sent me his classic look of long-suffering; the look that said, *I'm going to be patient, but you're not making it easy.* "That's not going to happen, don't catastrophize."

"Have you forgotten that I nearly died from Burning? Nicodemo *did* die, and Ryan *would* have died if I hadn't found him in time? No, Tomio. The answer is: no freaking way."

"That was then. This is now. Please, just hear me out without losing your mind or getting all emotional?"

I set the glass down harder than I'd intended and glared, heat flickering along the stems of my eyes. "How exactly am I supposed to *not* be emotional about this insane request?"

He put out a palm. "Okay, that was a bad way to start. But please, just hear me out."

I pinched my lips together and shook my head, but Tomio forged on, talking fast, like he was afraid I'd go deaf in about fifteen seconds and he had to get it all out before then.

"I won't die. Not only did the formula that Ryan got from Nero work, you said that by using evanescent vision you could see at what point his insides had been volcanized, but his heart hadn't yet stopped. You'll know exactly when to give me water. I am sorry that you almost died, and I am very sorry that Nicodemo did die, but that was then. This is now. We know what we're doing, and if you don't do this for me, then you're letting me walk into a gunfight armed with only a knife.. A gunfight I might not come back from."

I gasped. "That's a low blow. Shame on you."

"It's not a low blow, Saxony." Tomio's eyes turned pleading. "Can't you see? You and Ryan and Basil have all these amazing abilities. If you see me through a Burning... just imagine. Please. Imagine my skills backed up by the kind of power and ability you yourself now possess."

I hated that Tomio's request was making sense. I opened my mouth to protest further, but only a choked sound made it out. "But—"

Tomio sensed the break in my resolve and went for the jugular. "You know I'm right."

Fear slipped its freezing, skeletal fingers around my throat. I shook my head, my vision blurred. "Don't ask me..."

But even as my determination to prevent Tomio from taking such a risk increased in response to my fear, my heart whispered that he was right. I had seen Ryan through his Burning, I had known what to do and when to give water. Things *were* different now, even if the process wasn't any less appealing. Letting Tomio go into this fight as an Unburned mage was probably more of a risk than a Burning was.

I felt like I couldn't breathe, and stepped back until I felt my bed. Sitting on a lump of clothes, I put a hand over my racing heart. Images of Tomio's agonized eyes battered me, the agony I would have to watch him endure surged into sharp, painful details in my mind. My breath hitched on a sob.

Tomio unleashed a curse and was at my side in a moment, his arms around me. "I'm sorry this is so upsetting. I was hoping you'd think of it on your own."

I squeezed my eyes shut and let my head fall on his shoulder.

"You finally asked her, I see."

Ryan's voice at my door made my eyes fly open. I gaped from him to Tomio. "Ryan knew you were thinking about this? When did you have time to discuss it? He only just woke up!"

Tomio looked guilty, but Ryan scoffed.

"I'm the one who told him, days ago, that you'd never think of it on your own. You'd rather send Tomio into this fight unprepared than watch him Burn because you're too sensitive. Do you forget how hard I had to work to get you to help me?"

"That's uncalled for," Tomio said to Ryan, his voice calm.

Ryan leaned against the doorjamb, relaxed, holding a glass of water. He looked almost bored. It annoyed me how fast he'd bounced back from his traveling experience. Why did he appear to be so much more resilient that I was?

"It's your fatal flaw, Cagney. You're the second-most powerful mage I know, but you let your emotions control you. Your fear. Everyone knows it. Just ask Basil."

I grit my teeth. "At least I don't manipulate and lie to get what I want."

Ryan's eyes flared. "If you were a little less fragile, then you wouldn't have to be manipulated or lied to."

My jaw dropped as I gave a squeak of indignation.

"I'm not manipulating her," Tomio protested, his arm tightening around me. "I'm asking her outright."

I brushed Tomio's arm off and stood, moving away from the bed so I could see both men easily. Cocking my hands on my hips, I seethed, "I. Am not. *Fragile.*"

"I know," said Tomio.

"Yes, you are," said Ryan at the same time, clearly enjoying himself.

"Prick," I spat.

"Invertebrate," he spat back.

"Asshat!" I half-screeched, enraged but also knowing Ryan was inflaming my temper on purpose, and I was letting him. Truth be told, I needed the outlet, so I gave myself a length of leash I rarely allowed.

I sucked in a breath. "You walk around this place like you own it, you always have, ever since the first day when we lined up for the fair. You stand around with your arms crossed, judging everyone, looking at everyone like they're beneath you—" I mimicked Ryan's snottiest snarl, the one where he cocked both the side of his lip and the eyebrow above it at the same time, and exaggerated it as much as I could.

Ryan didn't miss a beat. "That's because they are."

"Don't you even care that no one likes you?"

"Not really, no."

"Don't you care that Gage got all the likeable characteristics of your mother, while you got stuck with all the genetic refuse and tragic flaws of your father?"

"My father has his faults," Ryan said, patiently, "but my mother, lovable as she is, is also flawed. She has zero talent for teaching simple skills like how to properly load a dishwasher. There's bound to be screaming."

"The screaming is fully justified, I'm sure. The poor woman can't bear how obtuse you are. I'd like to get through one day, a single bloody day, without having to look at your replicant face. It's like you stole it off someone nice and then corroded it over time, with the poison of your soul."

Ryan gave a loud and obnoxious laugh but with genuine mirth, I noticed with satisfaction.

Tomio looked mystified. "How did we get here? I'm so confused. You two are usually so civilized. Well, Saxony is. To be frank my expectations of Ryan are pretty low. But still..."

It was like he hadn't spoken at all.

"At least I don't suck up to the headmaster," said Ryan, throwing his weight into one hip in an effeminate gesture that I assumed was supposed to mimic me. "In plain view of everyone. I mean, *come on*, it's so obvious. Have a little self-respect."

I squeezed my eyes shut and wrinkled up my nose like I was facing into a strong wind. Waving a hand in front of my nose, I blinked at Tomio. "What was *that*? Weird. A huge blast of hot air just hit me in the face, and man, did it *reek*. I mean, it was *rancid*."

Tomio ran a hand down his face and groaned. "Will you two quit it! What are you? Twelve? This is serious and we are running out of time."

That shut us up for a few long seconds. The fear was back, lacing itself into my muscle fibers like an invasive species.

Ryan's look turned smug, and oh how I hated that look. It was the look that said they were right and I was wrong. They had me backed into a corner. As he opened his mouth to make some final damning statement or hurl some last insult. I resisted the urge to clamp both hands down on my ears and scream, like a kid having a tantrum. Whatever he was about to say, I wouldn't like it.

And it was even worse than I expected.

His lip lifted in a snarl of contempt. "Even if you don't agree to it, Cagney, he's only asking you as a courtesy. We don't need you. I've got evanescent vision now, too. So, if you won't do it, then I will. Be there, or not. The choice is yours."

With those final stinging words, Ryan disappeared from my doorway, leaving me gaping at Tomio.

Tomio looked like he hoped a hole would open in the floor beneath his feet. "I wish he hadn't said that."

My heart ached with the pain of betrayal. "But it's true? You already agreed to do this without me? You and Ryan? You colluded behind my back?"

He stood, then shuffled awkwardly, appearing sheepish

but speaking without repentance. "I can't face what's out there as I am, Saxony. Why go into battle on a burro when I can go on a warhorse? I'm sorry it's happening like this, but it is going to happen. Tonight. Starting now." His features softened. "And, I really want you to be there."

IT TOOK another half hour of pouting and dithering before I tracked the men down in the fire-gym. They were near the rear wall, bent over a table with pen and paper discussing something. When I strode over, glowering, they looked up. Tomio's gaze skimmed my face and body language. I was in such a tangle of emotions that I didn't know what he was seeing, but whatever it was, it made them stop talking to watch me approach. Their faces mirrored a hopeful caution.

I stopped in front of them and forced my fidgety hands to my sides. "I hate the way this all came about, but I am sorry that I didn't think of it myself. I honestly didn't, because putting my loved ones in danger doesn't come naturally to me. Not like it clearly does to you, Ryan." I glared at him. "But, since it's going to happen with or without me, I'd rather be here."

Tomio swept me into a hug, whispering thank you into my neck.

I pulled back and took his cheeks in my hands. "If you die from this, I'll kill you."

His eyes crinkled. "I'm not going to die, but duly noted."

"Touching. Can we focus please?" Ryan gestured to the paper. A calculator sat beside the page and a couple of formulas had been scrawled down in long-form. The number 17.75 was written in a large size and circled vigorously.

I moved closer to look at the formulas. "What's seventeen point seven five?"

"The number of hours Tomio has to Burn for," Ryan explained. "The formula in the diary wasn't complete, but what was there was authentic. Nero gave me the rest. It's a basic calculation taking Tomio's blood volume in liters, divided by the golden ratio without a decimal, that spits out a target temperature in Fahrenheit. This gives us our first metric. Tomio's fever has to hit three-hundred-thirty-five. This number is then multiplied by the golden ratio with a decimal placed two points in, which gives us the next metric, which is time. Tomio's personal Burning time is seventeen hours and forty-five minutes."

My head spun. "I didn't get all that, but I'll have to trust you did the math right." I'd rely on my vision to tell me whether Tomio was in danger or not, not math.

"We've done the calculation five times, it always comes out the same," added Tomio.

"Seems like a long time, though. Doesn't it?" I peered at the mess of calculations on the page, feeling uneasy. "Nicodemo died after nine hours, I think it was."

"Yeah, but we don't know if that was nine hours from the last drink he had, or nine hours from when Dante locked him in the cell. There're too many unknowns to bother considering Nicodemo's case. It has to be from the point of Tomio's last drink." Ryan circled the number once more for good measure. "This is when Tomio will need water, either three-hundred-thirty-five degrees fever, or seventeen and three-quarters of an hour, whichever comes first. In a perfect Burning, they happen at the same time."

"Starting from when?"

Tomio fished his phone out of his pocket and showed me the timer he had running. "I had tea with the sushi, so less than eleven hours to go." He set his cell on the counter. "I won't have any fever for another two and half or three hours, going from past experience. Long enough to watch one of the *Lord of the Rings* movies."

I noticed the hafnium cuffs sitting on the table. "I'm not going to ask if Basil gave you permission to take those."

"That's probably best," replied Ryan with a saccharine smile.

I wondered if Basil would in fact stop us if he knew what we were up to. Given what was at stake and the fact that Tomio had two Burned magi monitoring him, there was a chance he might not protest, even though he'd been adamantly against students attempting Burnings when I started my first year. Still, in this case it was better to ask forgiveness than permission. Tomio only had one shot at it before we got on a plane for the Arctic. That thought led me to another, which made me feel slightly better about the situation: if Tomio and Ryan had genuinely thought I would rat them out to the headmaster, they would never have told me anything until it was all over. Which meant that they knew me pretty well, or at least Tomio did. Ryan had made it clear he didn't care one way or the other if I was involved. I didn't doubt for a second that Ryan had pressed Tomio not to let me in on their plan.

"I don't think we'll need them, though." Tomio gestured to the cuffs. "The two of you are more than enough to keep me away from water, plus I've got a high pain threshold. All those years of getting my ass kicked were good for something."

Tomio had had his ass kicked far less than he'd kicked asses himself, but I didn't doubt his tolerance for pain. I'd thrown him across a dojo several times, only to watch him bounce back like he was made of rubber.

"Don't underestimate the agony coming your way," Ryan told Tomio as he went to a storage unit in the wall that contained gymnastic mats.

"Yeah, it's too bad there isn't an anesthetic you can take." I matched my tone to their casual ones, but the thought of watching Tomio writhe in agony made my stomach do slow, nauseating summersaults. This was going to suck.

As the boys set out some mats for us to lounge on, I fetched my laptop from my room and queued up the movie to pass the initial stages.

Tomio and I lay sprawled on a gymnastics mat on our stomachs, my right thigh pressed against his left. I wanted to feel his body temperature as it rose. Ryan had stolen a pillow from a nearby lounge and lay on his back with it under his head. I couldn't focus on the film to save my life. Tomio's body temperature began to climb toward the end, and I knew the pain was setting in when he put his face down into his forearms. I put a hand on his back, feeling his fever coming through his t-shirt. I wouldn't ask him if he was okay. There was nothing I could do about it if he wasn't, and I already knew he wasn't.

"Eight more hours buddy," Ryan said when Tomio lowered his head to the floor. "Just eight hours and you'll never have to feel that kind of pain again."

Tomio rolled onto his back on the mat and nodded. "Yeah." His voice came out dry and raspy. He looked at me and, incredibly, found a smile as he put a knuckle against my cheek. "Don't look so worried, I know what's coming. I'm concentrating on what will come after, and that is helping."

We played the second *LOTR* movie, but again I couldn't focus. Normally I enjoyed a fantasy escape, but all of my attention was on the Burning man at my side.

We were prepared to handcuff him when the first cracks

in Tomio's resolve revealed themselves, but he never whined or begged. Moving made the pain worse, I remembered this from when I threw fireballs at the prison door in the basement of Dante's villa. So Tomio remained mostly still, sometimes on his stomach, at times rolling slowly onto his back.

We abandoned the last *LOTR* movie half way through, when the smell of burning flesh began to taint the air. The sun was well into the sky when Tomio looked at me with glowing eyes and opened his mouth to speak. Only smoke issued from between his lips, and a soft moan of pain. His eyes, always so keen and perceptive, were glassy and bloodshot.

My own eyes misted up and before I could gather any rationality into my thoughts, I got up and headed for the door, unable to bear the sight and the smell. I used the washroom near the lobby, splashed cold water into my face, had a good cry and then headed back.

I did this twice more over the next several hours, while the smell of smoke and charred meat grew worse. Tomio's fingertips began to smoke. I used evanescent vision on him and wished I hadn't. The line of fire creeping through his insides and leaving charred ruin in its wake was moving far too slowly. I left the fire-gym for a third time, but when I returned to the double doors, I found them locked. Frowning, I knocked. "Ryan? It's me."

"I know," he said from somewhere on the other side. "Go away."

My gut cramped with worry and I felt like I had to go the bathroom again, though I'd just gone. "What do you mean? Why?"

Ryan's voice came closer to the door. "Nothing has happened. You're driving me crazy with all the histrionics; back and forth and huffing and puffing. Your eyes are all red and you can't stop sniffing. You're seconds from falling to pieces. I can't keep an eye on Tomio and you, too. It's better if you let me take it from here on my own."

I opened my mouth to give him a piece of my mind when his dig about fragility echoed from the halls of recent memory. Turning my back to the doors, tears dripping down my cheeks, I sank to the floor and allowed myself another silent cry. Maybe I was fragile at times, but so what? When it came to the people that I loved, maybe a little fragility wasn't a bad thing. Maybe suffering alongside those who were in pain, whether it was physical, mental or emotional, was actually a little more of what the world needed.

Exhaustion crept into my bones as I wiped the tears away from my face and began to feel a little better, now that I wasn't watching Tomio roast himself into Burned status. Maybe it was better to let Ryan help Tomio creep up to the finish line. But just to be sure, when the deadline was closer, I would break down the doors if Ryan didn't let me in. There was no way I would miss giving Tomio the life-saving, Burn-halting water, the first drink of his Burned existence.

I lay down on my side and curled up in front of the doors with my back against the metal.

THE SOLID SUPPORT moving away from my back woke me as I rolled over the threshold into the fire-gym. I suppressed a groan at the stiffness in my shoulder and neck. I felt like I'd been lying on the floor for days.

I blinked as my eyes adjusted to the sunlight flooding into the lobby from the gym's skylights. Tomio and Ryan stood there looking down at me.

I rubbed my eyes, certain I was dreaming, then blinked

up at them again, wondering if I was hallucinating. How could Tomio be on his feet already? And what time was it? I didn't have my phone and there was no clock in the gym to reference, but all that daylight suggested high-noon.

"Tomio?" I croaked.

He held a hand down to help me up. Feeling his palm against mine yanked me the rest of the way into lucidity. He pulled me to my feet as I drank him in from head to foot.

"You're...up!"

Ryan patted my shoulder and went around me, his footsteps receding.

I took Tomio's face in my hands. He looked tired and moved a little stiffly, but seemed otherwise fine. "I can't believe it. I slept through the hardest part."

Tomio smiled, his eyes flickering momentarily like the eyes of a Jack-o-lantern on a dark night. He took me into his arms. "It's over now. We did it."

Tomio's selflessness made me feel ashamed. I shouldn't have allowed my fretting to get so obvious. It's no wonder Ryan locked me out. Tomio had enough on his mind without worrying about how I was coping, while he snuck right up to the edge of death.

"How do you feel?" I hugged him but didn't squeeze too hard, remembering how tender my innards had been for a day after my Burning. I was amazed Tomio was standing already. Even Ryan had been unable to stand for a day after his Burning.

"I'm sore, but otherwise I feel absolutely fine." He buried his face in my hair and inhaled. "Better than fine."

6

INSIDE THE ARCTIC CIRCLE

I gripped the armrests of my seat as our eleven passenger Bombardier Challenger skimmed off the runway at the London City Airport. The small transcontinental jet—piloted by a former non-supernatural colleague of the agency—was set to take us on a direct overnight flight to Yellowknife. It required the maximum endurance of this aircraft, but meant the agency wouldn't have to rent the larger Gulfstream G450, the next step up and too big for our needs. From Yellowknife, we would fly a much smaller Embraer Phenom 300 to the landing strip at Mahoney Lake. We'd been warned that the strip had only ever been used by small bush-planes, and to expect a bumpy landing. We'd given Ms. Shepherd our passports and she would deal with all the red-tape of international travel so we didn't have to; a plus of being part of the intelligence community.

Tomio sat in the single seat facing me, gazing sleepily out the window as the city dropped away into oblivion. Basil had scheduled our flight to Yellowknife for 9 p.m., which meant leaving the academy around supper time, so I'd taken over packing Tomio's duffle bag while he guzzled water and lay on his bed directing me.

I was thankful the plane's seats were comfortable and reclined almost all the way. The moment the plane hit cruising altitude, Tomio adjusted his seat back, propped a pillow under his head and closed his eyes. Ryan sat across the narrow aisle from me, while Mehmet, Ms. Shepherd and Basil occupied a table with four seats nearest the cockpit.

Still stiff from napping in the lobby of the fire-gym, I rolled my neck and stretched my arms overhead. Ryan looked up briefly from his cell phone to glance at Tomio, who let out a quiet snore.

"Too bad we can't teach him alchemy on the plane," I whispered. I was still so relieved Tomio had survived his Burning that I felt giddy when I looked at him.

Ryan snorted. "No flight crew worth their salt would let most of those chemicals on the plane, let alone allow us to play with them."

"Plus, it's probably best for him if he just sleeps." I sat back against the cushy seat, finding the button to recline it. Just watching Tomio sleep was making me want to sleep.

Basil had told us on the road to the airport that he had Burned magi meeting us in Yellowknife, though there wasn't time to explain much more than that, let alone discuss a plan. The headmaster and Ms. Shepherd had assured us that a small team of competent naturals had been recruited and were working on a strategy. Since the physicist had narrowed our target to a point on the map that was less than a quarter-mile wide, the most important thing was to get to this location before Nero did. The last known sighting of Nero had been at the Verona airport where he'd boarded his own private flight to Yellowknife. He was ahead of us, and that had everyone on edge, but Nero's flight had been scheduled to make a stop in Montreal—whether to refuel or for passengers, we didn't know—but it was the reason Basil had booked the Challenger. It was the smallest, fastest aircraft which could manage the distance without having to stop for fuel.

How Nero planned to get from Yellowknife to the incredibly remote epicenter of supernatural effluent wasn't as clear. How *we* were going to get there from the bush-plane landing strip hadn't been made clear either, and I figured that was part of what Basil, Ms. Shepherd and Mehmet were whispering about up at the front.

The headmaster had given us a very important directive just before we'd taken off. All three of us were to get as much sleep as possible while the plane was in the air, because once we landed, there wouldn't be time for rest. Basil had been so distracted that he hadn't even noticed Tomio's lower-than-usual energy level. Tomio had told me that he'd tell Basil that he'd joined the ranks of the Burned, but when I'd asked him when he planned to do that, he'd only shrugged and said, "When the time is right."

I had argued that the sooner the better. Basil and Ms. Shepherd were making plans, wouldn't it be best to let them know that they could factor another Burned mage among our assets? Even if he hadn't had much time to exercise his new-found depth and powers. But Tomio had whispered back, as we'd thrown our duffle bags in the back of the black cab parked outside the academy, that at least it would be an addition of fire-power and not a subtraction, and to leave it to him. It was his secret to tell, not mine.

Fair enough.

We had additional questions for the headmaster, but he'd told us that we did have a plan to set in motion when our boots hit the ground on the other side of the Atlantic.

Until then, there were some details that needed ironing out and we'd be briefed once we'd arrived.

So, with the hushed murmurs of the headmaster and his aides drifting to my ears from the front of the plane, I closed my eyes and let the white noise of the Challenger lull me into something that loosely resembled sleep.

Four trips to the bathroom, and two meals consisting of cold sandwiches and juice later, we began our descent. Our pilot's voice came over the intercom about the local time being four am and the temperature being a balmy thirteen degrees in Yellowknife. The disorienting Arctic sun was so bright it almost hurt when I lifted the shade over my window, although the ground was still in twilight. Gaping down at the terrain of my home country, my heart cramped briefly with a strange combination of excitement and dread. This whole thing hadn't felt real until I saw the small city banking into view.

I looked at Tomio to see how he was feeling, and gaped again. His cheeks were flushed with pink, his eyes were clear, the whites very white. "You look...amazing."

He ran a hand through his thick, black hair. "Do I? Thanks. I slept hard." He turned down the volume of his voice. "Kind of can't believe I didn't do the Burning thing sooner. Why didn't you tell me it felt like having your batteries super-charged?"

I gave him a bemused smile, casting my mind back to the bedroom in Raf's villa where I had woken up and explored how it felt to be Burned. "I've been so prejudiced against the process that I put the reality of how it feels out of my mind. I mean, something that could kill people isn't something that should be glorified. You know what I mean?"

Tomio propped his elbows on his knees, letting his

hands dangle between them. I did the same, which brought our faces close enough together that we could talk without being overheard.

He whispered, "You sound like Basil. I get it. A huge number of mages have died in the past. But, with Ryan's formula, and with evanescent vision, no mage ever has to die again. Nor do they have to live with the daily pain of carrying a fire around in Unburned insides."

The plane tilted as we headed for the runway.

I took Tomio's hands. "Let's first make sure there are magi left to Burn."

Tomio's eyes flared and he squeezed my hand in answer.

Yellowknife had a small and quiet airport, the only part of which I saw was the lady's bathroom, a coffee kiosk, and a statue of a polar bear chasing a seal. After we were ushered off the plane we were given fifteen minutes to be present on the tarmac and ready to board the Embraer Phenom.

As Tomio, Ryan and I approached the Embraer, our eyes were captured by two burly men arrowing for the small plane from the terminal. They were dressed in black cargo pants and vests, wearing black ball-caps, and carrying black duffle bags.

"Who're the special ops?" Tomio murmured, as these men stopped in front of Ms. Shepherd to exchange a few words.

I appraised the strangers, thinking these must be the Burned magi Basil had mentioned would be joining us. The men looked to be Basil's age, and moved with confidence. But where Basil was refined and well-dressed, with nicely coiffed hair and a posh British accent, these men were tanned, scarred, and craggy-faced in a pleasant way. I had just managed to tear my eyes from the men, wondering what Ryan and Tomio thought of these strangers, when a third person approached. She was taller than both the men, and reedy, but with super short hair and cool gray eyes she was just as intimidating.

"How many mages does it take to stop one super-charged psychopath?" Ryan said, under his breath.

I shot him a glare, a rebuke coming to my lips, when I registered the obvious pleasure on his face. He was pleased to see our ranks bolstered by these additions. I'd thought he was being sarcastic and macho.

All three of our new teammates headed toward us, followed by Ms. Shepherd, whose expression was inscrutable.

"I'm Greg," said the one in front, holding out a hand to Tomio.

Thus began a flurry of handshakes and quick first-name-only introductions. The men were Gregory and Frederick, the woman was Shereen. Their expressions were unguarded and unassuming. If they were concerned about going into this mission with three teenagers, none of them showed it, and I appreciated that. They were professionals, that meant keeping their emotions under wraps. It inspired me to do the same.

My resolution lasted approximately half a second, until a blast of heat flared up my arm as I shook hands with Shereen. I couldn't stop the huge grin that split my face.

She chuckled at my clear acknowledgment of our bond and grinned back, highlighting an arrowhead shaped scar at the outer corner of her right eye. She held my hand in a firm grip and shook, letting heat swirl and flare back and forth between us. "Nice to meet you, Saxony."

"Pleasure is all mine, Shereen." I hoped she could see I meant it. Having grown up with two brothers, it didn't bother me to be the only female mage in the group, but damned if it didn't feel great to have another woman join the team besides Ms. Shepherd and her stress-rash. I briefly conjured the faces of Targa and Georjie, and felt momentarily consumed by a strange combination of longing and gratitude. I missed them, and it would have been amazing to have them here at my side. But flying made Targa feel ill, and Georjie—as amazing as her abilities were—wasn't fireproof, neither of them were. No, they were better off safely away from Nero, and out of the kind of danger that fire presented to all living beings who were not magi.

The three new soldiers ducked into the plane's open door, and we followed. Ryan ahead of me and Tomio behind.

I felt Tomio's breath against my ear as we climbed the stairs and he leaned in close to whisper, "Feel anything?"

I nodded and smiled at him over my shoulder. "Yep. Shereen. You?"

Tomio shook his head, puzzled. This was anomalous. There were only two idles left, and if I had a bond with Shereen, then Tomio should have a bond with Fred and Greg. Unless they had some way of keeping a bond from flaring, but as far as I knew, that wasn't possible.

Basil was already on board, and clearly knew our additions. He greeted them like they were old acquaintances, if not quite friends. I wondered if they were Arcturus assets or if they'd come from some other agency.

As we settled into the bucket seats in the cabin of the Phenom for the over two-hour flight to Mahoney Lake, my heart expanded with an eager hopefulness I hadn't allowed myself to feel since Naples. Witnessing the way Nero had so easily kept Ryan at bay as they danced across the molten heart of Vesuvius gutted me whenever I replayed it. But the addition of mature magi sewed up that feeling with a strong thread of hope.

The little plane was packed with fire-power. Unless Nero had recruited magi to his side (and what magi would want to aid a madman who was bent on snuffing the fires of one's own people?) this fight would be seven Burned against one. Surely the odds were for us. The unknowns were: first, would we arrive at the next location before him, and second, if we did, was our collective fire-power enough to stop his unquantifiable abilities?

I THOUGHT I was prepared for the wilderness. I was wrong. Watching hundreds of thousands of miles of coniferous forest, then tundra, whiz by beneath the Phenom made me feel tiny and insignificant and awed. There were lakes as far as the eye could see, in every direction. I expected to see life forms and plenty of them, perhaps a herd of caribou, a wolf or two, maybe bear or a musk-ox, but there was nothing.

Stepping off the plane on the narrow strip of packed earth beside Mahoney Lake made my eyes water and my mind stagger, as I strained to take in the seemingly endless land- and lake-scape. The sky overhead was vast and clear. And the smell of the air was indescribably pure, so clean and fresh it tasted sweet when I sucked it in through open lips, like it was laced with honeysuckle.

"So, this is where the world's oxygen comes to vacation," Tomio said, as he came to stand beside me, clearly as in awe of the vast wilds as I was.

Inhaling deeply made me feel deliciously dizzy, and even my fire seemed to flutter with pleasure as I soaked in the pristine environment.

Apart from a few white buildings with red steel roofs, the camp at Mahoney Lake consisted of the old airstrip, a hangar, and a lakeside lodge. Where the logs that formed it had come from was beyond me, there wasn't a tree in sight, only a few scrubby bushes, bent and gnarled but waving green leaves. A narrow, rutted road arrowed its way through the camp and disappeared around the edge of the massive lake.

I was utterly enchanted by our new environment... until the mosquitoes found us. They were enough to drive even the most hardened of us indoors. The only other sign of life was a middle-aged man with a kerchief hugging his head, Bruce Springsteen style. He emerged from the hangar as our party disembarked using the set of narrow, in-built steps. He introduced himself as Arnold Crupps and told us the lodge was open. There were sandwiches in the fridge, and we were welcome to claim any room we liked. We were the only party currently occupying Mahoney Lake, which was a fishing lodge in its heyday, but had been closed for repairs and upgrades.

"Dump your stuff in a room and meet us in the hangar in twenty minutes," Ms. Shepherd said to the magi gathered on the tarmac. "Get some food into you and wear your fireproofs."

Carrying our duffle bags, Tomio and I followed the rest into the main lodge. We passed a couple of fire pits and a shed with an old riding lawn mower parked beside it. Aluminum boats lay upside down along the nearby beach, their silver bellies reflecting sunlight. A wind chime tinkled from beside the lodge's door, and wooden masks carved into animal heads had been nailed over the doorways and windows.

Passing through a huge kitchen with an industrial dishwasher and three side-by-side gas stoves, we entered a large open space with huge windows overlooking the lake. To the left was a living room with furniture that looked vintage sixties. A fireplace and shelves crammed with cracked and faded books kept company with stuffed fish trophies and the head of an enormous caribou. To the right were long tables with benches for communal eating. Red and white checked plastic table covers were pinned down with aluminum clips. Beer bottles containing artificial crocuses gathered dust in the center of each table.

"Clearly decorated by a man," said Shereen, pausing briefly to view the dining area before disappearing through another doorway.

Down this hall were several bedrooms containing single beds with bare mattresses. I chose a room between Tomio and Ryan. Dropping my duffle on the floor, I checked the wardrobe and found clean bedding in plastic wrap , as well as two flattened pillows. I'd worry about making the bed later.

Rooting through my bag, I pulled out a black fireproof shirt with long sleeves. I tossed it on the bed and went back for a fireproof sports bra and slim fitting pants. My fireproof boots were new from the academy's shop, a gift from Basil. They were heavy, with thick and chunky soles and zippers running from the instep to mid-calf. I'd never worn such sturdy footwear, even during the games, but Basil had said the terrain was rough. What he hadn't needed to say was that these boots could withstand twenty-five-hundred degrees worth of heat before the soles softened and the neoprene began to smolder. They were called Fire Stalkers and had been designed by a genius mage from Norway. They were worth a small fortune. Basil had given Tomio, Ryan and me a pair without even flinching, which said as much about what we were up against as it did about his generosity.

On top of this all-black getup, I pulled a thin fireproof motorcycle-style jacket, and added a black fireproof toque over my low braid. A glance in the mirror confirmed it, I looked like a bank robber.

I met Tomio and Ryan in the kitchen, also dressed like a couple of thugs, stuffing their faces with tuna and egg salad sandwiches. The kitchen smelled like farts and fish, but we hadn't eaten since before landing in Yellowknife, and I was starving—and grateful it wasn't just Wonder bread and peanut butter.

Gregory, Frederick and Shereen emerged as we were washing down the last of our sandwiches with over-sweetened iced tea. They looked a lot more badass than we did in their fireproof kit. They looked like experienced agents, and we... well, we still looked like senior high school kids. I half expected one of them to tease us, but no one said anything as they started in on the remaining sandwiches.

Ryan, Tomio and I left by the back door and headed across the yard for the hangar. Immediately we were plagued by clouds of mosquitoes.

"Damn," Ryan muttered, slapping at his neck, "mozzies are attracted to black."

"Put fire under your skin," Tomio said, waving a hand in front of his face and blowing the insects away from his lips. "They can't handle much more than forty-five degrees."

As we clomped over the rough dirt with our heavy boots, I drew heat from my core and sent it oozing under my skin like a layer of fat. I watched in mild amazement as the mozzies searching me for blood took off. They didn't go far, still whining around and hoping for a meal, but they didn't land anymore. "Clever lad. How did you come up with that genius idea?"

"I can't stop fiddling with my fire now that I'm Burned," Tomio said with a smile as we approached the hangar.

Voices issued from within.

We rounded the steel-clad wall to pass through the hangar's enormous doorway. The smell of grease, oil and dirty metal was strong in the air. Two small bush-planes sat side-by-side with their noses angled for the exit. Across from them were three mystery vehicles covered with tarps. They weren't tall or big enough to be SUVs or trucks. Other than the one road going through this place (which I'd overheard led to a dump) the only way in and out of this camp was by plane.

Arnold, Basil, Mehmet and Ms. Shepherd stood around a large square worktable. Basil wore fireproof gear and had replaced his glasses with custom-made heat-resistant contact lenses. From the way the rest of them were dressed, they were not planning on coming along. And why would they? They'd only be a liability out there. I had been curious about Arnold, as he hadn't shaken anyone's hand when he introduced himself, but guessed from his grease-stained hands, and dirty plaid jacket and jeans that he wasn't a mage either, he looked like a mechanic.

Fred, Greg and Shereen entered the hangar and we gathered around the worktable. Spread out on the table's surface were a couple of maps and a few devices I hadn't yet identified.

"Right." Ms. Shepherd bent over to smooth the wrinkles out of the map sitting on top. She pointed to various blobs. "Here is Mahoney Lake. Here is the camp. Your target is the epicenter, or Nero, whichever comes first. The epicenter is here." She swept her finger in a straight line toward the mountain range in the west, stopping where an 'x' had been scrawled on the map in black marker. "We've taken some aerial photos by drone. The terrain is rough. You'll probably have to stop here"—she pointed at a ridge just east of the epicenter—"and hike in the rest of the way."

About a million questions burst into life to flap wildly around in my brain like panicked bats, but no one else had asked any questions, so I held my tongue and waited, trusting that they'd worked out the details as best they could.

While Ms. Shepherd talked about splitting us into three teams, Arnold crossed to the covered lumps and pulled the tarps away. What lay beneath were amphibious vehicles. Two of them were identical except in color: one red, the other black. They were little more than boat-shaped bowls balanced on eight tires, two-seaters with enough room in the open box for a couple of people and some gear. The third vehicle was like a small tank, complete with a steel track and a bumper running around its perimeter, marking its waterline should it be required to float. This one also had two bucket seats and the same kind of open box in the back. None of the vehicles had roofs or windows.

"Greg and Fred will drive the Argo Auroras," Arnold explained as we moved closer to inspect our modes of transport. "And Shereen will operate the Tinger Track. You kids..." he paused and held out a hand. "Sorry, no offense, but you look so bloody young."

"None taken," I said.

Ms. Shepherd actually clapped her hands twice. "Nice of you to consider their feelings, but a certain mage won't be so considerate. Can we move this along, please?"

Arnold complied. "Like I was saying, you kids will each ride with a driver. Basil, it's probably best to ride with

Shereen on the Tinger Track. It will handle the terrain slightly better than the Auroras."

Arnold went over the basic capabilities of the vehicles. The Auroras were fast but the Tinger Track topped out at only twenty-two miles per hour. The Auroras were to circle the ridge from the north then park behind it, and the parties would continue to the epicenter on foot. The Tinger Track would arrive after the Auroras, so the plan was for Shereen, Basil and me to make the approach through a narrow strip of valley that Ms. Shepherd described as full of "baby heads"—small, round rocks that would make the going difficult. We would be connected by wireless radio earpieces but if fire started flying, we were to take them off, as the technology didn't respond well to excessive heat.

Mehmet looked up from his laptop to add a vital piece of information: "I've got a drone with a heat-camera ready to go. I would have circled the area once already but Ms. Shepherd said it was too noisy, didn't want to alert Nero to our presence."

"The moment he hears anything outside of mosquitoes and ducks, he'll know we're on to him, so keep our presence under wraps until the last possible moment," she said. "I'd send you in by helicopter, which would be faster, but the region is too windy for that, and there's nowhere safe to land. Mehmet will pilot the drone out just ahead of you."

"Do we know for sure that Nero is alone?" Greg asked, tapping a finger on his whiskered chin.

Ms. Shepherd's lips pressed into a line. "We have no evidence that he has help, but we can't guarantee that he doesn't have a partner or partners with him. So be careful out there. As far as we know, Nero is the only mage to have achieved the extraordinary level of power that he's gained from whatever it is he's doing, but if there are other mages with him, it's best to assume they might have leveled up as well."

"No," Ryan said, speaking confidently. "There won't be any other mages with his abilities. He would never share. If he has help, the best they could be is Burned, but based on what I know of him, he'll be operating alone."

"Why?" Fred pierced Ryan with a calculating, inquisitive look.

"For just the same reason. Nero is closing in on his finish line. No sane mage would agree to work with him, because in the end they'd be helping Nero stomp out their own fires. He's either operating alone, which is most likely, or he's got paid goons, humans, which makes them easy enough to take care of."

"Thanks for that, Ryan," Basil nodded. "Anything else you can think of?"

Ryan shook his head. "Let's get this party on the road."

7

BLAST SITE

I stepped into the back of the Tinger as Shereen got into the driver's seat and Basil got in the passenger's bucket. The engine rumbled and the whole vehicle began to vibrate. She tucked her wireless earpiece into her ear canal, though I wondered if she'd be able to hear much over the Tinger's growl. Basil grabbed his door handle as we lurched forward with a rocking motion.

Behind us, the Auroras roared to life. Half a moment later, Tomio and Greg zoomed past us, out the open hangar doorway, followed by Ryan and Fred. The Auroras made the Tinger seem like a caterpillar next to roadrunners.

Heading straight west for the mountain range in the distance meant passing directly through one corner of the lake. Standing in the back of the Tinger and gripping the roll bar, I watched as Greg piloted the black Aurora straight into the lake. With a spray of mud and a splash that sent ripples across the surface in all directions, the vehicle's nose dipped, bobbed, then righted itself. The eight black wheels spun, the deeply grooved tread working like paddles. The red Aurora followed suit and the amphibious vehicles buzzed across the lake toward the swampy western shore. Mehmet's drone buzzed overhead like an oversized hornet, until it flew too high to see or hear.

The Tinger took to the water like a champ, although I had to hang on to keep from being pitched straight into Basil's lap. By the time the Tinger righted itself in the water and burbled in the right direction, the Auroras were climbing out the other side. By the time we hit the shoreline, they'd disappeared over a crest and were completely gone from sight. The only clue given that they were still motoring their way to the mountains was the occasional burst of birds winging their way skyward, en route to somewhere less offensive.

The Auroras left four lines of flattened marsh grasses and mud pressed into the tundra, so Shereen didn't even need to check our GPS until we hit the foothills. This was where we would head south and the Auroras would continue north, circling the ridge.

Climbing to the Tinger's top speed, we left the clouds of mosquitoes and the cluster of buildings that made up the camp behind.

The morning sun was bright yellow, reflecting in silver puddles as it journeyed above a horizon it never touched all summer. I'd read about the midnight sun of the Arctic and was interested to see what it would be like to have the sun still hanging in the sky at two a.m.

Shereen pointed to something on a low hill to the north. A herd of caribou, visible as small dark dots against the silver-green Arctic grasses. Basil pointed out a large gray hare as it darted from behind a shrub and zigzagged his way wildly left and right before diving out of view. Finally, some wildlife! But after that there was nothing. I wondered if they steered clear of the effluent on instinct. The immensity of the Arctic wilderness swallowed us up, and even the hum and squish of the Tinger seemed greatly diminished in the vacancy of the tundra.

With the Auroras tracks as our constant guide, the Tinger rolled over the marshy, uneven ground, the mountains loomed ever closer.

A sudden movement from Shereen yanked my eyes from the horizon as she touched her earpiece. I had planned to put mine in when we got closer to the ridge, since there was no need to communicate just now, but it appeared someone was talking to her.

She sent a look at Basil and raised her voice over the Tinger. "Did you get that?"

The Tinger rolled its way up a steep slope, but as we crested the hill, Shereen slammed on the brakes. If I had still been standing I would have flipped over the roll bar. Seated behind the headmaster as I was, I slammed up against the back of Basil's seat, my right shoulder jamming painfully as the left side of my neck over stretched.

Basil and Shereen were out of the Tinger and running across the saturated tundra, their feet churning up mud, before I had even figured out why she'd halted. Mehmet's drone hummed somewhere overhead. Rubbing my neck, I stood and took in the scene before me, my heart stomping around in my chest like a startled bull.

The black Aurora lay upside down, its tires spinning. It looked like a dying beetle. The red Aurora had slid to a halt several feet away leaving skid marks lashed through the ground. The wet scars were evidence that there'd been a collision and the vehicle had gone for a wild ride before it had come to rest. The red Aurora's right front light was smashed and the corner of its body panel cracked and dented.

Leaping from the Tinger's box, I landed in three-inch-deep water and almost fell as my boots slid through mud. Righting myself and trying to keep control of my panic, I ran toward the black Aurora, calling Tomio's name.

A head appeared just behind the vehicle. He was mud-covered and looked shaken, but alive. Tomio lifted a hand, dripping brown slag. "Saxony, here!"

Relief rushed through me at the sight of him, making my knees feel weak.

Basil and Shereen had reached the red Aurora and had already lifted the vehicle to its side. It teetered there for a moment before falling onto its tires with a squeak and a bounce. The sound of it splashing down was accompanied by a masculine cry of distress, though I couldn't yet see Ryan or Fred, I didn't think it had sounded like Ryan. I hadn't yet laid eyes on Greg, either.

"What happened?" Rounding the black Aurora, I discovered Greg on his knees in the water, head down. Blood dripped from a cut in his forehead onto the front of his jacket and into his hands. His posture scared me. He was not unconscious, but seemed unaware that he was bleeding. His hands lay palms up and open in his lap in a gesture of surrender, his head drooped like someone in prayer. He was utterly still in what looked like a pose of resignation, or even devastation. Tomio had a hand on Greg's shoulder, his face in a contraction of pain. Combing him again for injuries, I could see nothing obvious. No broken bones, no blood. Other than being dirty and upset, Tomio looked whole and unharmed.

"It happened so fast," Tomio half said, half choked.

Another cry from the red Aurora pulled my gaze there.

Shereen knelt in the swamp, blocking our view of Fred. Ryan was holding a towel to his own forehead and wincing, but I was glad to see him on his feet. He was so covered in mud it would have been impossible to tell them apart save for Fred's bulk. Shereen moved and I could see Fred crouched on his knees and bent at the waist in a version child's pose, his face so close to the water that the tip of his nose was in it. It was from this hardened agent that the hair-raising cries of distress had come.

"We're too late." Greg's voice cracked.

For a second, I was utterly confused, but as Tomio and I made eye contact and his features communicated a horrified understanding, I understood too.

"Snuffed..." I whispered, unable to vocalize more than that.

Tomio nodded. I studied him, my mind reeling, wondering if he'd lost his fire, too. He seemed more concerned about Greg and Fred than himself.

"We were going along just fine," said Tomio, "then all of a sudden, there was a scream. It was horrible. I was still trying to figured out who'd screamed when the Auroras lurched toward one another, like they were attracted by magnets. We hit. They swerved and must have hit a bump or something, because they bounced like they'd hit a trampoline, and then rolled. It was nuts to watch." Tomio's eyes widened further. "Do you know how hard it is to roll these things?"

"Tomio," I croaked, my heart breaking for him. He had to be in shock.

"No, I'm fine. See?" Tomio lifted a hand and in his palm sat a small orange flame; the mud on his hand began to sizzle. "Nothing happened to my fire."

My mind whirled as I stared at his flame, unable to compute. It made no sense.

Shereen came tromping over, expression resolute. "Fred's out. Greg?"

Greg just shook his head without looking up.

"Tomio?" Shereen snapped, grabbing a box from the back of the Aurora and setting it on the vehicle's truncated hood.

"I'm fine," Tomio repeated, his words just as short and clipped as hers were.

We watched her, wide-eyed and wondering what to do next. She unearthed a first-aid kit and pulled out a bottle of clear liquid. Opening a plastic bag containing a bandage, she glanced at her hands to make sure they weren't too dirty, then sent me an inquiring look. "Saxony?"

"I'm fine, too." I felt anything but fine, but if Tomio could say it, then I could say it.

"Ryan still has his, as well."

I could have told her that of course he did, he had a green idle, same as hers and same as mine, but I held my tongue.

"Listen." Shereen whipped the top off the bottle and dabbed the liquid on the bandage before splashing through the water to Greg, where she began to clean his wound. Greg didn't react. Other than his head bobbing with her ministrations, he didn't wince or cry out. He was like a zombie, but based on the few words he'd said, he knew exactly what was happening, what had happened.

"The four of you have to go on without us," she said. "These men can't continue. Take one Aurora and the Tinger, I'll take the other Aurora, which still works, thank God, and get them back to camp. I'll drop them off and come after you as soon as I can."

At the red Aurora, Basil and Ryan helped Fred get into the box. When they got him seated, Basil stayed with him and Ryan came splashing over to us. An impressive goose-egg had already formed over his right eye.

"We're too late." His eyes flashed. "Too late to stop this snuffing, but not too late to stop the next. The bastard is only nineteen kilometers from us. He's there, right this second. We can't waste any time. Come on, Greg. On your feet, buddy."

Ryan's movements as he crossed to Greg to help him up were tightly controlled. He snapped off his words the way Shereen did, all action and intention. His gaze flicked to Tomio as he gave him a once over, head to foot, then back to his face where it gobbled up Tomio's expression and body language, like he was starved to understand. His eyes widened. "You're okay?"

Tomio nodded.

"Thank God for that." Ryan bent to help Tomio get Greg to his feet. The newly bereft mage could hardly put one foot in front of the other. They escorted him to the Aurora where his comrade sat, slouched like a beaten boxer. Basil opened the passenger door and they somehow got the wide man into the front seat.

Grasping my arms, Shereen pulled me to face her. Her gaze was molten. "You go on. You get him," she whispered, squeezing my biceps, her fingers biting into my flesh. "You kill him. You *end* him for what he's done to our friends, for what he intends do to you, and me and them." She jerked her head toward Basil, Tomio and Ryan, who were making their way back to us. Every expression was stiff and grim.

She released me and stormed through the mud to the Aurora with the damaged ex-magi. The way they sat there--slouched and broken, like they'd just had news that their entire family had been killed in a plane crash--was heart-rending.

I looked toward the mountain, my mouth tasting metallic. Nero was on the other side of that ridge, but he wouldn't be for long. Our window would close fast.

The drone was nowhere in sight. It would be circling the ridge, looking for Nero. Now that we were too late, we didn't have to care about alerting him.

I made sure my earpiece was on and jammed it into my ear canal, but Mehmet was silent.

Basil got behind the Tinger's steering wheel as Tomio took the passenger's seat. Ryan climbed into the black Aurora's driver's seat and I got in beside him as the engine rumbled to life. Looking back over my shoulder, I watched the red Aurora make a circle and head up the short embankment where it had tumbled, leaving a muddy gash in the tundra; a small spot of tragedy marring an otherwise perfect and endless terrain of marsh grass and reflected pockets of sun.

"I DON'T UNDERSTAND," the headmaster said, toeing his fireproof boot through the blackened rubble.

None of us did, and none of us had the energy to say me either, as we moved through the crevice in the rock.

We'd found the epicenter. It hadn't been difficult given that we had precise coordinates, but we'd had to slide through a crevice in the mountainside and hike over rough, rocky ground.

It looked like a blast site. The same stones that were mottled gray and covered in moss *outside* the blast site, had turned black *inside* the site. Everything seemed dusted in a coating of sparkly charcoal. The red rubble of the mountain ridge where we'd parked the amphibious vehicles was also turned black, as were all pockets of dirt.

"It's like Vesuvius." I squatted and scooped up a handful of what looked like volcanic sand. Black, and glittery where it caught light, the larger pieces made a clinking sound like glass, when they were tossed against one another, or kicked. We spread out within the blast circle, inspecting it. No blast had actually taken place, not one that we'd heard or that Mehmet had seen by drone, but I couldn't help but assume there had been an explosion of some kind, or in the very least, an event.

The site was cradled in the mountains, partially hidden under an overhanging rock and partially open to the sky. Whatever had happened had caused a ring of black some eighty feet in diameter. Where the black stuff met the unaffected rock and ground, it was jagged with outwardly shooting marks, like a starburst. The charcoal-like substance wasn't a coating, either, or if it was, it ran deep. Digging through the crumbly, now-fragile rock—so brittle it could be broken and crushed by hand—revealed only more layers of it.

"Any ideas, Ryan?" The headmaster had been kneeling, and let a handful of the stuff fall to the earth as he got to his feet.

Tomio and I looked at Ryan, who had so far said nothing.

Ryan tossed a volcanic rock to the side in an irritated gesture, clearly annoyed. "Why does everyone think I know everything?"

He turned his back and toed through the rubble like that was the end of it.

Tomio caught my eye. All I could muster was a shrug.

Basil let out a pent-up breath. "Let's go then. There's

nothing else we can do here. He's obviously gone. How? No idea. But we'll soon know where. We have one more shot at this."

Ryan threw his head back and screamed at the sky, making me jump. Then he stomped away in the direction we'd come, disappearing through the gash in the rock.

"Yes. Precisely," Basil said, his voice even. The headmaster began to follow Ryan, but moving slowly as he studied the blast marks.

I moved to join Tomio when a glint drew my eye to a low overhang, and the rubble beneath it. When light caught the rubble or dust, it did glint, but this had been a different kind of reflection: larger and brighter, like there was something smooth and irregular there. Squatting at the overhang and peering beneath it revealed more broken, blackened stuff. Tomio came to join me as I pawed debris and fragments away from where I'd seen the gleam.

"Find something?"

His question brought Basil back to us. He stood over us with his hands on his knees, watching as I pulled away refuse for a better look. When I'd revealed what had reflected the light, we leaned back in unison, staring.

The headmaster was the first to speak. "Looks like part of a huge broken egg-shell, sort of."

It did look a bit like that, albeit not as even-surfaced nor as neatly oval as an egg. Tomio picked up a shard. It was curved and smooth on the convex side, like it had once been part of a sculpture, or a vase. Basil straightened, bumping his head on the overhang. He took off his toque and shoved it into his pocket, wiping his brow with his inner elbow. "We might have to admit that we'll never know what happened here."

I scooped up a handful of the broken stuff. "Yes, we will. We will know exactly what happened here."

I took off my own toque and began to fill it with shards and debris. When I had filled the hat, I took off my ponytail elastic and put it around the opening, pinching the toque shut and making a perfect little sack.

"Come on." I crawled out from beneath the overhand, took out my phone and snapped a few photos, then headed in the direction of the vehicles. "I need to get to a phone, stat."

PART II

MESOPOTAMIA

8

A REMOTE VIEW

Tomio rested a foot on the open door of Basil's Evoque. His eyes were far away and troubled. I checked the time on my phone, though I'd checked it only two minutes ago. The train from Blackmouth was due in six minutes.

"I hate when things are inconsistent," Tomio said.

"In this case"—I let my head rest against the headrest, knowing he was talking about being an exception to the snuffing rule—"I'm relieved as hell that things are inconsistent."

"Yeah, don't get me wrong. I'm thrilled my fire hasn't been snuffed, too. But it's so weird."

We'd returned to the UK in a reversal of our outbound trip, except that Shereen, Fred and Greg had come with us. Once we'd landed, the ex-magi had been taken to the agency to convalesce, while Shereen had returned to Dover with us.

When we'd returned to the Academy, Tomio had phoned his old sensei and gotten Junko's parents number, the natural-born mage who had passed him his fire when he was nine. Junko's family and Tomio's sensei, as well as Tomio himself, had made an agreement to go their separate ways after the endowment. They had wanted as little as possible to do with the supernatural heat that had tortured Junko and nearly killed her as small child. But learning the color of her idle fire, if possible, had become important. Maybe Tomio *was* green after all, somehow. Maybe we were soul mates and that was precisely why we had no mage bond. Maybe my fire had simply wanted to keep me away from anyone I had lusted after who *wasn't* Tomio, and flared up in protest every time I touched non-Tomio in a romantic way.

Maybe.

But I didn't think so, because a bond went both ways. And it wasn't like there was any danger of lusting after Basil, for example, or Shereen, so I hadn't fully bought my own theory, even if the idea of Tomio being my fated soul mate was romantic. I wished I'd had another crush that hadn't been Gage, if only to have more data to work with. My father liked to say that answers presented themselves after enough data had been gathered, and if one didn't have answers, it was simply because there wasn't enough data.

Well, here was another bit of data: When Tomio had called Junko's parents, her mother answered. They spent some time doing a rapid catchup of the last decade, but the most dramatic change in their lives had been the loss of fire Junko's father had endured. Tomio wasn't permitted to give them information but he sympathized. When asked, Junko's mother couldn't recall Junko producing any colored flames, but Junko's father contradicted her. He had in fact seen Junko's idle when she'd been only two and a half years old, while his wife had worked her usual shift at the hospital.

It had been late afternoon after a spring rain. He had

held Junko's hand as she'd toddled through the green space, following the winding sidewalk through thick sparkling grass. She'd been delighted by the earthworms, the way they squirmed and writhed across the walkway. She had given a squeal, the kind of squeal only a young child discovering something new and exciting about the world could emit. Along with that squeal had come a flash of fire from her fingertips, making the worm she'd squatted to touch writhe away. The worm's obvious pain from the fire snuffed the child's delight instantly, and snapped the idle off the way a lighter can be snapped off, but not before he'd gotten a good view of its startling hue.

Red. Like a candy apple.

Which meant Tomio's fire should have gone out with the third batch, the one that took place while Nero had been in Yangjiang. Liu Xiaotian had lost her fire along with that group. While I hadn't had much time for Liu, I still felt bad for her and wondered how she was coping. She had struck me as someone with a lot of pride in her capabilities.

"Did you ever touch her?" I'd asked Tomio, meaning Liu. He hadn't.

The other mage who'd lost his fire while Nero had been in Yangjiang was Mehmet, who had confirmed that his idle fire had indeed been candy-apple red. No one doubted that the fires were being snuffed by idle any longer, but Tomio was the exception.

"The exception that proves the rule," I mused, as I watched the tracks. We could hear the train now, its whine ushered to us on a wind gusting from the north. We got out of the Land Rover as the train slowed and came to a stop at the platform.

My stomach was full of butterflies, not only for what Georjie would be able to do for us, but just to see her. I had visited her in Blackmouth at Easter, but that visit felt like ancient history. So much had happened to both of us since then.

"What does she look like?" Tomio came around the Evoque to stand beside me, scanning the passengers as they stepped through the train's open doors.

"Brown eyes. Blond. Slender. Six feet tall. So pretty, it's painful."

"Six feet?!" Tomio's eyes nearly fell out of his head.

"She's half-fae." I said this like it explained her height, but I'd never seen any other fae and neither had Tomio, so I elaborated. "Georjie's mom, Liz, isn't particularly tall. She's a hotshot lawyer, and as human as humans get. Up until recently, Georjie thought her dad was some dude named Brent, who wasn't particularly towering himself, so Georjie was always conflicted and confused about her height. I mean, it can be handy, you know. She's got exceptional reach, looks slim in every photo, and her legs go on for days. But kids used to make fun of her in elementary school. They called her Skeletor. Isn't that brutal? Kids can be so mean. Anyway, Liz never bothered to be straight about her paternity, at least, not until recently, when Georjie learned the truth on her own. I hope Liz feels rotten about that, honestly. Turns out, her real dad is as fae as fae can get, and even glamoured her mom into getting pregnant because he himself was bewitched by a..."

Tomio was looking at me like I'd sprouted two more heads, and neither of *them* would be shutting up anytime soon either.

I wrapped up. "It's complicated. There hasn't been time to tell you much about my friends. We've been so focused on bringing Nero down. Sorry."

"But half-fae—" He looked poleaxed, and I enjoyed it. Tomio wasn't easy to impress.

Georjie's pale blond hair grabbed me by the eyeballs. She emerged from the train behind an elderly couple wearing tweed and moving at the pace of tortoises, which they--now that I was looking--shared similarities with. Maybe it was the matching berets. Georjie held up a long arm, towering over them, a grin splitting her face.

"Yep, she looks fae," Tomio observed.

Georjie glowed with good health and was exceptionally beautiful. If she'd wanted to be a supermodel, she could have done so. But she'd been clueless about her beauty until she was sixteen, mostly on account of jealous girls tearing her down to make themselves feel superior. She'd been painfully shy and nerdy, obsessed with photography and books, and complaining about her mother. But now she looked like a woman who knew who she was, a woman who liked herself, a woman who had seen trouble and dealt with it, a woman of substance, and confidence.

Not to mention magic, and scads of it.

Once she'd freed herself from behind the tortoise couple and stepped through the gate into the parking lot, we flew at one another. Tears threatened to spill from my eyes just from the warm, amber smell of her. She lay her cheek on the top of my head as she pulled me close; being five inches over me, that had become the way of our hugs. I wondered how Targa felt when Georjie swallowed her in a hug. Targa was another three inches smaller than me.

Georjie released me and looked at Tomio, extending an elegantly formed hand. "You must be Tomio."

He shook with her and deadpanned, "Great to meet you, Georjayna. Saxony has told me nothing about you."

Georjie's laugh tinkled out as I loaded her luggage into

the back of the Evoque. "Well, sounds like you've been a little busy. I'm boring by comparison, I'm sure."

"Well, I know *that* much isn't true." Tomio gestured that Georjie should take the passenger side. He got into the back as I slammed the trunk closed, then slid behind the wheel.

"Thank you for coming," I breathed at her, exhilarated that she was here. I started the Evoque.

Georjie waved a hand and pulled a pair of sunglasses out of her pocket. They made her look more effortlessly glamorous than should be legal. "Happy to be of service. How far to the academy? I'm dying to see it."

I shot her a grin. "Less than ten minutes."

A stab of fear lanced through me that Georjie wouldn't be able to read anything from the dirt we'd gathered, that it was too damaged to hold memories, and that she'd traveled down from Blackmouth in vain. Well, almost in vain. Seeing her had done miracles for my mood. I swallowed down my fears and put the Land Rover into reverse. We had no data until she tried, and even if it failed, we had to exhaust all options.

Piloting the Evoque out of the train's parking lot, I steered us for Arcturus.

BASIL, Ms. Shepherd, Mehmet and Shereen were waiting for us on the front steps of Chaplin Manor as I piloted the Land Rover down the drive. They all knew what Georjie was capable of, I'd given them the best explanation I could. So, naturally they weren't going to miss her arrival.

Ryan was nowhere to be seen.

"The handsome chap with the perfect hair and glasses has to be Headmaster Chaplin," Georjie said, gripping the dashboard as we took the steep downhill. "Who are the other three?"

"The lady in the suit is Ms. Shepherd, she used to head the agency. She's ex-military, and a natural. The other woman is one of the magi who met us in the Arctic. Her name is Shereen. The tanned guy is ex-mage, his name is Mehmet. He's a tech-wizard."

"Poor guy, and she looks pissed." Georjie undid her seat-belt as we came to a stop in front of the academy. It was clear who she was talking about. Shereen hadn't cracked a smile since the accident on the tundra.

"Yeah, that's her face nowadays. Fred and Greg were friends of hers," Tomio explained as he got out of the back seat.

I introduced Georjayna to everyone. She shook hands and gave her sympathies.

"Where's Ryan?" I asked as we climbed the steps and passed into the lobby.

"I'm here." Ryan looked up from a sofa and stood, putting his phone into his pocket. His eyes fell on Georjie and he extended a hand. "You're obviously Georjayna. Thanks for coming."

I was proud of Georjayna for not hesitating. She was cool but polite as she doffed her sunglasses and told Ryan it was good to meet him, too. She knew about all the conflict between us and had vented her frustration and anger on my behalf. I'd told her on our way through Dover how badly Ryan's family had been impacted by Nero's actions. She gave a grunt that could have been sympathy or could have meant he deserved it. It was hard to say.

Georjie stood there in the lobby taking in the antique furniture, the old phone-box, the elegant second and third story railings and the chandelier. "I'm dying for a tour, but let's do the remote viewing first. Where's the sample?"

Ms. Shepherd picked up her red satchel and produced the pile of rubble and debris that I'd collected. It had been transferred into a sturdy clear bag with a zip closure. She handed it over with a thinly veiled look of hopeful desperation. Georjie took the bag and examined the dirt through the clear plastic, a frown creasing her brows. The lobby went dead silent as she made her inspection, holding the bag up to the natural light streaming in through the lobby's windows. All gazes were locked on the half-fae woman.

"Looks volcanic," she observed. "I've never looked into volcanic soil before. This should be interesting."

"Do you think it'll be a problem?" I sounded calm but my pulse was jumping. I uttered a silent prayer that she'd be able to tell us something. Anything.

She let the bag drop to her side and smiled. "Only one way to find out. I assume this place has a back yard? Outside is always best."

Like the perfect host, Basil gave a little bow and gestured to the hall leading to the nearest lounge, which had French doors opening to the rear terrace. "This way."

The headmaster and Georjie led the way, the rest of us following like ducklings. On the rear terrace, Georjie kicked off her sneakers and left them sitting on the pavement. She walked out onto the Academy's lush grass, closing her eyes as her bare soles sank into the lawn. I could have imagined it, but I thought the leaves of nearby trees rustled more vigorously as she did this. We watched her, not sure what to do with ourselves.

She looked up at the line of curious faces and laughed. "You can relax. This'll take a few minutes."

She beckoned me over as the rest of our party sat on the

stone benches. Georjie took my hand when I got close. She spoke quietly, so only I could hear. "Fyfa taught me something called endowment."

I gave a little gasp. "We have something called endowment, too."

Her brown eyes widened a fraction. "Does it mean you can temporarily share power with someone else?"

"Sort of. Well, there's two kinds. A Burned mage can pass fire into another mage for them to use, so yes. But there's also plenary endowment, which is permanent."

"That's what happened between you and Isaia?"

I nodded.

"We have a similar principle to the first version. Do you want me to endow you with whatever this dirt reveals, so you can see it too?" She held up the bag of volcanic rubble.

My stomach fizzled with excitement, like I'd drunk too much soda pop. I hadn't dreamed this was a possibility. "Absolutely."

She squeezed my hand. "I thought you'd be up for it. But be prepared. I've been told it's disorienting to be on your end of it, especially for someone who's not fae or Wise."

"What does it feel like?"

She opened her mouth but hesitated, her gaze wistful. "I can't tell you, especially since you're a different species. Your experience might be completely different to mine. Fyfa endowed me to show me how it works, but it was really just like doing the viewing myself. No big deal." She cocked her head and thought of something else. "I already told you I can now see them in color sometimes? It flickers in and out, I'm still working on it."

A burst of pride swelled in my chest. "You're progressing."

"That's what Stavarjak has done for me." She dimpled. "And Lachlan, not to mention a few other things—"

She halted, glancing briefly at our audience, and evidently decided now was not the right time to elaborate on the things Lachlan had done for her. We'd already been standing here with four pairs of eyes patiently—or impatiently, but they were quiet, so it was hard to tell— waiting for her to get information out of what was in the bag.

"Take off your shoes." She unlocked the zip-top. A fine puff of black powder, as light as air, emerged from the sack.

Kicking off my sneakers, I peeled off my socks and stuffed them in the toes of my shoes, enjoying the damp, cool feeling of the well-tended grass.

Georjie scooped a handful of the stuff out of the bag, then let the bag drop. She held her other hand out for me to take. Her eyes were already illuminated by a soft, white light.

I took her hand...

And went immediately and completely blind.

"Georjie," I gasped, clenching her hand. But I could no longer feel her hand in mine, or the academy's lawn beneath my bare soles, which went so much deeper than the grass now. I stiffened and my eyes stretched wide as grays and blues and blacks swirled and flecked in front of me. It felt as though roots had shot from the soles of my feet, thrusting deep into the pedolith, searching, probing, sucking up information.

A slender form took shape beside me, wavering and flickering in hues of white and pale blue.

"Georjie?"

"I'm here." Her features sharpened, every detail of her now as clear against the backdrop of grainy texture as my own when I looked in a mirror. But there was something different about her.

"Your ears."

Georjie had told me her pointed ears only manifested when she was in Stavarjak. I had never seen them for myself.

She smiled. "Look around you. Do you know where we are?"

I pulled my eyes away from her to focus on the setting, feeling a wave of vertigo as our location flickered in and out of focus.

It was the blast site, only there were no black marks or darkened surfaces. I recognized the location by the cleft in the rock, the overhang, and the stones themselves. There was no rubble, but beneath the overhang, where we'd seen what looked like the remains of the broken sculpture, the rocks were large and whole. They were also hiding something smooth and shiny, the only black thing against a field of gray.

Nothing moved, and there was no sound. I looked at Georjie, standing beside me, waiting.

Her eyes glowed with that ethereal light. "Time is stopped. When you're ready and you can see well, I'll let it go on."

"How do you know where we are in time?"

"I don't, exactly. But the soil knows whatever it is that we are seeking to learn. It wants to give up its secrets."

I tried to take a step, but at first, I couldn't lift my foot off the ground. Then, like parting magnets, I dislodged myself and moved closer to the overhang for a better look. The background flickered in varying shades of gray, like an old damaged film, making it hard to walk without shooting my arms out for balance. The smooth black shape revealed itself as I went around the rocks. Georjie walked with me, holding my hand. I had to sit down hard as the blood rushed from my head and my vision dimmed at the edges.

"Are you alright?" Georjie's voice brought me back.

I nodded, but couldn't find words as the hairs on my arms and legs stood on end.

It was a sculpture, we'd been right about that. But it was not a large egg, or a vase. It was a man. He lay reclined in the dirt, in a relaxed position. He was naked, totally unfettered by so much as a loincloth or an earring, with smooth and perfect limbs. He appeared to be carved of obsidian or onyx, but neither was quite right. His shoulders were narrow but ropy and taut with muscle. His stomach had more fat than a typical sculpture might have if it was made to capture male beauty. It hadn't been made for that purpose, though, that was obvious by his posture. It looked like some artist had seen a sleeping man, and had been inspired to sculpt a rendering of him just as he slumbered.

But it was his face that took my breath from my mouth and set electricity shooting through my nerves. It was fierce and familiar, even while it was relaxed, a slight smile curving the generous lips. The eyes were open, solid black and glinting. His hair was long and wild, half tied back, revealing a thinning hairline. Lines ran through his forehead and cheeks, bringing age and character to his features.

Here was the prominent visage I had seen while traveling through the orb, at the end of my journey, looming like an exclamation point or the crescendo of a symphony.

When I found my voice, I told Georjie: "This is the sculpture of a man I saw when I heated the orb. I don't understand what it's doing here, or what it's made of. Do you know?"

She crouched, observing the sculpture through a soft,

respectful gaze. "If he's made of the same stuff you gave me, it's unique. A bit like charcoal, only it has more energy."

"Supernatural effluent," I murmured. "Maybe it has permeated the stone, whatever this was carved from. It was obviously carved by a mage."

This sculpture lay at the epicenter of the effluent we were using to track Nero. It wasn't the place, leeching elemental magic, it was this perfectly formed piece of art. When I thought of it as art, my mind veered to the orbs, and I wondered if they'd been made by the same artist. I thought it possible, maybe even likely, though the orbs had not been manufactured from this shiny, black stuff.

"Are you ready to see what happens?" Georjie asked in a low voice.

A deep sadness came over me, because I already knew that this priceless creation would be destroyed. How didn't seem to matter as much as why. "I'm ready."

Moving away from the sculpture and the overhang it hid beneath, we retreated to the clearing.

Little tufts of grass began to move with a breeze, as Georjie let the timeline play. Wind whistled over and through the rocks. Illumination appeared in the cleft between the rocks, brightening. A figure followed, a figure on fire with unnatural flames. Nero. His whole body was ignited, his eyes were two white windows, not soft white like Georjie's, but sharp, like lit fuses. He wore black clothing I recognized as fireproof. It too, was alight. Nero's face was smooth, his expression calm, and his walk into the clearing, confident. No, he didn't walk, he *seared* his way into the rocky glade, scorching the air with an unnatural, caustic heat. He knew exactly what he was doing and precisely what he would find here. He crossed the clearing. There was a momentary flicker of color, and I took in a breath. His body was consumed by licks and flashes of orange, pink and yellow. If I hadn't been observing my enemy, I would have been awed by the rainbow beauty of his appearance.

He made a sound like high winds as he passed us by, like a lot of air compressed through a small open door, heading straight for the sculpture. Wherever he stepped he left black footprints, the edges of which seeped outward, expanding as puddles of obsidian dust.

I wanted to scream as he stopped at the overhang, looking down at the sculpture with those blank, blazing eyes.

Georjie moved with me so the rocks didn't block our view. I wanted to look away. What Nero was about to do seemed so much more horrifying than someone simply destroying art. I began to shiver and quake as the desire to stop Nero became nearly overwhelming. Georjie's hand tightened around mine and she murmured something in a soothing tone, though I was too disturbed to pay attention to her words.

Nero made a fist, and cocked it.

I sucked in a breath and winced, wishing I could tear my eyes away.

He rammed the fist into the sculpture's chest. A fracture appeared there. He struck the same place, again and again, tirelessly, brutally. He did not stop until the chest contained a jagged hole. Using his fingers, he pried away shards, revealing a thick-walled but hollow interior. A new glow sprang up against Nero's face, an illumination flickering from within the sculpture's chest. Nero himself flickered in and out of color, and so did the light licking out from inside the form.

It was violet.

I felt like crying. My throat closed up, my eyes stung.

Nero reached into the cavity, his hands disappearing behind ragged, broken edges. When they emerged, they held a beautiful violet flame, the size and shape of a heart. It pulsed in his grip, just like a heartbeat, bright then soft, bright then soft.

"Oh, Saxony." Georjie's whisper made me choke back a sob.

I understood what was happening to my people, what had happened to so many of them already. As Nero held the violet fire in his hands, its pulses slowed, a heart being drained of blood. The violet light infused his hands, then traveled up his arms. It reflected in his eyes. Two points of dying purple light.

It was like watching someone kill a helpless animal.

At this very same moment in time, we'd been rolling across the tundra on those amphibious vehicles.

The violet light shrank and diminished, growing ever weaker, ever smaller, until it was completely gone, absorbed by the mage who'd destroyed its immortal resting place.

The sculpture had not been a sculpture. The sculpture had been a mage. A progenitor, and the father of all the violet magi who'd come after. His remains had held the source if his offspring's fire for centuries, maybe millennia. And now that source was gone. Swallowed up. Eliminated, and with it, all those flames who'd come after.

When there was no trace that there had ever been a violet fire save for the occasional flickering addition of its hue to Nero's dazzling form, Nero used his foot to stomp out the rest of the sculpture. This time it fractured to pieces like glass. It was brittle, fragile, so easy to crumble, now that its fire was gone.

"Take me back," I choked out, tearing my eyes from Nero and the remains of the violet father. "I've seen enough."

Georjie tipped her hand and let the dirt fall.

I fell with it.

My senses sharpened as color and present reality washed over me like ice-water. The ground released its hold on me and the feeling of my legs and feet unexpectedly liberated made me lose my balance.

Georjie caught me as I fell, my face hot with tears. "I'm so sorry."

I sobbed into her shoulder as she lowered me to the ground. I felt as if my heart was breaking. I felt somehow, that I'd known the violet progenitor. He'd once been alive, powerful, he'd loved and lost, had been a father, and a chieftain or a leader. His demise represented the violence that every mage whose fire had been snuffed had suffered. I tried to control my weeping but it was futile, my body wracked with sobs that would not be held in. I'd witnessed something more horrible than anything else I had ever seen. There'd been no blood, no gore, no pain for the victim, yet it had been indescribably, unbearably brutal.

"It was awful," said Georjie softly, as she held me, speaking over my head to the others.

My friends gathered around where we'd collapsed on the grass. They were upset by the spectacle of my emotions spilling out all over the lawn. They whispered words of comfort, but had no clue as to what Georjie and I had seen. They were confused and at a loss.

Tomio was there, I felt him touch my shoulder, and rub a hand across my back. I felt the care in his gesture, his intense desire to make everything ok. But it wasn't okay, because there was no way to put that violet fire back, or any of the other idles that Nero had stolen.

9
___

MYSTERY DELIVERY

"This came for you." Tomio, carrying a box, entered the first-year student's lounge where Georjie and I were having coffee and catching up.

While Basil and Ms. Shepherd worked with their people to nail down the location of Nero's next target, Georjie distracted me with stories about her friends in Stavarjak, Fyfa and Laec. She told me how amazing it had been to be get to know her father and her fae heritage, and waxed mournfully about the history of the Wise and their persecution as witches in the middle ages. But mostly she talked about Lachlan, and as she did, her face and tone took on the trappings of love; her eyes shone, her lips curved in a sappy smile.

I was happy for my friend and her new life away from Saltford, but it was difficult to allow myself to be fully absorbed by her amazing descriptions of the fae realm and its queen while my own people were under such threat. It felt like watching a hurricane barrel down upon us, watching it gather force and knowing it would hit with biblical-level fury, and there was nothing that anyone could do about it. Indeed, the storm had already struck the majority of us, the damage already done. How bereft magi reacted to the loss was difficult to predict, I'd explained to Georjie. Some ended their own lives while others seemed almost grateful to have been unburdened of their searing internal presence.

I took the package from Tomio and looked at the postage. "It's from Venice, express post, but there's no return address."

Georjie gave a quiet gasp and moved from the chair, where she'd been sitting, to beside me on the sofa. "Could it be from Dante?"

I frowned, hefting the weight of the box. It wasn't light.

Tomio perched on the coffee table across from me, knees almost touching mine. "This ain't Christmas, quit guessing and open it."

Tearing the tape off the box, the packing slip fell out of its plastic envelope and into my lap.

Georjie snatched it up. "Hmm. It's insured, but there's no value listed."

Inside the box was bubble wrap and layers of crumpled up craft paper. Underneath that lay a small white envelope. I recognized the handwriting which spelled out my first and last name. I smiled. "It's from Elda."

"Isaia's mom?" Georjie's brows lifted.

We hadn't talked about the Baseggios in a while, and I had only ever referred to my previous employer as Mrs., until after we'd become friends. Georjie knew her as Signora Baseggio.

I nodded. "Color me intrigued."

Opening the letter, I scanned the note. "Even more intriguing."

I showed it to Tomio and Georjayna.

Georjie read aloud: "Call me when you get this, ideally before you see what's inside. I need to explain."

Tomio handed me my cell.

I dialed Elda's number, and got her almost at once.

"Hello, Saxony." Elda sounded like she had just woken up, even though it was early evening. "The package has been arrived, I see."

"Yes." I was too distracted to correct her English. "I haven't looked inside yet. Can I put you on speaker phone? Tomio is here, you met him when you visited the academy, and one of my good friends from Canada is also here, Georjayna Sutherland."

"As you like," Elda replied. "I'm sure this will be of extra... ultra interest to Tomio, given that he is one of yours."

Interesting that she was referring to our kind. This wasn't just a late birthday present, then, or a random gift.

Pressing the speaker button, I set the phone on the arm of the sofa. "Go ahead."

"First, I have some bad news." She sounded melodramatically sad as she said this. "This is why I didn't want to say you in a letter. I'd prefer to say in person, but you're there. I'm here. And here we are."

I cocked an eyebrow at the phone as Georjie covered a smile. It wasn't just me, Elda's English had deteriorated since I'd last seen her. Like, *a lot.*

"Dante is dead."

Wow. Okay. That came out perfectly. There was a beat of silence that covered us like a layer of new-fallen snow. Georjie lost her smile, and Tomio's head recoiled. I searched for words and came up blank. Mercifully, Elda continued.

"Last week a courier delivered a package from Enzo. The note told that the contents had belonged to Nicodemo and were found in his room after his death. He explained, Enzo did, not Nicodemo, obviously, that his son arrived home in horrible pain." Elda hiccupped before continuing. "Suffering from the curse that also plagued Nicodemo. There was nothing any of the best doctors of Italia could do for Dante. He didn't recover. He is gone, and Enzo wants nothing to do with any magi. He believes his line has been cursed, because his son interfered where he should not. He apologized for not giving Nico's things to Isaia sooner, and told me that he kept nothing. In his words, 'with this final transaction, Isaia and the Baseggio famiglia will be pulito'd from memory.' It will be for him as though Nico and his kind never were."

This speech hammered me with blow after blow. Emotions as mixed as a mutt rose unbidden: sadness for the father who'd lost his only son, vindication that a crime had gone punished, shock that Dante had not survived the process that I and Tomio had both survived, and anticipation for what could possibly be inside the box.

After that, my armpits felt positively swampy.

"I'm sorry to hear about Dante," I said, when no one else spoke. "I didn't like him, obviously, and I'm not fond of Enzo either, but death isn't something to celebrate."

I was lying, though. If the news had been that Nero had died instead of Dante, I would have popped some bubbly, even if only to watch the snuffed magi enjoy it.

"Yes, well I'm not sorry," said Elda, as flat and blunt as you'd expect an offended mother to be. "We endured molto years of aggravation from Enzo. If the death of Dante's son brings an end to that, then I shall celebrate it with a glass of wine. In fact, I already have. Two. No!" There was a pause. "Three." She trilled the 'r' in 'three' as beautifully as any Italian could. "And, I don't need anyone to celebrate with. I'm perfectly ability, all for myself."

Clearly, and her solo celebrations also explained her English.

I tried not to let the symmetry of her proclamation with my own thoughts about Nero's potential death bother me. Georjie and Tomio's faces were carefully blank. I felt like they were watching me for my reaction before they'd commit to their own.

Elda took an audible sip of her wine, then cleared her voice. "I went through Nico's things and took what I thought Isaia would want. I'll give them to him when he's older. I don't want to upset him, you understand. Anything to do with the magi, I have passed on to you. I want as little to do with it as Enzo does, and I figure it's correctly yours now anyway. Do with it as you like."

"Thank you," I said, involuntarily. "How is Isaia?"

Elda let out a breath, like she was relieved to have done her duty and happy to be moving on to her favorite topic. "Bene. He's wonderful. He's growing too fast, and playing soccer. He always wanted to play."

"Yes. I know." In her libations, it seemed Elda had forgotten that I looked after Isaia for a full summer.

"He's still nowhere able to keep up with Cristiano, but in a few years, he'll be very good. He's also fallen in love with… what, it's called… parkour?"

"Street acrobatics?"

"Si. He has strong of a monkey now. I try not to hover like a scared mama, but some habits die hard." She smacked her lips. "I always liked that saying."

I grinned, imagining my dark-eyed little friend bouncing around the Venetian Calle and bridges. "Cool."

"He still asks about you. All the time. In fact, since we saw you at the academy, he's only asked about you more often. But, he's not worried about you anymore, so that's good."

Tomio lifted an eyebrow at this and I thought I knew what he was thinking. I was in more danger now that I'd ever been. The Baseggios didn't need to know that.

"That's lovely." It was on the tip of my tongue to say that I'd come visit when I could, but it seemed a better idea not to get Isaia's, or my, hopes up.

"I have to go pick Cristiano up from English," Elda said. "It's nice to hear you, Saxony. Now when you visit Venice, you know Enzo won't bother you. I don't think he'll be in the market for a magus again. Penso di non."

"Thanks. Nice to hear your voice too, Elda. Give the boys and Pietro my love."

We said goodbye, and I hung up the call.

"Well, that was enlightening," said Tomio, then cocked an eyebrow. "Wait, did she say she was going to pick up her boy? With all that alcohol in her system?"

"She'll stagger there on foot," I said, "there's no cars in Venice." Elda would likely embarrass herself in the process, showing up half-cut and breathing wine fumes at the other moms.

"Hopefully she doesn't fall into a canal." Georjie moved to the floor. "Can you *please* open it now?"

I took a breath before lifting out the first bubble-wrapped item. Unraveling the protective layer revealed a small leather-bound journal. It smelled of decades passed somewhere damp. It was plain brown, a little damaged at the edges, and wrapped closed with a leather thong. Opening it revealed brittle, yellowed pages, and hand-written entries in a language I didn't recognize. Further in, there were entries by a different hand. Those I recognized, because they were in Italian.

"Those must be Nicodemo's notes," Tomio guessed, his head and Georjie's bowed over the journal as I paged through it. "But whose are the first ones?"

"Whoever passed the diary to Nico, I guess. Maybe an ancestor." I flipped a page open near the front. "What language is that?"

Tomio grabbed his phone. "Let me search it. Those are Latin letters, but with a hell of a lot of accents. Hang on." Tomio's fingers flew over the keyboard as his eyes flashed back and forth from the diary to the phone. His brows cocked again. "It's Turkish."

That brought back a memory. "Dante told me Nico's grandmother had been Turkish. Interesting. Maybe the diary was hers."

Georjie nudged my knee. "What else is there?"

Setting the diary aside, I lifted the last item from the box. It was heavy. It was just under a foot long and a slender, rectangular shape. Removing the bubble wrap revealed a cardboard box with two characters on the lid. I showed them to Tomio.

"Is this Japanese?"

He squinted at it, then his expression brightened. "Nope. It's a form of old Chinese. I can't read the first character, but I can tell you that the second one means 'steel' because it's very close to the Japanese character for steel. My guess?" He pointed at the box, his eyes bright with intrigue. "That's a blade."

Tomio was right.

Beneath the lid, a shiny black handle protruded from a paper sleeve, into which the blade had been slid. Sliding off the sleeve elicited a gasp from all three of us.

"What the hell is it made from? Porcelain? It's doesn't

look anything like steel. Weird that's what it says on the box." Georjie shifted for a better look.

The blade was a bright, pure white. There was a single character embossed into the blade, just below the haft.

"That's the name of the metalsmith." Tomio pointed at the character.

"But it's not metal." I held the blade up in the poor side-lighting of the lounge.

It wasn't porcelain, there were flecks of something reflective in it. I didn't recognize it from my metal studies. Past experience told me that the best way to identify a metal was to handle it. Touching the blade lightly with my fingertips, I jerked my hand back in shock and hissed as pain seared the sensitive skin of my forefinger.

"What the hell? It's freezing!"

Tomio frowned. "Can I see?"

"Be careful." I handed the blade over to him.

Tomio pressed his thumb to the blade lightly, and pulled back as fast as I had. We exchanged a shocked look. What kind of blade could harm someone with a single touch?

"It feels like it's coated with nitroglycerine, or something," Tomio said.

"May I?" Georjie held out her hand. "I have to see this for myself."

Hesitating a moment, Tomio handed the blade over. "It hurts like hell." He looked at his thumb. "I've got a blister."

My fingertip still throbbed and I looked at it, dismayed. "Me too."

Georjie gingerly touched a fingertip to the blade, but didn't pull back her hand. She frowned, then pressed the blade against her palm. Her brown eyes found mine, then Tomio's. "Nothing. I don't feel anything."

"Bloody hell," Tomio breathed, alarm rising in his face. "It's made to hurt magi. Do you think it will melt?"

Georjie looked confused at how Tomio got from his initial observation to his question, so I explained. "We're trained to melt blades on contact, so they can't hurt us."

"Oh." She looked duly impressed.

"I'm not sure I want to try, though." I ran a hand across my brow, feeling the damp that had gathered there. There was something niggling at my memory, something that reminded me of this blade. Something I had seen in the academy.

"What are you thinking?" Georjie slid the blade back into its paper sleeve and set it in its box. She put the lid on, like she didn't want Tomio or me to inspect it any further.

"I've seen that substance somewhere before, only not in knife form." I sat back against the sofa, wracking my brains.

Georjie got to her feet and stretched her back. "In the library, maybe? Or Basil's office? You said it's full of cool stuff."

Tomio grabbed my knees. "The professor's lounge!"

We exchanged an enlightened look and got up at the same time, bumping chests.

"Bring that," I called to Georjie as we bolted for the door.

THE PROFESSOR'S lounge was unlocked and needed airing. No one had used it since the Fire Games, and a layer of dust had been allowed to collect on the light fixtures and desks. We made a beeline for the glass case under the window where a collection of raw minerals and rocks lay under cover.

"There." Tomio jabbed his finger against the glass. A few

inches down, a white chunk of jagged rock sat benignly on a bit of tweed, laid within a wooden box. "Is it the same, or is it the same?"

We bent our heads over the unlabeled item.

"It's the same," Georjie pronounced.

"It's too hard to tell in this light," I said.

Even the overhead lamps only threw a muted amber glow. It was atmospheric but terrible for identifying a lump of mystery rock by its finer details.

"Here." Georjie reached up and scraped back the drapes along the narrow, attic-style dormer window above the case.

Natural light swept into the room, reflecting off the little particles embedded in the pale substance. My heart thudded hard with recognition, but there was only one way to be sure. I found the latch keeping the lid closed and lifted the cover back.

As I reached a finger out to touch the lump, Tomio's hand snaked out and stopped me. "Let me do it."

Before I could protest, he tapped a finger against the top of the rock, then brought it to his mouth. "Yep. Same. Ow."

I let out a harsh breath. "What the hell is this stuff? And why hasn't Basil told us about it? Why does he have a chunk of it sitting here in the library?"

"Given that Nicodemo had a whole blade made of the stuff, I wish we could ask him instead." Tomio frowned at his second blister, and somehow also managed to look impressed at the damage a simple touch could inflict.

"Seems like this might be something worth disturbing Basil for," Georjie said. "But it's up to you guys. I'm just the peanut gallery."

"You're hardly that," Tomio said. "You're the one who showed us what Nero was really up to."

"I agree. Let's bust up the party. Come on." I took the box containing the murdery rock, and led them from the lounge.

We'd been given a directive not to leave the academy until we'd had our next location target. Basil wanted us all in one place and ready to go when the time was right. He'd also asked not to be disturbed as he, Ms. Shepherd and Mehmet closed themselves in his office with multiple computer monitors, connected to scientists from multiple locations across the world. In some ways, Tomio, Ryan and I were treated like equals, and in other ways we were treated like students who would just get in the way. After listening through the keyhole, I surmised Basil was right to kick us out. There was a lot of incredibly dull, academic conversation going on in there.

I rapped on his door with a knuckle.

"Come," answered Ms. Shepherd.

I opened the door to see Basil and Mehmet bent over a computer monitor. They had glasses perched on the end of their noses, which made them look distantly related. To my surprise, Ryan and Shereen were seated on the couch, and from the looks of it, quite cozy. I assumed that Ryan was ingratiating himself to an agent, the clever weasel. I wanted to ask him what he was doing in here when the rest of us students had been banished, but didn't want to sound petty. I was fine with sounding petty when we were alone, but not in front of adults.

"Can you zoom in?" Basil glanced up briefly, not upset to see us. In fact, he looked almost jovial. They must be hot on Nero's heels.

Timing was everything.

"Hi, kids," the headmaster said.

Yep, he was excited. He never called us kids unless he was feeling upbeat.

"We're getting close. We know it's going to be Turkey, just haven't nailed the coordinates quite yet."

That comment knocked my peevishness about Ryan right out of my head.

"We figured it would be Turkey," said Tomio, a bit peevishly himself.

Ryan scoffed. "You did not."

"We did, actually," I lied, ignoring Georjie's look and keeping the box containing the lump of white rock behind my back so I could refresh Basil's memory with it, if need be.

It *hadn't* occurred to me that the next location would be in Turkey, but that's because I'd been distracted by the freezy white blade. Given a bit more time, I would have come to that conclusion. I was sure of it.

"How did you figure that?" Shereen appeared much less annoyed and skeptical than Ryan, which made me like her a little more.

I wondered if I needed to warn her against dating my semi-deranged frenemy, but dismissed the thought as her ferocity on the tundra came surging back to me. A woman like Shereen could eat Ryan alive. She didn't need any help from me.

"Saxony got some interesting items in the mail, from Nicodemo," Tomio said.

I appreciated his abbreviated version events so we could get to the point faster. "It contained that."

I pointed at the box in Georjie's hands. She stepped forward and lifted the lid.

At the mention of Nicodemo's name, Basil stood erect. At the revelation of the blade, he came around his desk, fixing his glasses more firmly into place. He made a move to take the box, but Georjie held it back.

"Let me show you," she said. "You'll understand why in a second."

She set the lid on the table by the carafe of water and lifted out the knife. As she slid the paper sleeve off the blade, Basil and Shereen gasped.

Shereen practically crushed Ryan in her quest for a closer look. She closed in on the blade but didn't make any move to touch it. Her reverence made it obvious, I thought, that she knew what it was, or at least, what it was capable of.

"But Nicodemo is dead." Basil's eyes were wide and glued to the blade.

"Elda sent me his things. Dante is also dead."

Another hush went through the room. Even Ryan looked shocked.

I explained what the note had said, and the room was so quiet when I finished you could have heard an ant marching across the floor. Basil and Shereen seemed incapable of drawing their eyes from the knife, but neither moved to touch it.

"So, what is it?" Ms. Shepherd asked, her voice filled with impatience.

It was clear from Mehmet's expression that he didn't know what it was either.

"It's ghost steel," Basil said.

Tomio glanced at me. "That's the other Chinese character: ghost."

I looked at Basil. "What's ghost steel?"

Ryan finally got up and came over to look. "Can I see it?"

"Don't touch it," Georjie emphasized again, patronizing Ryan on purpose, like he was five. I almost threw an arm around her for that. She handed the blade to him so he could take it by the handle.

He took the knife, and immediately touched the blade

with a finger. He snatched it back, cursing but also looking elated.

Georjie sent me a half-lidded look of bored disbelief. "Seriously?"

"He's not the brightest," I told her.

But Ryan laughed, too amazed to care about my insult. He handed the blade back to Georjie. "That's incredible."

"It is," Basil agreed. "Remarkable. I have a sample, somewhere."

"You have some of this? Here? In the academy?" Ryan looked like he was torn between throttling and hugging the headmaster.

"Just a small chunk," Basil admitted.

I produced the box.

"Yes, there it is. Thank you, Saxony. Quite so. I found it at an estate sale in 1990. In fact, I'm ashamed to say I never paid for it. I'm not entirely sure it *was* for sale, but I wrapped it in a kerchief and pocketed it, intending to take it to the proprietor to make an offer. But an emergency came up, one that your father, Ryan, had something to do with, and I forgot all about it until much later."

"Was that the estate sale where my dad set fire to the drapes? I've heard that story a million times," Ryan said.

"The very same. How remarkable to see something actually forged of the stuff. For a time, I tried to learn whatever I could about the substance. I sent samples to geologists, who could handle it without being hurt by it, and *they* claimed it was simple quartz and suggested I was obtuse for wasting their time. Can you *imagine*? Quartz!" Basil looked appropriately scandalized.

"Clearly, it's not quartz," Shereen said.

"No. It's called ghost steel, but in fact it's not steel at all. It shares precisely zero properties with steel, well, other than being hard. It doesn't respond to any level of heat, but it is on the brittle side. It can be broken by a strong enough mage, if only touching it could be endured." Basil's amazed gaze drifted back to the box. "How diabolical to have made a weapon from it."

"It's genius," Ryan observed. "Don't you see the serendipity? It makes what happened to my brother worthwhile."

We stared at Ryan in open bewilderment. Even the background conversation from the monitors seemed to have subdued itself in confusion.

Basil finally broke the silence. "Good heavens, man. What a thing to say."

Ryan rolled his eyes heavenward, then looked at me. "And you call *me* the dense one?"

"Humor us," Georjie ventured, gently.

"If Dante hadn't taken my brother's fire, Dante wouldn't have died. If he hadn't died, Enzo wouldn't have sent Nico's stuff to Elda. Elda's a decent chick, obviously she thinks highly enough of Saxony to send it here. Putting that," he jabbed a finger at the box in Georjie's hands, "into our possession." He stopped there, waiting for us to get to the conclusion he'd obviously reached.

"Are you saying, this is the weapon we need to stop Nero?" I asked, slowly.

"Well, duh." Ryan returned to the couch and plopped into it, like he'd solved all our problems, and the rest of the world's besides.

"Ryan," Basil began, "I don't entirely disagree, but I think it's dangerous to assume that this little creation, as dastardly as it is, will be sufficient to stop a mage who has now absorbed six out of the seven original idle fires. What we're dealing with is a supernatural beyond our comprehension.

Getting close enough to pierce him with it would be challenge on its own. Whether its magic would even affect such a powerful mage, who—let's face it—might as well be labeled a demi-god now, is completely unknown."

Ryan stretched both arms out then laced his fingers over his head, letting them rest on his skull as he tilted his head back. He eyed the headmaster with disdain, which made me want to smack him. "You have a better idea?"

Shereen took a gleeful stab at a few: "A bomb? Semi-automatic weapons? Anything we might fire from a distance?"

Ryan frowned. "You're not getting it. That thing is the reason Gage had to lose his fire. That thing is what will stop Nero. We're supernaturals, that means supernatural serendipity conspires to help us when we need it. Gage's sacrifice has to have meaning, and this gives it meaning. If you can't see that, well, I don't know how to help you."

I thought about the fight with the storm-demon in Saltford, and the fact that Akiko had been a demon-hunter and willing to sacrifice herself for us. I thought about the crystal of Atlantis that Targa had described, and how Petra had unearthed the ancient ruins in a single night so it could be located, and the curse broken. I thought about the fae queen called Elphame who was now in possession of an apparently harmless rosebud that held trapped within it the spirit of a malevolent witch who could be buried no other way, and only a Wise as powerful as Georjie could have contained her there.

The expressions on Basil, Mehmet, Shereen and Tomio mirrored doubt, but as I looked into my fae friend's eyes, I wondered if Ryan might prove to be right. I understood the need for tragedy to make sense, really, I did. Did that mean that tragedy always made sense? I didn't know.

The fuzzed and distant sound of an electronically filtered voice drew our attention to Ms. Shepherd, who put her fingers to her earpiece.

"They've found it," she said, moving to where she could peer over Mehmet's shoulder.

Her words had the effect of an air raid siren on everyone except for Georjie. We bolted into a cluster behind Basil's desk, cramming together to get a view of the screen. Georjie wandered a little further into the room, watching us with a bemused expression, holding the box at her side.

Mehmet clicked on the link which had popped into his messaging feed. It opened a neon yellow outline of a map of Eurasia against a black background. A small green dot blinked, sending green ripples outward from its center. Mehmet's fingers skimmed over the keys and the trackpad, zooming in. "This is it," he breathed. "The point the radiologists and linguists have narrowed to. Here we go."

The map was too blank to hazard a guess about the dot's precise location. I could find Turkey on a world map, but if you asked me to point to Ankara or Istanbul, I'd be at a loss.

A satellite image, starting out blurry and pixilated, sharpened into a topographical overhead view.

"There." He jabbed a finger at the green dot, then made a line toward another dot with a name beneath it in small letters. "Closest airport is Nevşehir."

Ms. Shepherd snatched up her phone and dialed. Holding the mobile to her ear, she moved away from Basil's desk and put her back to us. A moment later she turned and glanced up, seeing us watching her expectantly. She snapped her fingers and barked. "What are you doing? We leave for the London Airport in fifteen minutes. Now! Move, move, move!"

10

IT IS WHEREVER THEY ARE

We were somewhere over the Mediterranean. Ms. Shepherd had told us to get sleep while we could, because the moment we got off the plane, we'd be hustled into choppers and headed as-the-crow-flies for the epicenter. By the time we'd lifted off the tarmac at London City Airport, it was nearly ten that evening, which had made Ms. Shepherd crusty as she muttered about incompetent fools.

There'd been no news from any of the contacts at the world's airports, small or large. No sightings of Nero. I wondered if by this point he had some ability to travel without a plane. For all we knew, the man might be immortal by now. A scary thought that kept me from sleeping.

Tomio sat beside me in an aisle seat with a sleep mask on, but I didn't think he was having much success sleeping either. The seats were soft and as comfortable as plane seats could be, but the grim reality—the grim unknown—of what we were headed into had a disturbing effect on slumber.

Ms. Shepherd had procured the smallest plane available

that could make the journey without requiring a fuel-up in Istanbul, which meant it was much too big for our small party. When we landed, it would be in Nevşehir.

Georjie had not been invited. She'd volunteered to come, but neither Ms. Shepherd nor Basil would take responsibility for her, and in my heart I was relieved. Georjayna though, had decided that rather than jumping on the first train back to Blackmouth, she'd wait a few days for us to return to Dover, in case it was all over quickly. She wanted to be there to receive us. She had books, a beautiful garden, and claimed to be perfectly happy to house-sit the academy.

I slouched in my seat with my knees propped up. My reading light was on, illuminating the pages of Nico's journal where it lay open against my lap. I'd been skimming the pages of the Italian entries for the last ten minutes, wishing for a functioning Wi-Fi connection so I could translate it. I'd half expected Ms. Shepherd to snatch it away and send it to a lab, but either she wasn't interested in anything additional since we had our target, or she'd forgotten about it.

I spotted words here and there that I recognized. No coherent picture had formed, though. Most of the entries weren't even full sentences but bullet points, some ticked with checkmarks. I could translate a few of those. They were things like deliveries of packages at locations in Venice or nearby Mestre, or offers that had been made, and subsequently accepted or denied. It never gave much detail about to whom these offers were made or what they were for. It seemed that Nico had been using the journal as a catch-all for day-to-day information about his activities.

I flipped through the pages faster, wondering why Elda had sent it to me. Surely it would have been better left in Isaia's hands. Then again, Nicodemo had worked for a crime boss, maybe Elda didn't want Isaia knowing too much about his father's doings.

Then there was the Turkish section. A flip through that was basically useless. I had zero understanding of the language. As the pages flew past, my eye caught on a drawing that made me pause and sit up. It was a small, poorly done sketch in black ink, smack in the middle of a written entry. It looked like a cluster of eggs that someone had draped shoelaces over.

My heart skittered and picked up speed as I found an entry above the drawing, written in Italian. It was a simple phrase, one I had enough of the language to understand, though it didn't entirely make sense. I reached over and pressed on Tomio's knee.

He made a soft grunt and shifted up his sleep mask enough to peer at me from beneath it. "Trying to sleep, here."

"Look at this," I whispered, holding the drawing under the reading light.

He peered at it from underneath his mask, his head tilted back. As the importance of it registered, he slid the mask to the top of his head, making his hair stand up around it in spikes. Then he took the journal from me and stared at it. "What is *that*? Are those what I think they are?"

"Look at the caption." I pointed at the Italian entry, which had clearly been added by Nicodemo at some point later.

"I see it. *È ovunque si trovino*," he read aloud. His gaze flicked to mine. "What does that mean?"

"It means: *It is, wherever they are.*"

I watched as this took time to sink in, my heart knocking blood audibly past my eardrums. Tomio's gaze drifted back to the drawing.

"What is *it*?" I asked, my voice fluttery even through my whisper. I was afraid to venture an opinion first, because my opinion seemed too far-fetched. If Tomio's thoughts hadn't immediately jumped to the story that Basil had told us while we were in Naples about the original fire, then I didn't want to prompt it. He might have some other idea of what "it" was talking about, but there was no mistaking what those egg-like objects were, and he knew it as well as I.

Tomio sucked in a breath and looked at the top of Basil's head where the headmaster was asleep a few rows up. "Should we wake him?"

"I think he'd kill us if we didn't."

Nodding, Tomio scrambled out of the seat and I tumbled after him. We scampered up the aisle to Basil. I flicked on the reading light over his seat as Tomio slipped through the seats ahead of Basil to come around to his other side. We woke him, pincer-style.

His eyes came open immediately. Seemed he was having trouble sleeping, too. "What is it?"

"Look at this." I thrust the drawing beneath the light's glare.

Like a man not quite sure if he's dreaming or not, Basil rubbed his eyes, sat up, and took the book with one hand. He patted his chest, looking for his glasses, and found them in his inside jacket pocket. The headmaster was the only person I knew who still dressed posh when everyone else around him had opted for t-shirts and sweat pants. He put the specs on and inspected the drawing with clearer vision. It took a few seconds before he reacted, but when he did, it was an artfully crafted curse word. He glanced at Tomio, then to me, then down to the page.

"Where did you get this?" His finger shook a little as he pointed at the drawing. "These are the orbs!"

"It came in the box Elda sent. We were so hung up on the knife that we didn't talk much about the journal." The words tumbled out of me. "You see the Italian phrase?"

"In among all the Turkish? Yes, I see it. My Italian is rusty, please humor an old man."

"It means: *it is, wherever they are.*"

Basil's eyes looked the size of saucers, being behind the strong lenses of his glasses practically made them pop. His cheeks looked pale beneath his hours-old stubble. "All this time. It was right under my nose."

Tomio braced his shoulder against the back of the seat in front of him, getting a better view of Basil's face. "What do you mean?"

Basil lay the journal open on his lap and took off his glasses. He rubbed the bridge of his nose, taking a moment to gather his thoughts. "After I came into possession of the first orb in 1990, I spent the next three years searching for more. I knew from the myths that there were supposed to be seven. It wasn't until 1994—when a progressive friend of mine convinced me to have dial-up installed—that I was able to locate another one through a website that sold unique items. Of course, I bought that one immediately, and paid a small fortune for it. The owner, a Brazilian art collector, had no clue what it was, but knew it would be valuable to someone. It didn't come with any information, no story on where it had been found. In fact, I had to sign an agreement before using the site that was like a non-disclosure. Buyers could make any purchases they wanted, and sellers could peddle whatever they wanted, as long as they agreed to operate under a blanket of universal anonymity."

He put his spectacles back in place, his expression turned sheepish. "I kept looking, but after that I never found any more. I used to dream about them, vivid, disturbing dreams. There was always this feeling that if I didn't get my hands on the orbs, all of them, that something terrible would happen."

"In your dreams, you had this feeling?" I asked. "Or in waking life?"

"Only in my dreams. As soon as I woke, the feeling would fade. I ignored it, but the dreams intensified. I was beginning to feel as though I might go crazy if I didn't try to do something about it. I found a therapist. She suggested that since I couldn't find the rest of the orbs, that I make them instead, that having a complete collection, which my subconscious so desired—even if the collection wasn't authentic—might make the night terrors go away."

I hardly breathed. *This* was the story behind the secret studio. Finally!

I sensed a presence behind me and looked up to see that Ryan had slid into a seat ahead of us.

He peered over the seat back to look into Basil's lap. "Can I see that?"

Basil lifted the journal into Ryan's hands, who stared at with glassy eyes. "Holy shite."

"Did you do it?" Tomio prompted Basil.

The headmaster nodded. "I was embarrassed about it, though. I was raised never to show weakness, and by that time I had students wandering every nook and cranny of the academy. I would have been horrified if they stumbled across my artsy-fartsy activities. Which were more fartsy than artsy, let me tell you. I never did have much in the way of creative talent, though I tried my best."

"Don't say that," I urged, recalling the drawings in the greenhouse. They weren't brilliant, but they weren't half-bad, either.

Basil waved a hand. "I've made peace with it. As it

happened, there was an empty cellar beneath my office. During the renovations, its access got closed off, so I had a stair built that led down to it from my storage closet. When I had time, which wasn't often, I would go down there. I would listen to music and try to imagine what the other orbs might look like, based on the differences between the two that I had acquired. I started by doing paintings, then moved to plaster and molds. Got quite good at that, better than I ever was at painting, in point of fact." Basil chuckled self-consciously.

Ryan was staring at the drawing, but he was listening, and glanced at me surreptitiously. I gave him a warning look. Basil was on a roll, there was no need to confess that we'd known about his studio since first semester.

"And did it work?" I asked.

"Not at first, but eventually. Yes. Maybe it was because I got quite good at making the replicas, or perhaps the dreams would have gone away on their own. Either way, by the turn of the century, the dreams ceased completely, and the arts and crafts phase of my life passed. I got rid of most of the art, not wanting to explain it to anyone who might find it. But I never totally cleaned up my studio. I kind of forgot about it. And never once, in all that time, did it occur to me to do *that* with them." He gestured at the cluster of orbs, as tightly packed together as newly hatched chicks in a nest.

"Well, even if you had thought of it," Tomio said, "seven orbs with lines like those don't look like they'd snap together easily. It defies the laws of physics."

"Ah, but this is magic we're dealing with," smiled Basil.

"Excuse me," Ryan said with strained politeness. "What does this mean." He pointed to the Italian phrase.

I told him.

"And what is *it*, exactly?" Ryan's gaze darted around, a little defensively, I thought.

He hadn't been there when Basil had told Tomio and me the story of the legends, the Tunguska-like event that had led to the seven sacrifices. It hadn't occurred to me to tell him about it. Maybe because everyone was always turning to him for answers, since he knew Nero better than anyone, and he was always acting like a know-it-all.

Basil rubbed a hand across his jaw as he looked up at Ryan, peering at us over the seat like a precocious child. "The 'it' the saying is referring to, cannot be anything other than the Source Fire. The original flame from the legend."

NEVŞEHIR AIRPORT WAS a small facility placed well outside the city of the same name. It was early morning when we stumbled out of the plane and onto the pavement, but already heat waves baked the air over the tarmac, as the sun peered over the horizon.

Ms. Shepherd, Basil, Mehmet and Shereen were in rapid-fire conversation as they strode across the concrete toward a set of small black helicopters, the blades already whirring.

Ryan, Tomio and I shouldered our backpacks, which was all the personal luggage we'd been allowed to bring, and jogged to keep up. Both the ghost-steel blade and the journal were tucked into my bag.

This part of Turkey was flat and dry; a lazily rolling, tree-less terrain that looked as though it went on forever. We were a forty-five-minute drive from one of the world's wonders, Cappadocia, but there'd be no time for sightseeing.

I turned my phone on as we walked to see if I could get a signal. I wanted a map so I could see where we were headed. The intel was that the epicenter of the supernatural effluent was a mountain north of a village called Aladag. Punching it in called up a grid dotted with crooked roads and undeveloped terrain. Rolling over the names of places on the map triggered memories. Demirkazik. Yeniköy. Murtaziköy.

"Hey." I bumped against Tomio and showed him my phone. "Check out these names. Remind you of anyone?"

The party ahead of us had come to a stop near the choppers, where two men wearing pilot's gear stood waiting. One of them I would have recognized by his eyebrows alone if he hadn't been wearing a helmet. But he was wearing a helmet, so I recognized him by his hulking presence, and the familiar aura of still waters running deep.

"Davazlar?!" I blurted, interrupting Ms. Shepherd mid-yell. She sent me a look of annoyance. She hated disorganization, especially in conversation.

The game-maker spotted me and quirked a smile. He had to call over the chopper, but even so, he was difficult to hear. I read his lips easily enough. "Hello, Ms. Cagney."

"Didn't know you were going to meet us here." I looked for Basil so I could send him a withering look for not telling me, but he wasn't paying attention. We were already loading our gear into the choppers.

Davazlar moved closer. "I'm originally from Ankara," he said in that low, grinding voice of his. "Welcome to my country."

The other pilot, who hadn't introduced himself yet, was in conversation with Basil and Ms. Shepherd as they threw their bags into the helicopter's small rear hatch. Basil's expression seemed brighter than it had in days as the pilot yelled at him over the sound of the blades. Ryan was already seated and doing up his belt when I ducked in and took the middle seat. Tomio took the seat on my right.

"They had the whole plane ride to tell us," Ryan groused, pulling a helmet over his head.

"Tell us what, exactly?" I picked up the helmet that had been sitting on the floor in front of my seat. It was neon yellow with an attached mouthpiece. Settling it on my head, I then fumbled in between the seats for the straps to my harness and belt.

Tomio pulled on a black helmet. "They already found it."

I froze as I was buckling my chin strap, staring at him. "What?"

"Her." Ryan added, fastening his own melon cage. "I overheard the other pilot refer to it as 'she'."

"I'm sorry," I said with artificial brightness as I swiveled my head to look at Ryan. "But you couldn't possibly be referring to the volcanic husk of the last progenitor, could you?"

Ryan nodded, still looking annoyed.

My heartbeat picked up a notch at the possibility. I hoped Ryan and Tomio hadn't misunderstood.

Davazlar slid into the pilot's seat as Shereen took the passenger side. She really rocked gear, no matter what it was; this time, a white helmet and black, bug-like, reflective glasses.

There was a staticky sound from my headset, then Davazlar's voice came through the speakers. He began flicking switches and doing other piloty things. "Shoulder straps, everyone. We'll be there in less than an hour."

Tomio squeezed my knee as the chopper took flight and we swung out over the now sunlit, arid terrain of central Turkey.

My mind tumbled and reeled at the speed we were

moving, not literally—I'd ridden in a chopper before—but at everything that had already happened if the epicenter had been located. Ms. Shepherd must have had fit and able agents on the ground near the epicenter who'd been deployed the moment she'd made that phone call in Basil's office. For all the complaining about incompetency, her team seemed pretty efficient to me. Why she hadn't bothered to update us about these developments—especially if Ryan had understood correctly, and they really had found the seventh shell already— spoke volumes about what she saw as our position on this little team. A little more respect for what we'd accomplished in Naples, even if we'd later failed to protect the violet fire, would have been nice. Once more, I wasn't sure I liked the idea of being an agent low in the hierarchy. I wanted to know what was going on, and have some say in the plan of attack.

Rather than moaning about this into everyone's earpieces, or harassing Shereen or the boys for details, which was what I really wanted to do, I watched the sky and land swing by the windows and let my mind wander. It wandered back to Dover where Georjie was waiting to hear from me. I really hoped we didn't regret not allowing her to come. I'd seen her in action, and she'd only grown stronger since then, but earth was earth, and fire was fire. If she'd been hurt—

"There!" Davazlar pointed a thick finger at a peak reaching into the sky from an otherwise mostly flat surface.

Where the terrain we'd covered was dusty ochre with the occasional splash of brown and gold, the mountain we approached was a mottled gray, yellow and green. A blue snake of a river wound its way around the base of the range, pooling into sparkling lakes then dwindling to multi-layered threads. We passed over the water and into the mountain range, where farms and houses ceased and the earth grew rocky and treacherous. Another twenty minutes of swinging through the airspace above the valleys, and Davazlar began to slow our chopper. He spoke to the other pilot, who flicked switches as we spiraled toward a large relatively flat area, cradled between the mountains.

Before the chopper touched down, I caught a flash of two human shapes waiting at a distance. Davazlar settled the bird and killed the engine. The blades gave a slow whine as they came to a stop, and we scrambled from the helicopter in a symphony of metallic clicks and snaps. Leaving our helmets on the seats, our boots hit cracked, rocky earth as the other chopper touched down a short distance away.

Davazlar and Shereen were already jogging toward the people who were waiting for us, both men, both darkly tanned and dressed in khaki clothing. They wore dark sunglasses and pale hats. Matching sweat stains ringed their armpits and blossomed at their necklines.

I jogged beside Tomio, not bothering to wait for Basil and Ms. Shepherd, who I guessed had decided this mission was somehow safer than the other. Probably because our target had already been located, the progenitor acquired. But if Nero did show up, it would be up to us to protect her, and that made her a liability. I scanned our surroundings for sign of Nero, but there was nothing. There wasn't even wind, only the calls of birds, the buzz of insects, and the occasional rustle where little geckos darted across our path.

Davazlar and the other men spoke to each other in Turkish as they headed up our crew, leading us on an angle up the mountainside. Clusters of prickly pear and cacti dotted the rocky landscape. Lonely old olive trees thrust from crags in the rocks, their silvery-green leaves still in the airless morning.

Tomio, directly behind me as we kept to the narrow path through the inhospitable topography, brushed my shoulder. "Saxony, look."

Following his gesture, I looked up at a nearby rock face to see small square windows cut into the sandstone surface. Nearby, a section of rock had broken away, revealing a hollow space within, including a set of shallow steps and what were—unmistakably—the rooms of some ancient home. A feeling of awe came into me, but it vanished again as the men led us into a shaded cleft, and down an embankment covered with small stones and loose shale.

In a pocket near a yawning black cave, sat a perfect, black statue. My heart jumped when I saw her.

Davazlar and the men got there first, still talking at the speed of light. Heart pounding and pulse jumping, I stopped near the volcanic shell, crouching for a better look. She was dusty and covered in handprints. They'd clearly unearthed her from somewhere and then carried her here.

She was an older woman, with sagging jowls and low-hanging breasts. But she had wide, beautiful eyes, and a broad forehead and mouth. She had hardened in a fetal position, lying on her side with her left elbow cushioning her head. Her left hand had been broken off—exposed, perhaps, to a rockfall—leaving the raw substance of which she was made, naked to the light. As the sun slanted overhead and the shadows crawled back, she glimmered in the places where she was clean.

The rest of our crew arrived, and as I glanced up to see Shereen, Basil and Ms. Shepherd slide down the loose stuff to join us, I caught a glimpse of Ryan's expression. His gaze was locked on her face, his cheeks pale and dark circles under his eyes, which I hadn't taken much notice of before, were pronounced. He was the one who had held the orb which had revealed the ancient language of this region, the clue that had led us to her. I wondered what his traveling experience had been like.

I moved closer to him, speaking low. "Do you recognize her?"

It was silly to worry that someone might overhear what I knew from experience was an intimate question, but our party were closed in around the statue now, some watching the surrounding terrain for signs of Nero, others absorbed with what had been unearthed and discussing how best to transport her. No one overheard, but Tomio noticed, and joined us.

Ryan seemed to tear his gaze away from her with effort. "Her face was the last thing I saw when I... traveled."

"You recognize her?" Tomio asked, as one of the men produced a large tarp from a backpack, and threw it over the statue.

"Only from the orb." Ryan rubbed at his eyes. "Come on, let's scout ahead while they bring her."

I'd been so relieved that she'd been found in one piece, I hadn't thought about what was next. Where would we take her? I had expected a battle, but the drone operators would have warned us if they'd seen anything strange within a five-mile radius. Nero wasn't here. We'd actually beaten him.

It only required two men to carry her. Davazlar and one of the men who'd been waiting for us when we arrived, set her on a collapsible stretcher with aluminum bars and a tough, nylon surface. Half our party followed behind and the rest of us went ahead, eyes peeled for anything alive that wasn't an insect or an animal.

It wasn't until she'd been secured in the back of the larger chopper and the helicopters were in the air that the tension drained out of my body and exhaustion washed over me like a tsunami.

We'd removed her from the predator's path. She was mostly in one piece. Now we just had to hide her somewhere Nero could never find her, and pick up the pieces of our ruined species.

11

ABSOLUTION

The large van that had picked us up from the London Airport hummed along the curvy, forest-covered roads leading to Dover. Ms. Shepherd and Mehmet had gone their own way from the London Airport: Shereen and Mehmet to the agency to visit friends, and Ms. Shepherd to her flat in London, claiming that all the stress was wrecking her immune system and she felt like she was coming down with something. When she'd rested, she'd visit Basil to discuss the long-term home of the sculpture.

We called it a sculpture, but only because there was no better word for the remains of the final progenitor. She sat on the van's floor, cradled inside a lined wooden crate, hidden from view. I was glad I couldn't see her. Tracing her features made me feel a sadness I didn't have the energy to cope with. It was the stamping out of the majority of idle fires, yes. That was a burdensome reality I knew would hit me when the madness of these days passed. But it was more than that. This mage had lived a full life, maybe even much longer than your average life. The headmaster had confirmed that magi had normal lifespans, but this mage was not your average fire magus. She was an original. A mother to all those who carried a green idle. She was the matriarch from whom Isaia had sprung, and Gage and Ryan and Shereen.

That made her also my mother. Adopted, anyway. Chad and his twin sons were born with different colored idles. So, it was not genetics that determined a mage's idle, but something else, something more mysterious. Perhaps something in the nature of the person, rather than the blood. Perhaps the birth date, or the position of the stars when a mage was born. Whatever it was, it gave Basil's agency fodder for research for years to come, even if there were only green idles left to study.

I wondered how my progenitor had come to be in this state. Had she died a natural death, but her body couldn't decompose in the way of flesh because of the heat? I pictured her slowly hardening into the volcanic rock-like substance of which she was now made. Her fire perhaps slowly, or maybe even quickly, baking her into her final form the way terra cotta solidifies in a kiln.

Ryan and Basil sat on the bench facing me and Tomio, our backs against the van's steel sides. The vehicle had been delivered by a rental company, the keys passed over to Davazlar, who'd opted to see the sculpture delivered to the academy before he parted ways with us. The game-maker was currently driving. He appeared immune to exhaustion.

We had reached Dover before I sent Georjie a text, letting her know we were back. She responded that she'd gone for a long walk down the beach. She'd return now that she knew we were home, but would arrive back at the manor after us.

Ryan was slouched against the van's wall, his head down. I thought he was asleep when he raised his head, eyes dark in the gloom of the vehicle. He gazed at the box. His voice was dry. Tired. "Nero might be able to track her. We don't know how the effluent works. It might take centuries to saturate the area around it, but what if it doesn't? What if he can track her wherever she is, in real time?"

Basil looked at Ryan. "That has occurred to me, too, but we can't hide her at the agency, there are too many vulnerable mages there, and too many eyeballs. I'll never get her inside a bank vault without arousing unwelcome questions. The academy is the perfect temporary hiding place, until Ms. Shepherd and I can locate somewhere more secure."

I lifted my head from Tomio's shoulder. "But he's been to the academy. That's where he found the diary in the wall. The one with the formula."

"Yes. Many years ago, he was there. But he doesn't know anything but the common rooms and the bedroom where he slept. Further, he doesn't know that I'm involved, operating against him. I'm sure he's arrived in Turkey by now. But our people covered our tracks well. He'll reach the epicenter, but there won't be anything there, and why should he have a clue as to who foiled him? It could be archaeologists who stumbled over her remains just as easily as it could be mages who got there before him." Basil waved a hand. "There are many hiding places at Chaplin Manor. And with all that neoprene and fireproofing, it should help to cloak whatever supernatural effluent she is leaking, too. At least for a time."

"Are you sure about that?" Ryan leaned his elbows on his knees but twisted his head to look at the headmaster, resting his chin on his palm.

Basil let out a long sigh. "My boy, I am sure of nothing. We are only doing what we can do. Our entire species is grieving and in a state of disarray. The agency, for all intents and purposes, no longer exists, not to mention all the agencies like ours around the world. We're at war. In war, nothing is certain. But we've finally gotten the upper hand, and I'll do everything in my power to preserve what few mages we have left. Over time, more mages will be born."

Maybe he was right, but from what—whom—would their idles spring? From Nero? With only a rare few springing from the shell in the crate? It wasn't a comforting thought.

The van slowed. I leaned forward to glance out the windscreen. "We're almost there."

Davazlar turned the van into the academy's driveway, to the familiar sound of the gates squeaking open. We braced the crate as the van took the steep, curving driveway and came to a stop in front of the manor.

Davazlar and Ryan carried the crate from the back of the van, and up the front steps as Basil unlocked the doors and held them open. Tomio and I stepped into the lobby after them and shut the doors.

"Where to, boss?" Davazlar asked.

Basil turned to address us as a group. "Before we secrete her away, I want you to consciously decide whether you want to know where she is, or not. I won't keep her location from anyone in this room who wants to know, but don't go into this knowledge lightly. Remember that it could make you valuable, not to mention, a target, if anyone were to find out."

His statement jarred me unpleasantly, and my skin prickled. I was suddenly very glad Georjayna wasn't here to greet us. It was better if she didn't know where the statue was to be kept. "Are you suggesting that this knowledge might be... tortured out of us?"

Ryan shot me an eye roll. "Duh."

Basil gave Ryan a weary look but went on to reiterate another point. "Also remember that she won't be here indefinitely. Her hiding place is temporary, until I can arrange something else. You'll only have to carry this knowledge for what should be a matter of days."

"I want to know where she'll be," Ryan said. His look darkened. "And, I would welcome an encounter with Nero."

Ryan had already shown that while he was more competent than the average Burned mage, he didn't stand much of a chance against Nero. If he ever did face Nero, I didn't think he'd come out of it as the victor, but I didn't say so.

Tomio nodded. "I want to know, too."

Davazlar didn't need to answer, it was already clear that this was why he'd come with us in the first place, to see her well-hidden with his own eyes.

All the men looked at me, waiting.

I frowned. "If all of you know, I don't want to be left out."

Basil jerked a nod. "Right. Step carefully, gents. This way."

"WHAT DO WE DO ABOUT JANET?" I asked as Georjie, Tomio and I snagged slices of the pizza we'd had delivered from our favorite place in Dover.

After Davazlar had left and Basil had retreated to his suite to make phone calls, we'd ordered pizza and taken it to the first-years' lounge to eat. Ryan had grabbed a slice and left, his phone in his hand.

Tomio took a bite, grabbing the gooey string of cheese running from his mouth to his food. He was so hungry that he barely chewed it before he swallowed. "I've been thinking about that, too. I don't know. She could be anywhere. She could even be de—"

"Please don't say that," I said, around my bite. "I refuse to believe he killed her."

"Why would he?" Georjie asked with alarm.

Tomio lifted a shoulder in an elegant shrug and took a sip from his glass of water. "Maybe for betraying him? For bringing a radio into his hiding place to tell his enemies what he's up to?"

I swallowed and waited as the lump of food made a slow, painful descent down my throat. When he put it that way...

Tomio didn't seem to notice my dismay, and continued. "What use is she to him now? The last idle has been located and moved. It's not like he'll bring her more artifacts to demystify."

"You're making me lose my appetite." I put my half-eaten slice in the box and fell back against the couch. Georjie put a hand on my shoulder and squeezed.

"Sorry," Tomio said. "Just trying to think the way Nero might think. It's a principle of combat." He crammed the rest of his slice into his mouth and picked up another one, his own appetite clearly unaffected.

"We have to keep looking." I stared at the ceiling, not seeing anything but Janet's huge eyes as we closed the door to her cell.

"Of course, you do, sweetie." Georjie was all empathy. She'd put down her own slice now, too.

Tomio talked between bites. "Where do you suggest we start? Not that I'm disagreeing with you, I want to find her, too. Just... Nero is an international traveler. Where do we look first?"

I rubbed my face. I had no answers. I could fill a library with the questions I had no answers to.

The hinges on the lounge door squeaked, and we looked over. Ryan had returned. He approached and held his phone out to me. "Gage wants to talk to you."

I took Ryan's phone as he picked up another slice of pizza and sat in a chair across from Georjie.

Tomio leaned over so he could see Gage's face on the screen. "Hey, how are you feeling?"

I smiled and waved at him. "You look much better. Wait. Are you... standing?"

On the screen, Gage seemed to sway, then sit down on his hospital bed. He smiled. The sight of it lifted my spirits. "Yeah, now that I'm awake, I'm healing really fast. We are flying home tomorrow."

"That's great," I said, blinking with surprise. "No, that's amazing!"

Gage's grin faded a little, but a crooked smile remained. "Yeah, I'm really missing my dad. I'm worried about him, you know."

"Of course. Seeing you will be so good for him."

"That's what we're hoping." Gage's gaze flicked from side to side, from my face to Tomio's and back again. "Hey, do you mind if I talk to Saxony privately, Tomio?"

"Oh. No, not at all. I'll go." Tomio made to get up.

"No, I'll go." I got to my feet faster. "You finish eating. I'll go down the hall."

Tomio nodded, expression inscrutable.

Leaving the lounge, I went to the nearest landing and took a window seat. With a quick glance into the front yard, I sat against the pillows and brought Gage into view. "What's up?"

"Listen, I just wanted to say a few things before I arrive home and get distracted by my dad, and old friends, and stuff. You know how Saltford is. Home town, and all that."

"Sure." My heart was pounding and my palms felt damp.

"I wanted to say thank you for everything you did for me, after... after Nero took me. Ryan told me that you and Tomio were kind of abandoned by the police, and even by the agency, but you never gave up."

"Oh."

Gage had already said thank you, he really didn't need to say it again.

"It's nothing you wouldn't have done for me. Plus, Basil did all he could, considering what was going on."

Gage dimpled and nodded. "Yeah, I'm sure he did."

"Now that it's just us, I want to know... are you sure you're okay? I mean, you look great. But, how do you really feel?"

He looked down momentarily, thoughtfully, then up. "Have you ever lost anyone close to you?"

Goosebumps swept across my legs and back. I didn't trust my voice, so I just nodded.

"It's like that," he said. "It's like a death. Maybe that sounds stupid, because no one died, but—"

"No, it doesn't sound stupid, Gage. It makes perfect sense. After all, a part of you did die. And I am sorrier than I can say."

"Yeah. Thanks. There're pros, though. Don't forget, it's good for perspective. I don't have pain. I never realized before just how much pain I was enduring until it was gone. So that's a silver lining."

"That's good. And have you thought about what's next? Besides healing, obviously."

"My dad is my priority now. He's not doing well. Mom said that Basil told her that some mages handle the loss really poorly, while others are mostly fine. Maybe I fall into the latter category, though I think it's too early to tell, since

I'm still in shock. But my dad… he's taking it really hard. So I want to help him get well. I guess I'll figure out what's next after that."

"That sounds like a plan. When I'm in Saltford next, I'll come see you."

Gage hesitated, and my heart gave an ache as I realized that he might not want that. I added hastily. "Only if you want me to."

His eyes and nose scrunched up for a second. "No. Yeah, of course, I would love to see you."

But he had hesitated.

I couldn't tell if his words were genuine. Given what he'd been through, both with Nero and with me, maybe Gage didn't really know how he felt. That would take time.

"So, you think you've saved whoever is left?" Gage set himself back against the pillows on his bed, shifting the phone to look up at it.

"I hope so, but we still have to find Janet."

Gage nodded, then yawned. "Ryan told me about her. Poor lady."

"I should let you go, you're yawning."

He nodded again, but his expression shifted gears. He looked pensive, uncertain. "Yeah. I am tired. But there's one more thing. I feel really weird saying this, but, here goes." He cleared his throat. "You and Tomio—"

My gut twisted.

"—it's okay with me. I mean, I'm okay with it." His expression cramped again. "Not that you need my permission, you can do whatever you want, but— Wow, this is so awkward."

I felt as though my chest was filling with helium. No, I didn't need his permission, but his words still had a remarkable effect on me. "Do you mean that?"

"Of course, I wouldn't say it if I didn't mean it. What happened between us sucked, but I don't blame you, and I've already forgiven Tomio. My mom thought I shouldn't go home without telling you that."

My eyes widened. "Your mom?"

Gage laughed. "Yeah, she's... she's kind of a fan of yours. She said that we'd both feel better if we talked about what happened and you'd feel better if you knew I wasn't angry." He shrugged. "And, I'm not. It seems pretty clear that we weren't meant to be together, Saxony. And I don't want to stand in the way of your happiness, if being with Tomio makes you happy. I mean, it's not my business, but just saying. My mom also said..." he paused, looking for words.

I prompted him when too much time passed. "What did the regal Angelica have to say?"

He spoke slowly, as though trying to make sure he paraphrased his mother well, which was probably exactly what he was doing. "She said that it's not universal, but almost everyone leaves their first love. And that it's that heartbreak that helps form the adults we become. It gives us a deeper capacity for love. She says, sorrow and loss are essential to growing up, and so is learning to forgive and let go."

My vision blurred and I ran a hand across my eyes. Yes, those were definitely Angelica's words, either that or Gage had matured considerably while he'd been comatose.

"Wise lady, your mom."

"Yeah." Gage let out a big breath. "We're lucky we have her. Speaking of we, I should talk to Ryan again before I sign off."

I got up and headed back toward the lounge. "Sure. Thank you for the talk, Gage. I'm really happy to see how fast you're healing."

"Thanks. Talk to you again soon, I hope. Or not. I know you're busy."

I smiled at my friend, feeling lighter and happier as I said goodbye and handed the phone back to Ryan.

"So, do you really think it's over now?" Georjie asked as she grabbed a throw pillow and hugged it to her stomach. "The remaining magi are safe?"

Tomio got up to stack the empty pizza boxes and take them over to the garbage bin behind the door. There was a cold slice sitting on my plate, but I didn't feel much like eating it.

"Basil seems to think so, although he's still taking a lot of precautions, which I say there can't be enough of." I took a drink of water as Tomio plopped into the sofa beside me.

"It would be foolish to think Nero is going to give up just because the statue isn't where he expects it to be," he said, letting his head lay back against the couch.

A sky dark with the colors of twilight peeked through the gap in the drapes. It was getting late. Ryan had excused himself, either he was still talking to Gage, or he'd gone to bed, or he was off doing mysterious Ryan stuff. Basil hadn't emerged from his suite since dinner. The academy was dim and still, save for our lounge where the sconces flickered with amber light and the air still smelled faintly of cheese and olives.

"How much power does one mage need?" Georjie wondered.

I took Tomio's hand and began to massage the fleshy pad between his thumb and forefinger absent-mindedly. My imagination went back to the rainbow-hued creature we'd glimpsed with Georjie's magic.

"I'm not sure he is just a mage anymore. What we saw was something new, something magedom hasn't seen in living memory."

"He's one idle away from possessing all of them," Tomio murmured, his eyes half-lidded with sleep and a full-stomach.

Georjie yawned. "What do you think would happen if he got the last one, too? He'd be like the original god from the legend?"

"Now, there's a scary thought."

My body felt flushed with heat, maybe from sitting too near Tomio, or just from wearing a thick sweater. I paused massaging Tomio's hand to pull my hoody over my head and set it over the back of the couch.

Tomio yawned and stretched, his back crackling audibly. "I don't know about you, but I'm bushed, not to mention screwed up from all the travel." He glanced at Georjie, then to me. "I'll let you two catch up. See you in the morning?"

"Good night, Tomio," said Georjie, smiling with her chin propped in her hand.

"Sleep well." I turned my face up as he leaned over to kiss me. It wasn't a lingering kiss, because of Georjie's presence, but it still made my toes curl and my belly unfurl like a stretching cat.

I watched Georjie watch him go, one fine, pale brow arching appreciatively as he disappeared. Her brown eyes flicked to me. "He's pretty dreamy, Saxony."

I couldn't stifle the grin that took over my face. "Right?"

"I'm happy for you."

"Thanks, I'm happy for you and Lachlan, too." I was

about to tell her what Gage had said, when her forehead pinched into two shallow lines.

"Do you think Basil will go ahead with the school year? Given everything that's happened?"

I sighed. "I don't know. We've lost a lot of students. I don't know how many, exactly. No one ever made a point of talking about idle fires before, so I don't know who is left unless I've touched them. Except for Tomio, of course."

"So weird that he still has his fire, but the two of you don't share a mage bond. Do you think it's because you love him?"

I lifted my head in surprise, feeling lost. "How did you get there?"

Georjie shrugged. "Love is the most powerful force on Earth. Maybe the fact that you—being part of the remaining green-idle family—love him, is enough to protect him."

"There's a thought I never thunk before." I didn't agree with Georjie's theory, since I hadn't been in love with Tomio when the red fires were snuffed, as nice a theory as it was. But she could put out any conjecture she wanted, I'd listen.

"You do though, right?"

"What?" I was feeling lost again.

Georjie rolled her eyes good-naturedly. "Honestly, you need to go to bed too. Love him, of course."

"Oh." I smiled crookedly as Tomio's features and character swam before my mind's eye. His beauty, his kindness, his strength, his calm demeanor but quirky sense of humor. "Yes. Yeah, I do. A lot. I never saw it coming, but what I feel for him makes me realize that what Gage and I had was on the juvenile side."

"He sounded nice too. But yeah, I guess we have to go through the juvenile ones to find the real deal. I sure did."

Georjie yawned again. "I guess... should I book my ticket back to Blackmouth?"

"You missing Lachlan?"

"No," she answered quickly, then laughed. "I mean, yes. Yes, I miss him, but that's okay. Missing someone is good. I don't want to leave if you need me."

I didn't want Georjie to leave. I felt better with her here, but I had no idea if her powers would come in handy again. It didn't look likely, and she had a life to get back to. "You should book your ticket."

Georjie got to her feet and stretched. "Okay. I'm glad I came. Not just for the remote viewing, but to see where you've been living and what you've been up to since we left Saltford. I've seen where Targa lives, but your life was a mystery. It's nice to be able to picture your surroundings, and meet the people in your life. Especially Tomio."

I got to my feet, grabbed my hoody and tied it around my waist as we headed for the door. I was feeling incredibly tired. More than tired, I felt downright sluggish, and my eyes didn't seem to want to focus. I rubbed them, trying to clear them, then reached for the light switch to turn off the sconces.

"Saxony," Georjie's voice drifted into my ear like a whisper, though she was right beside me. "Look at your arm."

Her features fuzzed then came into focus, her brown eyes concerned as she looked at my bare outstretched limb as my finger hovered over the light switch.

I pulled my arm closer to my face for a better view. All of the little hairs were standing straight up. I felt warm and exhausted, but I hadn't felt the goosebumps which usually accompanied hair spindling upright.

"Weird," I breathed. Twisting my arm and watching the

way my blond hairs stayed perfectly perpendicular to my body.

"It's like that on your face and neck, too," Georjie said with a mix of amusement and concern.

"I have neck hairs?"

She laughed. "Of course. They're fine, but they're there. I'm looking at them. Did you get a shiver?"

"No. Maybe it's the effluent leaking from the statue." I looked up at her, gaze sharper now. "How do you feel?"

"I'm fine." She pulled back the sleeve of her cotton t-shirt to show me. "No hackles here."

I flicked off the lights. "Maybe its static from my sweater. I'm fried. Let's go to bed."

I walked Georjie to her bedroom, one door down from Tomio, and two doors down from me. We whispered good night in the dark hallway, then slipped into our rooms.

12

BESIEGED

It began with a dark, horizonless void the color of an eggplant. Flickers of light licked at the periphery of my vision momentarily, there and then gone, making me wonder if there was something wrong with my eyes, or silent fireworks were going off somewhere behind me.

I'd gone through my bathroom routine and dressed for bed in a bit of a haze, the edges of everything blurry in the gloom, or blurry because I was just too tired to focus anymore. Multiple flights across several time-zones in such a short time were murder, even for a young person.

I was dreaming. I had to be, but it was so lucid. Was I traveling through space? The rainbow flickers of light were perhaps projected from passing galaxies?

I felt a psychic tug on my mind, like a toy boat on the end of a rope with a boy's gentle fingers guiding the vessel this way and that.

After landing in London, after the airport. What happened next?

The pull was gentle but insistent, and came with a flash of lemon yellow to my right. I turned, seeking a better look.

A light source could not be seen, but the movement kicked off a sensation that reminded me of the steady slide of a curling stone, a slide and a turn I was powerless to stop. It was a familiar feeling. But the yellow light ceased, and only that depthless purple-black presented itself, no matter which way I turned and drifted. Frustration glimmered deep inside my mind, but there was a flash of tangerine orange from above and the frustration was overruled in favor of curiosity. I wondered vaguely if this was how Alice felt after following the white rabbit into its hole: confused, intrigued, puzzled by the quaint place in which she found herself.

A sense of being gently redirected brought my awareness back to the topic at hand, with another inquisitive tug. Some force probed my mind for answers: *After the airport. Run it through your mind. Play it back, like a film.*

It had been raining, and the temperature was warm enough to leave a layer of mist over the tarmac as we stepped from the plane and waited for the van. I stood beside Tomio, his arm wrapped around my shoulders, his head against my hair, as we were asked to wait five minutes. The van would be delivered from the service parking lot. Someone had spoken in a strong East London accent. Not to me, but to Basil. Ms. Shepherd had gone already, Mehmet and Shereen had gone shortly afterward—her tall, slender frame disappearing against the glimmer of glazed illumination from the terminal building. Orange lights flashed, safety lights, or the ones held by airport personnel. I couldn't remember, and it didn't matter.

Another soft tap to send me in the right direction: *These details are unimportant.*

In my mind's eye, I watched as Davazlar and Ryan oversaw the extraction of the wooden crate. It emerged from the belly of the plane, slowly, gingerly, with the word 'Fragile' stenciled on the side. It was so bright, that crate, almost like the wood had been permeated by a reflective substance. Funny. I hadn't recalled it being so vibrant. Why had Basil chosen such an attention-drawing box in which to house—

My mind recoiled like a snail's antennae, suddenly shy. There was a nebulous, ill-defined sensation of danger being close. I pulled away from the memory, twisting and drifting again, like that curling stone swerving around its mark.

There came a flash of red on black on red, a full-frontal assault, accompanied by a throat-tightening, face-blistering feeling of rage that was not mine.

It was gone before I could linger on its origin, but not before I shrank away on reflex, sending my formless weight gliding in reverse.

Green threads emerged on either side of my vision, narrow rivers of emerald and lime, like the northern lights. So beautiful. So, comforting. A feeling of utter peace and sedation leeched into me. I almost felt numb.

Think of the box. What happened to the box?

My memory resurfaced as images appeared to be painted across a backdrop of heavily saturated pigmentation: the unmarked van, windowless, clean, and in pristine condition, had approached slowly. It had stopped, then reversed so its rear double doors were presented to the group standing at the foot of the plane, the box on the pavement between them.

The box.

Yes, the bright, glowing box with the letters stenciled on the side.

Keys had been exchanged, and some small-talk, between Basil, Davazlar and the driver, who seemed in a hurry to get on to his next task. He tipped a finger to the brim of his newsboy cap and loped toward the nearest terminal, moving with the boundless energy of youth. The mist swallowed him the way it had swallowed Shereen and Ms. Shepherd.

Back to the box. The delivery boy is of no consequence.

This thought was accompanied by a bouquet of pretty pink bubbles, inflating slowly and then bursting in slow-motion one after the other. The effect was mesmerizing. With the pop of each bubble, the visual of a bright wooden crate with the word 'Fragile' stenciled on the side became sharper. It sat on wet pavement, throwing a short confusion of shadows in the synthetic lights.

Well, the box. It had been loaded gently into the van, hadn't it? Why else had the van been necessary? It had slid perfectly between a set of bench seats, each bolted to the floor and facing the other. Tomio had held the van door open for me because it tended to swing shut. Then he'd followed me in and settled on the seat beside me. Basil and Ryan had come in after, and the driver's side door had slammed. Davazlar turned on the engine, and the van rolled.

Where did the van roll to?

My memory balked. I couldn't see, could I? There were no windows, and I had to crane my neck to look out the windscreen. And why would I bother when I was so tired?

These thoughts were petulant, annoyed, and ever so slightly tinged with something else. Rebellion? Deviousness? I tasted something sour in my mouth and wrinkled my nose, or tried. I had no hands, no face, but the sensation of wrinkling my nose was still there. The sour taste turned bitter.

Focus!

An explosion of teal lights, jagged and retina-searing, startled me, above and to my left. The sliding sensation increased as I turned for a better view.

Saxony. Wake up!

The words echoed as though shouted into a canyon: *You're in danger... anger... anger!*

This echoed too, only it came back to me changed: *I'm in danger... anger... anger!*

My skin prickled, and I became aware of my body, my weight, my breath. I gasped so harshly that my throat burned, and I came awake at once. Lying in my bed at the academy, I was safe in my bedroom, yet the feeling of being in danger yanked me upright, like I was tied to a ceiling fan by a rope. The sliding sensation sent me upward, straight through the ceiling. Alarm coursed through my nerves, hot and acidic. How could I still be sliding?

An equally powerful force pulled me the other direction, stretching and snapping me back, sending me sailing down through the floor.

The van. The box. Think of them. It's of the utmost importance. You must... focus. I demand it!

I.

One word. I felt as though I'd been slapped. This "I" was not me. This I was an invader.

My heart throbbed and my stomach clenched as a powerful, sickly-sweet feeling of being violated punched me in the throat. I scrambled for the surface of my consciousness, screaming, though there was no sound. A different scream echoed mine, a deep, evil-sounding howl from somewhere behind me. No. Not behind me, below me. It sent my body in a spasm of panic, my mind crawling desperately away, hand over hand, clawing into whatever I could hold.

I lurched upright for a second time, this time for real, dizzy and gasping. I clutched at my ribs, my arms. My body finally felt solid.

My sheets were soaked, my skin felt like ice—a sensation I'd not had since I was a natural. All of the hairs on my body pricked upright, and this time they were accompanied by goosebumps so strong they actually hurt. Panting like I'd just sprinted a hundred-meter dash, I raked my gaze around my bedroom. It was quiet and dark and empty save for me.

Rubbing my legs vigorously to get rid of the horrible gooseflesh, I swung out of bed and reached for my water glass. My throat and mouth were parched. Gulping the cup's entire content, I got to my feet and turned on the desk light, happy to see my vision was sharp.

But I was shaking and shuddering uncontrollably, as though hypothermia had gripped my nervous system and musculature. An absurd notion for a mage. Shock penetrated like a million tiny needles down my spine. I stood there in the middle of my room, holding an empty glass and looking around without registering what I was seeing.

What the hell was all that?

But I knew exactly what it had been: a full-on psychic attack, by a mage who must have gained access to the vulnerable sleeping minds of lesser magi. This was a weapon I had no idea how to fight. The thought of going back to sleep left me feeling weak with fear and shot through with adrenaline. Was this why the hairs on my body had stood upright in the lounge, when I'd gone to turn off the light? Had Nero been scoping me out, to see if I was asleep yet so he could make a move on my subconscious?

What would it mean if my memory had followed our van all the way here, to the academy? What if the psychic pressure had pulled the image of the statue's hiding place from my imagination, like a loose thread being pulled from a knit sweater?

Terror lanced through my stomach, and it gave an unpleasant heave.

Staggering into my bathroom, I flipped up the toilet seat and got myself positioned over the bowl, thinking I was going to throw up. But after a few seconds of deep breathing, the nausea passed, leaving me feeling trembly.

Going into my bedroom, I stood in the middle of the carpet casting about my room for an idea of how to defend myself. My gaze fell on the clock. It was nearly one a.m. Most of the night was still ahead of me. Raking a hand through my mass of curls, I let out a forceful sigh, then another thought struck me. If Nero could reach *my* mind while I was sleeping, could he reach *any* one of us, or was I just the most mentally weak of our group, the easiest subconscious to penetrate? Now that I was conscious, did that mean he'd seek out someone else's memories? Could he only search one mage at a time?

Shivering from stress, I snatched my bathrobe from the back of the door and peeked out into the hallway. All was gloomy and quiet as a graveyard. Bare feet padding on the hall runner, I went to Georjie's room and listened at the keyhole. Nothing. But Georjie wouldn't be a target anyway. Leaving Georgie's room, I went to the room Tomio had claimed before we'd left for the Arctic. He'd picked it to be near me, and I loved knowing he was close by.

His door stood open an inch. I pushed at it with a fingertip, peeking through the crack. He was a lump under a thin bedsheet, dark hair spiked out against his pillowcase. I crept in further, listening to his deep, even breathing.

He didn't look like he was under attack. He lay on his side with one hand tucked under his pillow and the other open against the mattress, his tanned skin dark against the white sheets. The muscles of his arm and shoulder were soft and relaxed with sleep. The skin of his back was bare. Tomio slept shirtless, I knew that from Naples.

I backed up, feeling like a creep, even though I'd only wanted to make sure he was okay.

A floor board creaked under my foot, and I froze with a wince.

Tomio shifted, the frame of the wooden bed squeaking softly. He raised his head, eyes still mostly closed. "Saxony?"

I waved my fingers and smiled. "Hi."

"What are you—" He sat up, rubbing the sleep out of one eye before peering at me with more focus. "Are you okay?"

Well, now that he was awake...

I padded forward until I was past the foot of his bed, not sure how to start. "I am, but... I wasn't. I think—"

I hesitated. Now that I was fully awake, I wasn't sure anymore that what I had dreamed had actually been an attack. What if it had just been a vivid fear-dream? But then again, what if that's what Nero wanted me to believe, so that I would lower my guard and brush it off?

Tomio sat up, the sheet falling away from his chest. He shuffled over and patted the mattress. "Whatever it is, I'm not going to go back to sleep until you tell me." He smiled crookedly. "Not that I'm complaining. You're welcome here anytime, day or night."

He lifted the sheet and it was all the invitation I needed. I thought no further than how it would feel to have his arms around me. I slipped off my robe and scooted onto his bed, turned my back to him and lay my head on his pillow. He lay behind me and put his arm around my ribcage. The feeling of his solid bulk against my body immediately soothed me and my eyes drifted closed.

He didn't push me to talk. Maybe he was too tired or

maybe he figured I'd talk when I was ready to talk, but he pulled me into his body, put his nose in my hair and inhaled.

"You smell so good." His voice was husky and the sound of it did something delicious to me.

Warmth and longing pooled in my stomach and pelvis, my eyes drifted open as Tomio ran his palm over the back of my hand and interlaced his fingers over mine. He drew a lock of my hair back from my ear with the tip of his nose and planted a kiss behind my ear—gentle, a question. It sent shivers down my spine and made my thighs feel weak. Rolling into him, I turned my face up to his.

That was it.

The world tilted on its side and every nerve ending came alive. The heat of his mouth soaked through the full length of me. I ran my hand around the back of his neck, deepening our kisses. I couldn't get enough of him and wondered if I might actually die if we stopped.

His skin was so soft under my hands, so smooth and perfect, encasing hard curves of muscle that fit perfectly under my palms. He was made for me to touch, to smell, to taste. His scent clouded my mind and blocked out everything else. His sounds, the little moans in the back of his throat and the deeper sounds, like growls, made my toes curl and my eyes roll beneath my eyelids. The feeling of his kisses, his lips, his hands gliding over my body and lifting off my shirt, skimming the sensitive sides of my breasts. I was consumed by him.

As air hit my naked skin, he stopped, looking me over and pausing so long that I felt I might melt away under his gaze, like candle wax. I held my arms up for him, realizing that I was on my back now, and wanting nothing more than to feel his weight on me. He tossed my shirt aside and came for me, blocking out all things visible and invisible.

There was nothing else but him.

IT WAS ALMOST HALF past two when a soft rain started. The wind picked up, blowing gently through the eaves. We were spooning again, breathing in time. I glanced at the clock on the desk and took a slow, deep breath. Tomio was relaxed, but not asleep. His thumb drew slow circles on the palm of my hand.

Sleeping with him had done wonders for my emotional state, but worries now crept in at the edges, like hungry wolves circling injured prey. If I let myself fall asleep, would it happen again?

"You going to tell me what's on your mind?" Tomio's breath brushed against the back of my neck, making me shiver.

"How can you tell something is on my mind."

His voice was a low, sleepy rasp. "As much as I would like to think you snuck in here in the middle of the night for naked hugs with your super-hot boyfriend, I'm not quite that cocky. Close, but not quite."

I smiled. "Well, even if that hadn't been my original intention, plan B turned out to be better than plan A ever was."

"What was plan A?" He dropped a kiss on the back of my shoulder.

"I'm not sure, but it involved making sure you weren't having an unpleasant episode in your sleep, and possibly not going back to sleep myself. At least, not alone."

He stilled. I could practically feel him orienting all his thoughts in my direction.

I cleared my throat. "There might have been a breach."

He lifted his head. "What?"

I turned my face in his direction, seeing the alarm etched in his eyes. So much for post-coital cuddling.

"In my mind," I clarified.

Dismay and confusion wrangled across his features as he sat up, gaze latched on my face. I straightened too, sitting with my back braced against his headboard. I wrapped my arms around my knees as I drew them up to my chest.

"The memory of it is faded now, but I think Nero got into my dreams."

"You had a nightmare?"

I shook my head, trying to recall the experience, which already seemed as unclear as a distant ship on a foggy, windswept night. "No, it wasn't a nightmare. Not exactly. There was no scary imagery or anything like that. There was a lot of colored lights, and I had no body. I felt like I was sliding through the universe on a sheet of ice, which, come to think of it, was a bit like traveling with the orb. But there was this other quality, too. A kind of internal pressure to go back over details in my mind and relive our arrival at the airport. And there was a lot of... compulsion to focus on the crate. Specifically, where it went after the airport."

Tomio's breath hitched. He had no trouble believing that it had been a psychic invasion and not just a dream, I could see it in his face. "Holy crap, Saxony. Did you show him where we are?"

"No, I woke up before it got that far. But, well, if that was him digging around in my mind"—I shuddered with revulsion at the feeling of being violated—"then he knows we landed in London." My skin prickled as something that should have occurred to me earlier now came into my mind with outstretched talons. "And, he knows Basil was there."

Tomio ran his hair into spikes with his fingers. "Damn it, Saxony. He'll come here for sure. Why didn't you tell me right away?"

He got out of bed, his beautiful form bare before my hungry gaze.

"I... hadn't thought about it in so much detail as to put two and two together like that." I rushed out of bed, casting about for my shorts and t-shirt. They were nowhere to be seen, probably tangled up in the bedsheets. I picked up the bedding and shook it out.

Fifteen minutes ago, I was in romantic bliss with my boyfriend, now I was scrambling to find clothes, and balancing on a knife's edge of panic.

"Besides, you kind of distracted me. Which was what I wanted, I just wasn't expecting to be so *well* distracted." I gave a goofy thumbs up, trying to bring some levity to the situation. I was still standing there naked. "So, good job, you."

Tomio wasn't in a joking mood. He tossed me one of his Arcturus training tank tops and shorts from a pile of folded laundry sitting on his desk. "Here."

I pulled them on, heart galloping. The shorts sat low on my hips, so I pulled the drawstring tight.

Tomio grabbed a pair of black climbing pants from the same pile and hopped around, putting them on. He got them into place and made for the door. "Come on, we'd better wake up Basil."

13

CONFRONTED

We jogged down the hall toward Basil's suite, passing Ryan's room on our way. His door stood wide open, and the bed—visible in the corner—was a mess of sheets. We paused.

"Where's Ryan?" I asked, my chest pumping air and my heart pumping overheated blood.

Tomio went into the room, looking around. He checked the bathroom and came out frowning. "Not in the toilet."

We looked at each other, eyes filling with dread.

"Nero got to him?" My whisper was hoarse.

We bolted.

If we were right, there wasn't time to wake Basil. If we were wrong, then we'd know it within minutes.

We ran through the second-story in the direction opposite Basil's suite, weaving around landings and passing many closed doors. We zipped through the hall overlooking the lobby, quiet and dark below us as our bare feet pounded on the carpet. Running through the arch leading over the driveway, we took the stairs to the fire-gym's lobby three at a time.

Tomio reached the gym doors before me and tugged

them open. I followed him through into the dark, cavernous space.

Ryan was on the other side of the gym, making a beeline for the control panel that would unlock the compartment where we'd secreted the crate. Hearing us, he stopped and turned, eyes wide with surprise. When he saw it was us, he visibly relaxed, but not much.

He beckoned. "Come on. Help me. I don't know how much time we have."

We caught up and flanked him. I peered up into his face. "Did he get to you through your dreams?"

Ryan's irises were black circles in a sea of white. "How did you know?"

"Because he tried to get to me, too."

His expression was lined with tension. "Did you give anything up?"

I swallowed. "Kind of. Not that we brought her to the academy, but he saw us loading the crate into the van, and…"

"And?" He bit the word out.

"And Basil. He saw Basil in my memory, too. But that doesn't automatically mean he'll come here."

Ryan gave a twisted, humorless smile as he rolled the cover off the control panel. "If he doesn't come because of what he saw in *your* memory, he'll definitely come because of what he saw in *mine*. When did this happen?"

We waited as he punched his code into the computer.

"Less than two hours ago."

He gaped at me again, his fingers pausing over the keys. "And you didn't think to wake me up?"

"She woke *me* up," said Tomio, without giving a hint about what had happened afterward. "She just took a little time to get to the point. We were about to get Basil when we saw you weren't in your room. Here's a question. Why didn't *you* wake *us* up? Why try and move her all by yourself?"

"She's not that heavy, Nakano," Ryan snapped. "I just want to get her away from here as soon as possible. Basil said I can borrow his car any time, so right now my plan consists of throwing her in the back and getting her the hell away from the academy."

"And go where?" Tomio fired back.

The panel beeped its confirmation that Ryan had the right to access the gym's high-tech equipment. All that remained was for him to key in another code and the door hiding the crate would unlock.

"I was thinking the old mine would be safe. For now."

I rolled my eyes. "You really like that place."

Ryan paused, his fingers hovering over the keys. "What would be smarter, would be for us to wake Georjie and have *her* drive away with the crate, somewhere none of us knows."

"No way," Tomio hissed.

"She's not getting any more involved than she's been already," I added, sending Tomio a look of gratitude.

"I figured you'd say that." Ryan finished entering the code. The sound of a bolt whirring back came from the back wall of the gym. He turned away from the panel, looking down at my body, all the way to my feet and back up. "Where are your shoes? And why are you wearing Tomio's gear?" His gaze flashed to Tomio's pants and bare chest.

My face flushed as a look of smug realization came over Ryan's face. "Oh, I see. I get it now. My brother forgives you for cheating on him, and right away you hop into bed with his best friend. Pardon me, ex best friend."

I made a sound of indignation. "That's not what—"

Ryan snickered. "Relax, Cagney. I don't give a crap who's

bed you've been in or what you did while you were in it. Learn to take a joke."

We were halfway to the hidden compartment, and I was about to tell Ryan where he could shove his jokes when the gym doors squeaked. I expected to see Basil in the open doorway, but the shape standing in the shadows of the fire-gym's lobby was distinctly female. Whoever she was, she just stood there, watching us from her hidden place in the darkness.

My first thought was Georjie, which I dismissed in the next instant. This woman was a foot shorter than Georjie. My next instinct was to call Shereen's name, but this woman had longer hair. Plus, Shereen wasn't anywhere near the academy, she was in London. There was also something familiar about this woman's outline.

There was a flash of bright violet around her head, the kind of corona you see in paintings of angels. It made me gasp and take a step back. The flash was there and gone so quickly I might have thought my eyes were playing tricks on me, except that the boys reacted to it as well. The three of us turned to face the woman full on.

Ryan swore under his breath. "We're too late. He's here."

I blinked in confusion. I didn't see Nero, all I saw was a strange female figure standing in the darkness, one hand holding a door open. She hadn't yet crossed over the threshold and into the soft moonlight falling in through the skylights.

"What do you want?" Tomio called, breaking the silence. He sounded so commanding, and not scared at all.

I, however, was totally creeped out.

The woman walked forward, passing from gloom into the pale light. The darkness covering her face drew back, and my heart skipped. Ripples of surprise marbled over my calves.

"Janet!" I made to bolt toward her but Ryan grabbed my arm. I was too confused to yank myself out of his grip. I was relieved to see her alive and in one piece, but what was she doing here?

Janet didn't respond when I called her name. Her face was a blank as she walked toward us. She moved like a robot, with perfectly even strides. That violet aura flashed around her head again. Her long braid was gone, her hair cut to a jagged bob and dyed black, or maybe dark brown. The light in the gym threw everything into shades of gray. She wore dark leggings and a plain black sweatshirt with black shoes. Her clothes had the texture of fireproof fabric. My stomach plummeted.

"Janet." My whisper was hoarse and plaintive.

What had he done to her?

As Janet walked forward a few more steps, another figure appeared in the doorway behind her, one whose hands flashed the same hue of bright violet as the aura around Janet's head. The purple glow briefly illuminated Nero's angular face and sharp widows peak, before it disappeared. His hands had flashed in the same moment as the aura around Janet's head, like the lights on the top of skyscrapers, there to warn planes and helicopters how much clearance they had.

He strolled across the threshold and into the gym, stopping several meters behind Janet.

It felt like all the oxygen had been sucked from the room. Ryan's hand still gripped my forearm. I hardly noticed.

"Nice to see you again, Ryan." Nero's words came out

almost gentle, and thickly lyrical with a strong Italian accent.

I shuddered and thought of Dante, who sounded similar.

Nero's gaze flicked to Tomio, then to me, but he continued to address Ryan without giving any hint as to what emotional state he was in or what he had planned. "You might have some elevated skills, Wendig, but you need to work on blocking your mind. I cracked you like an egg."

Ryan's fingers tightened so much around my forearm that I winced and finally yanked myself free.

"Unlike your friend, here." He gestured to me, an elegant movement that was in sync with another flash of violet. "She figured out pretty quickly what was going on. Though I'm wondering if she's as strong awake as she is asleep."

"What do you want?" Tomio barked.

Nero's lips curled. "Not too bright, are you, my boy. I want what's in the wall behind you. I'm not by nature a violent man. I don't feel the need to destroy others if it can be avoided. We can do this peacefully."

I let out a snort at this outrageous statement.

Nero's brows lifted. "Oh, I assure you it's true. Name one magus who has died as a result of their fire being snuffed. I challenge you."

My jaw dropped. "Thousands of magi, maybe even tens of thousands by now, have committed suicide thanks to you! Others have been killed in accidents caused by the shock of losing their fire, and many more are suffering with PTSD. You have a lot to answer for."

I felt waves of rage rolling off Ryan, but fear, too. Ryan was powerful, but we all knew who the most powerful mage in the room was. There was no way around that.

The three of us had had no time to coordinate a defense

or even talk about the possibility of having to confront Nero. We stood between him and what he so desperately wanted, with no strategy. Two of us weren't even wearing shoes.

Nero waved a hand. "None of that is my fault. Too many of you let the power inside define your identity. When they discover how little value they have without the fire, they crumble. *Tsk.* So sad."

I thought about Ryan's dad, about my classmates, and all the unknown magi convalescing at the agency and in their homes. Nero felt nothing for what he'd done to them. It was staggering.

Nero continued, moving a few steps closer. "Ask yourself a simple question. Who am I without my fire? Because one way or another, you will lose it. Better to prepare yourself now. But like I said, I am not unreasonable, and I abhor violence, so I'm prepared to offer a trade." He gestured to where Janet stood before him, quiet and complacent. There was no sign that she was aware of her surroundings or could even hear this conversation.

"You take her, and I'll take the shell. I know it's in this room. Not just from your memory, Ryan. I'm close enough to feel it now. So, how about we make a simple, peaceful exchange? Which is generous of me, under the circumstances. Decline, and I shall turn her to ash before your eyes, and take the shell anyway."

My tongue felt swollen and dry. Give up my fire for Janet's life? I could do that. I'd been born without it, and while I was attached to my powers now, I wouldn't be able to live with myself if I let Nero kill Janet just to delay him from taking the shell for a few minutes longer.

I glanced at Ryan, and Tomio, just beyond him. But would they? Not to mention we would be making this decision for all the magi with a green idle—the fourteen percent of our species left. If we did this, would we be on the run for the rest of our lives from vengeful ex-supernaturals? But no one needed to know. Most magi weren't involved directly with this pseudo-genocide, most magi didn't even know who Nero was, or that he was the cause of their loss.

I closed my eyes and sent Basil a request to wake up, to come to the gym and help us. Fire magi didn't have telepathy, but there was no harm in trying.

"Deal," said Tomio. My eyes flew open and I sent him another grateful look.

"No deal," barked Ryan. He put an arm out in front of Tomio's chest, and said under his breath, "He's bluffing. He won't kill her. He loves her, he told me so himself. We can take him, but we have to stand together. Please, trust me."

"If you love someone, you don't keep them in a cage," I whispered. "He doesn't give a crap about her."

Nero chuckled. The sound made my skin crawl. It was so utterly confident, so self-assured and all-knowing. He'd look like a regular guy if it hadn't been for the strange alchemy he was using on Janet, but he wasn't regular. Not anymore.

"Last chance." Nero raised a hand, fingers posed as if to snap. His hand flashed bright purple and Janet's feet came off the floor.

I gasped a deep inhale, and yelled. "It's in the wall behind us!"

Ryan's hand clamped over my mouth hard, bruising my lips.

"I already knew that," Nero replied, as cool as if he were remarking about the weather. "The deal is off. Too late, raggazzi."

He snapped his fingers.

Janet burst into purple flames.

Ripping Ryan's hand away from my mouth, I screamed

her name, my head pounding with heat and horror. Wanting to look away but unable, I saw her face contort with pain. She threw her head back and opened her mouth wide in a scream, though there was no sound. Her body, her clothes, her hair, turned gray then black as purple sparks seared through her. A pile of purple ash began to rise beneath her feet as her body dried out and crumbled from the bottom up.

There was a bright flash of orange, red and indigo to my left. There was yelling. Nero was gone, I couldn't see him anywhere, but I was too shocked to look for him. My eyes were glued to the ash pile that had once been Janet. Landing on my knees on the neoprene floor, I crawled toward the remains of the woman who had given up her new-found freedom so willingly for us.

Someone was saying my name, but I couldn't think about who it was or why. Hands gripped my upper arms, lifting me from the floor. Explosions of fiery colors in my periphery accompanied muffled blasts. It was like crawling through no man's land with a raging firestorm going on all around.

"Janet," I sobbed.

"Saxony!" Tomio's voice broke through.

He set me on my feet as I shuddered with grief and horror. His hands on my shoulders, he gripped and turned me forcefully away from the pile of ash. Putting a hand on the side of my face, he shielded my eyes from her, forcing me to look at him.

His voice sounded far away. "Look at me, Saxony. Sweetheart, focus on my eyes."

Shuddering and sucking in breaths, I forced my blurry vision on Tomio's face.

"Can you hear me?" he asked.

I nodded, feeling hot tears pouring from my eyes.

"Listen," he enunciated each word. "It was a glamour. Janet is fine. Look again."

I could hardly register his words over the sounds of popping, ripping, hissing, and yelling. Then his message penetrated my mind.

"Look." Tomio took his hand away from my face.

I turned my face, hope rising in my chest like a dove ascending.

Janet was indeed there, on her knees, her arms crossed over her chest, hugging herself. Her eyes were wide as she watched something going on behind me and Tomio, but she was whole. She was fine.

Relief made me sag against Tomio. He held me up until I could get my legs to flex.

Tomio said in my ear, "Get her out of here. I have to help Ryan."

Everything snapped into focus. The soundscape that been part of the background, came surging into the foreground with a vengeance. Looking over my shoulder, my heart almost stopped.

Ryan and Nero flew across the fire-gym's floor in combat, jetting colored flames at each other from afar only to tangle a moment later in a flurry of punches, kicks, and wrestler-like grapples. They moved like comets. The air seethed with chemical smells and smoke, singeing my nostrils.

In seconds, a pattern emerged in their aggressive exchanges. Nero advanced for the back wall, Ryan cut him off. Nero blasted Ryan with some alchemical-fire, filling the air with a strange hazy smoke. Ryan either absorbed it or deflected it, detonating in his joints to move faster than humanly possible. Nero, too. They moved like stop motion puppets in time-lapse, fast, then still. A blur between photographs. Their bodies became streaks of light as they didn't bother to internalize. My vision barely recovered from the resulting black spots before more colored blooms appear in front of my eyes, half blinding me.

"What—" I turned to Tomio, but he was gone. He swept into the rainbow battle and added his own explosive streaks of light, his form swallowed up by the pyrotechnics. I saw his shadow coil and spring, flying into a shape that had to be Nero, though by now he was barely identifiable in the melee.

All this happened in seconds, leaving me reeling and breathless. Janet was still on the floor. I ran to her and she saw me coming, her face lighting up with many emotions: relief, fear, hope, regret.

"Sax—" she opened her arms and got to her feet.

I flew into her embrace. "I'm so sorry. We failed you."

She didn't speak, only squeezed me, her body shaking.

I pulled her to face me, moving her toward the doors. "Listen carefully, go straight down the hall. Don't stop until you find the front lobby, it has an antique telephone box. Can you do that?"

She nodded, her fingers gripping my arm as we passed through the doors.

I tried not to talk too fast. "When you reach the lobby, take the stairs to the second floor landing. The first door on your left is the headmaster's office. It won't be locked. There's a phone on the desk. Dial one-oh-seven."

"One-oh-seven," she murmured, focusing all her powers of concentration on my words. "What's one-oh-seven?"

"Basil's suite. He'll come to you. Tell him what's happened."

Someone bellowed in pain behind us.

"Go!" I shoved her and she took off running.

Turning to the battle, my heart jumped into my throat. The back wall of the fire-gym was ablaze with lime green fire shot through with indigo streaks. The smell was dizzying. Bodies collided within otherworldly illumination: flashes, pulses, sparks, flickering lines of blazing alchemy. There was another cry of pain, and it sounded like Tomio.

Heat blossomed through my chest and swept into my limbs, catapulting me into the fray. Ryan's form was at the firewall, hands up and trying to absorb the supernatural flames before they consumed more of the gym.

Thuds and grunts came from my left, where Tomio and Nero attacked and deflected. Tomio's body moved through masterful sequences of detonations, while Nero's fists were ablaze with color, drawing shocked hisses of pain from Tomio as he seared him with chemical fire. Dodging fire was very different from dodging fists—to be precise, it was impossible.

When Tomio planted a perfect kick in the center of Nero's chest and the mage staggered back toward me, I saw an opening, and leaped forward, firing in both legs. Wrapping an arm around his throat from behind, I detonated along my spine, raked an ankle across the back of Nero's legs and slammed him to the ground. There was a flash of wide, surprised eyes and bared teeth before he grunted on impact. His dark glare gripped mine as I cocked back a fist and fired, popping in my shoulder and back and throwing redheat into my punch. Nero spat green copper-chloride-fueled fire at me as my blazing yellow fist cracked his head to the side. The green jet of flames sprayed wildly like a snake springing from a joke can, narrowly missing my face. Stinking sparks sprayed across the neoprene and smoke swirled over the floor, shrouding my feet and part of Nero's body.

With a violent roll to the side, Nero was out from under

me and up. I blinked to clear my stinging eyes. My skin burned where the green fire had touched me. I had to absorb what he was throwing, or it would hurt. But absorbing and detonating while in full combative motion was a big ask. I had no practice with this, only the theory Ryan had given me.

I bolted forward for another try as Nero came at me. We clashed in an explosion of light as my training swept its cold rationale over my mind like a veil. Heat and power banged off throughout my body, backing every shot I fired, every deflection, every block, without thought or hesitation.

When an open-handed slap caught me by surprise, I spun across the floor to my knees, left cheek stinging and vision whirling, my face flushed with fire and blood. An open-handed hit was somehow so much more humiliating than a fisted punch.

By the time I'd found ground again, Tomio was on Nero like a panther from jungle shadows. I caught a flash of bright red blood, moving too fast to know who it belonged to.

My nose was split and throbbed painfully with every heartbeat. I wiped at it, glancing at Ryan, who'd extinguished the chemical fire, but not before it had exposed the skeleton behind the folding wall and the gym's structural layers of I-beams and braces.

My heart jumped to my throat as Ryan tugged the wooden case, blackened and smoking, from its hiding place, moving it while Nero was distracted. But as he squatted to heft it, part of the crate broke and crumbled. The statue slid out and hit the floor as Ryan stumbled back.

All Nero had to do was look up for one second to see his prize, exposed and waiting to be plucked, like ripe fruit hanging low on the tree.

I sucked in a huge breath and spewed dense, boron-laced blue fire into the air, turning my head back and forth to spread it as much as possible. Ryan had told me that blue left the most opaque smoke, which could provide some level of cover. He shot me a grateful look when he saw what I'd done, picked up the shell and hefted her as the blue smoke enveloped him.

Turning to the battle, I saw Nero launch a kick at Tomio, catching him in the shoulder. Nero was clearly the less skilled at martial arts, but he had all that extra alchemy, all those idle fires, running through his body. He didn't even move like a normal mage anymore. His hands flashed violet as Tomio staggered back, but instead of gripping at his struck shoulder, he reached for his face. Tomio's eyes flashed purple and his teeth bared in a grimace. He started to cover his eyes but reversed the motion as his instincts kicked in. Had he been blinded? He had an unfocused look, and sank into half-squat, hands out, anticipating an attack he couldn't see.

Detonating everywhere, I barreled into Nero, flying at his ribs. We rolled over the floor. Gracelessly, firing at whatever I could reach, I pummeled his body as he pummeled mine. Pops and snaps of accompanied grunts and heavy, forced exhalations of breath. Blunt impact struck all over my body, leaving aching, sizzling and prickling sensations as I tried to absorb what I could, and then turn it back on my foe.

Nero hissed in Italian. Blood streaked across his cheekbone from a cut on the side of his head, and his lip was split.

So, he could still bleed.

I connected with the other side of his face, but he only snapped his head back, then planted a hand on my sternum, between my breasts. I made to knock his hand away when my entire body was consumed by a stretching, breaking pain. I screamed as every muscle went stiff, like I was being electrocuted. From its home in the center of my body, my fire bowed toward Nero's hand. I felt it shift off-center like it was being pulled by a powerful magnet. It was agonizing, like pressure on a joint to dislocate. I couldn't move, could only pant my breaths.

"P-p-p-ple..." I tried to beg, desperate for the pain to stop.

It felt like he was drawing my very heart out of place, stretching apart the very core of me. At any second I would break into pieces. My vision shrank to the size of a penny, black closing in from all sides. Much more of this, and I would lose consciousness. Through a small hole in a dark wall, Nero bared his teeth in effort. Like he was trying to remove the fabled sword from its stone. He redoubled his efforts, and I was certain my body would rupture. The sight of Nero came through a pinprick now. Moisture glinted on his forehead, his eyes narrowed to slits.

He meant to rip my fire from my body.

I slipped toward unconsciousness, losing all sight completely. The sound of my heartbeat echoed through my head, the only sign I had that I was still alive outside of the pain itself.

Then I hit the floor. Hard.

The wind was knocked from my chest, and my fire snapped back into place like it was fastened to my spine by an elastic. All the pain immediately stopped, leaving me stupid with shock. My vision returned. I sucked in air and staggered to my feet. My legs felt like they were made of pudding. Scanning for Ryan and Tomio, I saw that aside from the ruined crate and fading blue smoke, there was no one there.

Where was Nero?

At the sound of a thud and a grunt, I looked to the doors in time to see Tomio fly backward into the gym like he'd been vaulted from a cannon, straight at me. I barely had time to fill my body with fire-power in an effort to break his fall. He hit me full in the torso as I wrapped my arms around him, firing into my legs and hips. We staggered many meters back but managed to keep upright.

Ryan lay on the floor near the doors. He wasn't moving.

My blood turned to ice as I saw Nero standing over the statue, his fist cocked back. We were too far away to stop him, and Ryan was either unconscious or dead.

Nero slammed the shell in the chest. There was an outward blast of energy—absorbed by the neoprene—and a beautiful green flame was exposed, flickering inside the cavity.

I screamed and bolted forward, Tomio at my side, but I already knew we were too late. The gym was too vast to cross in time.

Nero's fist closed over the flame and snuffed it, as easily as blowing out a birthday candle. His arm and chest flashed with the power of the green idle, lighting his madman's grin. He glanced at Ryan with a predatory smile and had taken a step toward him when he looked up and saw we were upon him. His body rippled into transparency as we dove at him.

We flew through him and staggered into the lobby, barely arresting our momentum in time to turn and see a flickering human shape made of black fire as it passed through the wall and disappeared.

PART III

———

THE EIGHTH FIRE

14

CAUGHT

The world stopped.

All but our labored breathing seemed held in suspended animation. Tomio's hands flew to his chest, eyes round.

"Did you? Are you—" I could hardly think the word fireless, let alone say it.

He looked into his open palms and a moment later, fire danced there. "No," he croaked, clearly amazed. "You?"

I could feel the roaring heat of a fire recently engaged in combat, licking up my insides. I made a flame in my palm, just to prove it. There was pain in my side and the skin of my right forearm was red and blistered, and my jaw felt the same.

Ryan lay on his side, still and unmoving, facing away from us. We crouched over him. Gingerly, afraid of what I might learn, I pressed my fingertips to the place under the jaw where the pulse is easy to detect.

A wash of heat raced up my arm to my heart, making me cry out in surprise and snatch my hand back. It didn't hurt, but it gave me a hell of a start. I stared at Tomio.

"What?" His voice was shredded.

"He's still got fire, too. Our bond is intact. But, I can't feel his pulse with all the heat in the way. Can you try?" My mind raged. *Why*? I'd seen Nero absorb the green idle. Ryan's fire should have gone out simultaneously? So should mine, for that matter.

Tomio darted a hand to Ryan's jaw. His eyes drifted shut and he nodded. "He's alive. Should we move him? What if bones are broken? I read somewhere you shouldn't move someone whose been knocked out."

"Leave him." I sprang up, feeling dizzy and electrified with adrenaline. "I'll get Georjie."

I bolted before Tomio could say anything else, rushing through the empty corridors, past the lecture halls, through the lobby and up the main staircase to the block of private rooms. Skidding to a halt at her door, I rapped on it but didn't wait for a response before rushing through into the darkness of her room.

The lump on the bed moved as she rolled over. There was a click and the lamp on the bedside table flushed light across the floor. Georjie blinked in the sudden glare, her brows pinched, her hair a messy blond halo. "Saxony?"

"Sorry to wake you. You need to come." I located her sneakers, though I still had no shoes on myself, then dropped them as I remembered that she didn't like to wear shoes that much anymore, and maybe she was going to have to be barefoot to fix whatever was wrong with Ryan. I grabbed the cardigan draped over the foot of the bed as she swung her legs out of bed, fully awake now.

"What's wrong? You're bleeding!" She came for me, hands reaching. "Let me see."

"No time." I threw the cardi around her shoulders, and steered her to the door.

Once she got in gear and I'd told her where we were going and why, I almost had to use fire to keep up to her long-legged sprint. We found Tomio still crouched over Ryan, who now lay on his back, one eye open in a narrow slit. One side of his face was puffy, the eye swollen shut. Blood dribbled from his nose and lip, and his collarbone was raised under the skin, definitely broken.

Georjie knelt over him, putting a hand to his brow.

"An angel..." Ryan's voice was a dreamy, drugged murmur that might have been funny under other circumstances.

Georjie slipped a hand around the back of his neck to cradle his head. Her eyes drifted shut and all went quiet for several long seconds.

Ryan's eyes widened a fraction, then more yet. The swelling diminished and the flow of blood stanched. He moaned and jerked as the broken ends of his collarbone pressed down and back into place.

Tomio shot me an amazed look. I grinned, my heart doing somersaults. We were so lucky Georjie had decided not to go home. Too bad she wasn't able to return the bereft magi to their former glory, too.

When she was finished, Ryan sat up, gazing at Georjie like she was made of solid gold. "That's quite a trick."

Tomio helped him to his feet, though he clearly didn't need the help anymore. When Ryan's eyes fell on the blackened zone surrounding the broken pieces of sculpture, all the joy and relief that had been in his face vanished. The volcanic refuse and rubble clinked against our shoes. A set of legs, an arm, and part of her head were all that remained of the statue.

"We failed." He said this flatly, like he knew all along we would. A hand flew to his forehead and his gaze darted around, through the gym doors, around the lobby. "Where's Nero?"

"Gone," I told him, as Georjie ran her hands over Tomio, healing his bruises, cuts and chemical burns.

She came for me next, and I closed my eyes and stood still for her, relishing the feeling of her soothing magic filling my body. My nose tingled softly as the fae magic did its beautiful work. The ribs on my right side complained for a breathless moment, then the pain eased and I could breathe without pain. I hadn't realized they'd been broken.

"Where's Janet?" Tomio asked.

"I sent her to Basil's office and told her to call his suite. Come on. She'll be waiting for us. Basil too, by now."

We made our way to the headmaster's office and found the door open. A frightened, pale Janet lay curled up on his couch with her head resting on a throw pillow. When she saw us, she got off the couch, scanning us from head to foot. She hugged me, then Tomio. She didn't hug Ryan, but she squeezed his upper arms.

"I'm Janet," she said to Georjie, holding out a hand. "A friend."

They shook, and Georjayna introduced herself as an old friend of mine.

"Did you call Basil?" My guts tightened like an irritated garden snake when I saw that the headmaster was not present.

Janet nodded, then shrugged. "No answer. I wasn't sure what else to do."

Tomio and I had seen Nero absorb the green idle with our own eyes. It was gone. We'd been spared the loss of our fire, which had only one possible explanation. But Ryan had his fire too, which threw a wrench in my hypothesis. I was quickly forming a new one. Basil needed to be here for me to share it, and the fact that he hadn't answered his phone didn't bode well. I doubted the headmaster had been spared the snuffing as well. If he had, then everything I thought I now understood might as well get thrown into the garbage. As much as I wanted to grill Janet about where Nero had been keeping her, I couldn't focus on anything else until I knew Basil was okay.

Georjie stayed with Janet while Ryan, Tomio and I made our way to Basil's suite. As we turned the last corner to his hallway, the door opened. We froze, and for a second nothing happened, the door squeaked but no one came out. We stayed like that for long moment, barely breathing.

Walking like someone still asleep, Basil stepped into the hall wearing striped pajamas, no slippers or robe, and no glasses. His hair was disheveled and his cheeks pale under his stubble.

I felt Tomio grab my hand and squeeze it, hard. I took in a breath at the sight of the headmaster, and knew he'd not been spared.

The headmaster looked at us.

Something in my heart broke at the expression on his face. It hurt to see messy hair that I'd never seen mussed before, and feet I'd never seen bare before. I'd never seen the headmaster looking anything less than posh, even during intense combat training.

"Hello," he said, not looking surprised to see us. His voice broke. "I find myself taken back to the description Ms. Brown gave upon losing her... her. Well, she described it perfectly." He raised a hand, fingertips tented together, then opened them in a smooth, quick motion. "Poof."

"Oh, Basil." I closed the distance and threw my arms around him, my throat too tight to speak. The skin of his neck touched my cheek and I gave a sob when I experienced the sensation of normal skin-on-skin contact. No bond.

His hand drifted to the middle of my back and patted me gently. "There, there," he said. "I'm alive. We knew the risk of this was high. What I'm more shocked about is how it happened so fast. How did he manage to track us down so quickly? I'm quite flummoxed. I thought we might have a few more days, at least."

I drew back, wiping away tears and trying to smile. "You're so calm."

"Well..." He blinked, focusing as though seeing me properly for the first time since he'd stepped into the hall. "So are you, now that we come to it."

He looked at the boys. "Why do you two look like dogs that have done something bad?"

"We—we still have ours." Tomio lit the end of one finger with a teensy flame, as though he was worried the sight of too much would be rubbing it in the headmaster's face.

Ryan was looking more and more uncomfortable, like he was watching a noose being slowly tightened around his neck. Suspicion resurged with a vengeance. The misgivings I'd had that he was hiding something were back in force, and now I thought I knew what that something was.

Basil's expression brightened when he saw Tomio's finger-flame. He looked at me. "And you?"

"Same," I replied, though I didn't feel the need to prove it. My mind was a blender, in the center of which circulated Ryan's story about what had happened in Iran.

"Remarkable, and completely impossible. How? Why?" Basil lifted the heel of his hand to his forehead like he was worried his brain might fall out.

"I have a theory." I turned a cold look on Ryan. "But

before I share it, you should know that Ryan has also retained his fire."

Ryan bared his teeth and crossed his arms over his chest, appearing almost to shrink in size. "How do you know that, Cagney?"

"Because while you were lying on the floor unconscious, I felt for your pulse, you know, to see if you were still alive. Your fire said a very healthy hello to my fire. *That's* how I know."

Basil looked from me to Ryan in a species of dazed bemusement. Tomio shot Ryan a sideways glance that wasn't particularly friendly.

"So what?" Ryan asked, but took a step away from Tomio. "You have yours, Tomio has his, why is it so shocking that I have mine?"

I took a step toward him, half expecting him to bolt. Though I understood Ryan to have lied, I knew he'd done it out of shame, not because he was against us, so I didn't believe he would run. "There's a good reason why Tomio and I haven't lost our fire, but you? You have no good reason, unless you've been a very"—I took another step—"bad"—I stopped in front of him, looking him in the face—"mage."

His eyes flickered with fear, but he closed the distance between us, bumping his chest against me. The tip of his nose nearly touched mine. "How's that, omniscient one?"

"Plenary endowment."

He faltered. Confusion swept over his features. He stepped back, glancing from me to Tomio and back again.

Only I knew Tomio's secret, but there were only the three of us standing here in the hallway. I didn't think it mattered anymore given the circumstances. It was the clincher I needed to get Ryan to spill.

"W-what?" He stuttered, his indignance now gone.

"I never knew the idle color of the little girl who passed her fire to me," said Tomio, in a tone too gentle for my liking. "I suspected it was violet, but when I shook hands with Fred and Greg, I knew it couldn't be violet. So, I called Junko's father and he told me her idle had been red. I should have lost my fire along with the batch that was snuffed while Nero was in Yangjiang, but I didn't. I didn't know why, not until the green fire went out just now. Saxony and I both received our fire by plenary endowment. We weren't born mages, we were born human. We're like... adopted into the family. Somehow, that must have severed the connection our fires had with the original."

I poked Ryan in the shoulder. "But, you..."

Ryan's wide gaze whipped to me.

I felt Basil sidle up to join our group, listening.

"You were born a mage. You should have lost your fire just now, but you didn't." I put my finger in his face. "You have exactly one second to start talking."

AFTER WAKING Ms. Shepherd to update her—she agreed to send a driver to take Basil to the agency for an assessment—I filled the carafe in Basil's office and poured glasses of water for everyone as we settled into seats.

Ryan had agreed to explain what had really happened in Iran without embroidery or omissions, though it was apparent the prospect of this had him as nervous as someone going in for major dental surgery.

"I went to Ramsar with specific instructions," he began, sitting in one of the big wingbacks in front of Basil's desk, water in one hand and one foot tucked up beneath him. "Janet's work had highlighted a region west of the city, an area with a lot of archaeological ruins. One of Nero's contacts, a man at a university nearby, had found an orb and was willing to sell it. The transaction was illegal, but that's never stopped Nero from doing anything, obviously."

"The orb was in the university's possession?" Georjie hadn't left the couch beside Janet, who was eating a sandwich that Tomio had made after Georjie explained that Janet's current weakness was mostly low blood sugar. I suspected Georjie's healing presence also made the woman feel better, in addition to the food. Some of Janet's color was returning.

Ryan took a sip of water, then slid the glass onto the small table beside his chair. "It was, but this contact was almost as high as you could get at the uni, and was able to smuggle it out without being discovered. I don't know how, and I didn't ask, it's not relevant to the story anyway. I was to deliver the orb to Nero. In exchange, he would teach me more alchemy. At the time, I thought his enhanced abilities were all rooted in alchemy. I didn't yet know that it was idles he was after." Ryan's gaze went down to the floor. He scratched absently along his thigh as he talked.

"Along with the orb, this contact also provided an envelope, a certificate with basic information about the orb. It wasn't sealed, so I looked at it. It was like a receipt. It included the results of some tests that had been run on it. Those, I didn't understand, but I did understand that the GPS coordinates were where the orb had been found. I was curious about the location, and wondered if there might be other artifacts relevant to magi history. Since I had a little time before my flight back to Italy, and the location was not far from Ramsar, I rented a vehicle and took a little road trip."

"Did you know anything about the effluent at that time?"

I shifted as Tomio lay his arm across the sofa back behind me. He draped his hand over my shoulder.

"No, Nero hadn't put that together yet either, he thought that he was radioactive."

At this, Janet perked up. "He's not?"

Ryan shook his head. "The effluent registers as radioactivity, but that's not really what it is. My guess is that after he absorbed another idle or two, he could feel the effluent in his bones, and that's why he was able to zero in on the remaining idles so quickly." He waved a hand. "But back to my road trip. I had the orb with me, and carried it in my pocket because I was too paranoid to have it more than a few feet away from me. At the time, I didn't realize it, but now I believe that the orb led me to... it."

"A shell." I stared at Ryan, but he still wouldn't look up.

"Yes. I discovered it not even knowing what I was looking for or what I would find. I thought it was just curiosity, but it wasn't—some magic tethered the orb to the shell. It was hidden in a cave along a ravine that floods every spring but is dry the rest of the year."

"You say *it*, but was the shell a man or a woman?" Tomio asked.

"Honestly? I couldn't tell. It was already partly destroyed. Crushed over time, I guess. It had no face and part of its shoulder had been destroyed. The legs, too, were nothing more than rubble. If it hadn't been mostly caved in, I never would have spotted the idle—" Ryan's voice went froggy, then choked off altogether.

We waited, tension mounting in the office as it became apparent what was coming.

Ryan's eyes were red and tear-glossed, his lower lids rimmed with moisture. "If I had known what was going to happen, I wouldn't have touched it."

Tomio took in a quick breath.

I glanced at Basil, who was seated in his chair, still as a carving himself, his mouth half hidden behind his hand. He was listening, but it was also apparent that he was half elsewhere too. In shock, naturally. He didn't visibly respond or prompt Ryan with questions, just sat there. I dragged my attention back to Ryan in time to see him wipe away a tear. I knew this was what he had done. It was the only thing that made sense.

Ryan's bleary eyes found mine. The turmoil I saw there made my heart cramp. "When did you suspect me?"

I blinked, not expecting him to ask me this, but all attention was on me now.

"When I saw your skills on display inside Vesuvius, I knew something had changed you. At the time, I thought it was just Nero's coaching. Alchemy. I didn't know what Nero knew, and I knew nothing about alchemy either, so I suspected it was that. But then, when you taught me some, and I felt what it was like to have access to chemical fire, it became clear that simple alchemy wasn't enough to explain your increased abilities. It was like... you were a chip straight off Nero, a lesser being, sure, but cut from the same cloth. You move faster, like you can bend time. Even with alchemy, I can't execute the way you can. And then, when you had me travel with the orb..."

Ryan wiped a hand across his nose. "I thought that was it."

"You couldn't have traveled with the orb in Ramsar, not all by yourself, not the way you claimed to."

"Why not?" Janet asked, rubbing a fist into an eye. She looked better, but still like she needed to sleep for a couple of weeks.

"Because someone has to be there to facilitate. The orb

takes a hold of your imagination completely. It takes you on a kind of astral journey. You have no sense of your own body while you're traveling. There's no way you have enough presence of mind to take a pencil and put it to paper to capture the language. You have no awareness of making the scribbles at all." I looked at Ryan. "You were alone in Ramsar. You couldn't have done it yourself. Writing everything down is what ends the vision."

Ryan nodded. "You are right. The first time I traveled with an orb was here at the academy. I had only learned the principle of it from Nero, but there was no way he ever would have allowed me to receive the information the orb gives. He wanted that all to himself, because locating the shells was his main goal. Yes, he was willing to teach me alchemy, but he never intended for me to absorb an idle, and he hadn't explained to me that that was what he was after. When I touched the idle, I didn't know I was going to absorb it, and I certainly had no idea that it was going to snuff all the idles that ever came from it."

As annoyed as I was that Ryan made me handle an orb before him, like a human guinea pig, I believed his story. I suspected that if Ryan had known that absorbing an idle would make him super powerful, he would have gone out of his way to find one and take it into himself. But if he had known that absorbing it meant quenching all other idles of the same hue, he wouldn't have touched it. He wasn't *that* monstrous, but still, he had absorbed an idle. It was the only thing that explained why he hadn't lost his fire when Nero absorbed the green idle. Which led me to the next obvious question.

"What color was it, Ryan?" I asked, knowing this would be the most difficult part for him to admit. I didn't know for sure which color it had been, but given the timeline of snuffings and when Ryan was in Iran, there were only two possibilities.

Misery made an old man of Ryan's expression. His mouth drew down and his eyes filled with grief. But he looked me in the eye and didn't flinch.

"Pink."

Basil covered his eyes with a hand, making the first motion since he'd sat down in his chair. He pinched his eyelids and the bridge of his nose, the gesture expressed so much sadness and sympathy that I felt impaled by it.

"Oh, Ryan." Tomio lay his forehead against my shoulder.

Georjie looked around, confused. "What does that mean?"

Ryan couldn't answer. He put his face in his palms and leaned forward, his posture that of someone allowing themselves to feel the full weight of a tragedy.

I looked at my fae friend, wishing she could heal Ryan's pain, not to mention the pain that the rest of his family was in. "Ryan's father, Chad, had a pink idle."

Georjie's mouth opened a little. "Oh." Her soft, brown eyes went to Ryan in sympathy, but he was bent over and unable to look at anyone. "I am so sorry."

Would Ryan come clean to his family about what he'd done? If he hadn't gotten involved with a criminal of supernatural proportions, he would never have found that idle, never quenched his father's fire, or sent him into a crippling depression. Gage wouldn't have been put in a coma. Chad would have lost his fire anyway, as would all the rest of magedom who had not received their fire by plenary endowment, but at least Ryan wouldn't be at fault.

Ryan sat up suddenly, half laughing, half crying, eyes blazing in my direction. "How ironic. What a mockery you've made of our kind."

Tomio stiffened. "She had nothing to do with any of it!"

Ryan's wet gaze flicked to Tomio. "I know that, I'm not accusing her of anything."

"Sure sounds like it," I muttered.

"No, I'm not. I'm merely pointing out the great poetic justice. You, and apparently Tomio, too—nice job keeping that a secret, by the way—born human and given fire by accident or by providence, are now members of a very small, elite class of supernaturals. Fire mages—once the most populous species—are now rarer than sirens, maybe even rarer than Wise." He gestured at Georjie and then laughed again, but there was no joy or humor in it. Only bitterness.

Basil might have intervened to stop Ryan's acerbic tirade, but he didn't say anything. He probably agreed, since Ryan wasn't wrong, and it *was* ironic. The only magi left were those who'd stolen idles—and there was only two of those: Ryan being one—or those who'd begun their lives as naturals.

Briefly, I thought of Dante, wondering why he'd died. If he hadn't, he would have been counted among our number.

Ryan sniffed, calmer now. "I suppose, ironic though it is, you won't last long either."

"What do you mean?" Georjie asked, a wrinkle forming in her brow.

"He means that Nero isn't finished yet," I explained. "There is one last fire he wants to possess."

"An eighth fire?" She cocked a brow. "But there's only seven colors in a rainbow, what color is the eighth?"

An image of Nero's form, transparent and yet black, flickering like smoke as he passed through the walls of the school.

"It's white."

"The white god," Janet murmured, "from the original legend."

"He'll be back for my idle. I'm a walking dead man," said Ryan.

"You don't have to die," Tomio said.

Ignoring him, Ryan turned to Basil. "He'll be back for those two orbs as well."

Basil watched him with detached interest.

Ryan continued, "You won't be able to prevent him from taking them. He can feel them. He has six idles now, and five orbs. All he needs is those two, and..." Ryan put his fingertips against his lips and blew on them as he flicked outward, making the sound of a candle going out. "No more white god. No more adopted magi. Only a psychopath with unimaginable power—all the power of the original Source Fire."

15

THE BEST PLAN IS NO PLAN

Ms. Shepherd sent a car from London to whisk Basil and Janet off to the agency for care and safe-keeping. The headmaster had left the orbs with us before he'd gotten into the vehicle, insisting that he not be told what we planned to do with them. Which was good, because Ryan, Tomio, and I—the only soldiers left standing, with an earth elemental to back us up—hadn't a clue.

Georjie, Tomio and I stood around the orbs—nestled in their velvet beds and sitting on a table—brainstorming. Georjie had handled them gingerly, amazed that such small innocuous bits of art held the power to sweep one into an astral journey. Ryan hadn't stopped pacing in the lobby's hall, far enough removed from the rest of us to signal that he wanted time to think, but close enough that he could hear our ideas.

One thing was clear: time was running out. Nero hadn't made another appearance, but we doubted he was far away. Maybe he was waiting for us to go to sleep so he could dig around in our minds for the location of the orbs to make snatching them easier. That's what I would do if I were him. He professed to hate violence—not that I believed that for a second, but he did seem to be the type who only engaged in physical combat if he had to. His goal was supremacy, not murder. What he'd done to Bellamy years ago proved that he wasn't *above* murder, but the fact that he hadn't physically hurt Janet, or broken one of our necks in the fire-gym, was a kind of twisted testament that his intention wasn't to kill.

Could we afford the same luxury, though?

It didn't look like it.

I balked at the thought, my mouth souring with distaste. Some small part of me just wanted to let Nero have the orbs —he was already too powerful for us to beat. But what would we allow to be unleashed upon the world if we gave up? I wouldn't utter the words out loud, not when it was clear my companions had no intention of surrender. The expressions of determination on their faces made me feel ashamed for even considering it.

"We obviously can't keep hiding them here at the academy." Tomio picked up an orb and palmed its weight.

"It's no good," Ryan called from the lounge doors where he did an about-face. "He can feel them, anyway. He knows roughly where they are at all times."

"How do you know that?" Georjie watched Ryan through those keen brown eyes, taking in every movement, every twitch of an eyebrow.

"Because *I* can feel them, and I've only absorbed one idle. Imagine how good his radar is for anything remotely connected to fire mages. Why do you think he was so willing to dump Janet on us? She's no good to him anymore. He'll come for them, make no mistake, and there's nothing we can do to stop him."

"I wouldn't say *nothing*," muttered Georjie, crossing those long elegant arms.

"What are you saying, man?" Tomio shot Ryan a horrified look. "We give them up and be grateful to get away with our lives?"

The look on Tomio's face made me doubly glad I hadn't suggested it myself.

Ryan put a hand over his chest, where the pink idle lived. "He won't kill unless he has to. The person the most in danger here is me."

"He took Gage's fire pretty easily. Can he take your idle?" Tomio asked.

Ryan went back to pacing. "I don't know, but he's got blackfire now, so probably."

"What is blackfire?" Georjie asked.

"It means he can dissolve, walk through walls." Ryan scoffed. "I wouldn't doubt if he could fly by now, or maybe even teleport. How else did he come and go to the Arctic so quickly and without detection?"

"And what will he be if he gets all the orbs?" I asked.

Ryan snorted derisively but didn't answer.

Tomio let the orb roll off his fingers and settle on the fabric. "It won't be good for anyone, that much is apparent. We have to do whatever we can to keep these orbs from his possession. Should we split them up? Take them opposite directions?"

"That'll leave them both less protected," said Ryan.

"Why don't I take them to Stavarjak?" Georjie offered.

We froze, Tomio and Ryan in confusion, and me because at first blush, this was a stroke of genius. But a moment later, my stomach curdled. Georjie would be stepping straight into Nero's headlights.

"Where's that?" Ryan asked.

"It's a fae kingdom in another dimension. I can access it from places on Earth where the veil between the worlds is thin. I could take the orbs to Scotland and deliver them to Queen Elphame for safe-keeping, or Fyfa. The fact that they'd no longer be in this dimension should be enough to cut off Nero's psychic connection with them."

No one responded to this immediately, we were busy masticating the idea like it was overcooked steak.

"Shouldn't it?" she asked, tentatively, when no one said anything.

Ryan's expression turned skeptical. "Are you willing to risk your life on that? This is a supernatural being. We don't know what he's capable of. I'd wager he'll know where the orbs are even if we sent them to Mars, or dropped them into a bottomless pit. Also, making yourself their guardian puts you in the line of fire, literally. And fire—while it can't hurt us—can most definitely hurt you."

"It's a good idea, Georjie," I said, but in a tone that told her I'd already dismissed it, there was no way I'd let her put herself in danger for us. If Nero could feel the orbs, like Ryan said, she probably wouldn't make it to Edinburgh, let alone Stavarjak.

"Even if Nero can't trace them to a pinpoint, you just blew the plan," Ryan continued. "The truth is, no matter what we plan here, the moment we're asleep, Nero will root around in our minds like a pig after truffles. When he sees who you are and where you've gone, do you think a lousy supernatural border will be enough to stop him?"

Ryan said this with a little too much acidity for my liking, and I shot him a look of warning. "I don't see you coming up with any better ideas. In fact, every time one of us comes up with something, you shoot it down. You seem capable of coming up with elaborate reasons why nothing we've discussed so far will work, but incapable of coming up with any suggestions yourself."

Ryan didn't appear in the least bit reproached by this. "That's because no matter what we plan to do, Nero can see it in our heads. Don't you get that? The only plan that will work is no plan at all. And, I'll tell you something else." He pointed a finger at the boxes. "We need to get those things out of here, keep them moving until we come up with something that might work. As long as they are moving, Nero has to work to keep track of them. It probably won't be enough, and he'll take them from us sometime in the next day or two anyway, but it's a damn sight better than standing around here debating it."

As annoyed as I was with Ryan's attitude, he was right. "Let's go then. Pack a bag and let's meet at the Land Rover in ten minutes. We can talk as we drive."

"Drive where?" Georjie asked.

"That's the point. We don't know." Tomio closed the orb's boxes and swept them under his arm.

"We'll drop you off at the station so you can grab the first train to Blackmouth," I told her as we left the lobby, trailing the boys up the stairs.

Georjie whirled, eyes blazing. "I'm not going anywhere!"

Ryan and Tomio paused, looking down over the banister.

I didn't back down. "This isn't your fight, Georjie. And Ryan's right, fire doesn't burn us, but it will burn you. I can't ask you to put yourself in that kind of danger."

"You're not asking. I'm coming with you, and you can't stop me. Whether you like it or not, I'm involved, Saxony. Remember the promise we made back in Saltford?"

"The promise was that we'd come to one another if we called. You already helped us by showing us how Nero was taking idles. Thank you for that. Now it's time to get out of danger."

If anything happened to Georjie, I'd be crushed. Targa would be crushed. Her family would be devastated, both the fae and the human relatives. And Lachlan would have every right to blame me, because when I asked her to do a remote viewing for us, I knew she'd never say no.

"The promise was to help one another when we needed it," Georjie replied, "and girl, you need help."

"She's fae, right?" Ryan leaned his elbows on the banister. "Her skills so far have come in pretty handy, Cagney."

I glared daggers at Ryan.

Georjie looked up. "Half-fae, and thank you, Ryan."

"She's a Wise," I told him. "She's gentle and good, and highly flammable."

I was playing down Georjie's skill set. She could also split a gorge through the earth in seconds, vanish into the pedolith and travel through it like a ghost. She could pop up somewhere miles away. She could make a tidal wave out of soil, and probably throw full-grown oaks like javelins, but I didn't want to say anything that might encourage her to stay. I wanted my friend out of danger, and in spite of Ryan's complaint that he was the most at risk, I disagreed. Ryan was only at risk of losing his idle, which one could argue he didn't deserve to keep anyway. Georjie was at risk of getting burnt to cinders. Putting her into this battle was like putting a wolf on the front lines of a medieval war. Sure, he might cause some damage initially, but he'd be cut down by an arrow or a lance or a horse's hoof before the battle was over. His weapons were fierce but outmatched, and as powerful as Georjie's fae magic might be, she wasn't a soldier. She'd never had combat training, she was waif thin, and when she used magic, she shone so brightly that she might as well paint a target on both cheeks. I didn't want Nero to know she existed, let alone set eyes on her.

Georjie glowered. "Would you leave me, if the tables were reversed?"

In a battle between fae? I didn't know what that might look like, but of course I would never leave Georjie if she was in trouble. My inability to respond screamed more loudly than my vocal chords could have.

"Exactly." She smiled, turned, and tromped her way up the stairs. "So, I'm not going anywhere until we've put this mad dog down. Now let's move. If what Ryan says is true, then we need to be on the road to nowhere, as fast as possible."

As we threw our backpacks and duffels into the back of Basil's Land Rover, the sound of something heavy falling from a height and crashing to the ground from around the far side of the fire-gym reached us.

Georjie, who had her head stuck inside the open boot, extricated herself in one smooth, startled movement. She looked toward the fire-gym, although damage wasn't visible on the exterior. "What was that?"

"Nero," replied Tomio as he slid into the driver's seat. "He wrecked the gym. It's falling apart."

Ryan took the passenger's side.

I locked Arcturus Academy—hopefully not for the last time—with the keys Basil had given me, and put them into a zippered pocket inside my bag for safe-keeping, before sliding in behind Tomio. I took a look at the academy, with all its windows and blinds closed and its front doors shut and locked. It looked like it was going to take a long nap.

Pushing away questions about Basil's future, I turned to Georjie as she slid into the backseat across from me.

"I thought the gym was fireproof." She closed the door and pulled the seatbelt over herself.

"Against garden-variety fire, yes." Tomio turned the engine on and the Land Rover's powerful motor began to hum. "Not so much against alchemy."

"Not to interrupt, but…" I tapped Ryan's shoulder and he tilted his head toward me. "Where's the ghost steel?"

Ryan seemed to have an awe and attachment to the steel that made him want to carry it around all the time, so I'd let him take care of it. It wasn't like I wanted to touch it anyway—the thing gave me the heebie-jeebies.

"In my packsack," he said. "Why?"

I settled back. "Just wondering."

The most important articles to all of magedom right now sat with a trio of teenagers and one Wise: two orbs, a ghost-steel blade, and Nico's journal. And this quartet had no older magi on which to rely… and no plan.

I wondered if we should deliver the orbs to Ms. Shepherd, but she and her ilk had even less of a defense against Nero than we did. I thought of Shereen and Davazlar, and wondered how they were coping without their fire.

Tomio drove the Land Rover up the winding driveway and paused at the top, wondering which way to turn. No one volunteered a suggestion. He decided and turned left.

"So, what is alchemy, exactly?" Georjie asked, directing her question to Ryan.

While Ryan explained the art of incorporating chemicals with fire, and the differences between idle colors and chemical colors, I watched the English countryside whiz by and contemplated our predicament, itemizing what I thought I knew about the force we were up against.

No one was more adept at using fire and alchemy than Nero, that was apparent. If he could track the orbs as well as Ryan thought he could, that meant he knew that we were running away from the academy. It appeared that he could attempt to coax information from our minds while we were sleeping, but perhaps only one at a time, since I'd had the experience before Ryan, and Ryan had it while Tomio and I were... busy. Had the fact that he'd now absorbed the green idle given him additional skill in this area? He'd also performed a glamour on my mind, making me see Janet turn into ashes. He'd also glamoured Tomio at one point. Did the glamours work the same way as the sleep-stalking? He could only do it to one of us at a time? Could he do it from a distance? Was there a way to protect one's mind against these assaults?

When my mind had worn out those questions, it gnawed on others, like why Nero was doing this in the first place. I could see the attraction to becoming the most powerful mage our kind had ever seen. I had a competitive streak and loved to rank high in skills class, but I had no desire to wipe out my competition completely. That would be no fun. There had to be more to it.

Basil's story of how Nero became a mage revealed someone who was willing to hurt others to get what he wanted, willing to deceive and manipulate. So, this was more of the same, perhaps his early success fostered a desire to take more and more, no matter who or what stood in his path. In a way, this was a genocide. Even if magi didn't die directly from what Nero was doing, he was still destroying an entire species systematically, and he was almost through. It was similar among naturals. A small number of individuals, in this case one, could ruin everything for many when they became tyrants. That was how empires fell. Everything has a cycle, and perhaps it was time for the magi to end.

Tomio, Ryan and Georjie talked for a time, then fell silent and Tomio put on the radio. That was fine. I stewed in my mental juices, feeling like Nero was following us in his mind's eye, waiting for the right moment to pounce.

When Tomio gasped and swerved violently off the road for no apparent reason, Georjie and I screamed. Ryan cursed and grabbed the handle over his door as the Land Rover swayed and came to a screeching halt in a ditch filled with shrubs.

For a second, we just sat there, panting, Tomio the loudest of all.

"What the hell?" Ryan lashed the words at Tomio, who lifted his hands away from the wheel in a gesture of defense.

"I'm sorry! I couldn't help it, didn't you see—" but he cut himself off, shoulders stiffening as though taking a blow.

"See what?" I squeezed his shoulder, my heart beginning to slow. Georjie and I exchanged an uneasy look.

"A big animal, huge, like a moose or something, it ran into the road right in front of us. It was on fire."

"A moose? In England?" Georjie mouthed.

"It wasn't real."

Tomio nodded and put his hand over mine where it sat on his shoulder. "Yeah." He took a deep breath. "Yeah, I got that now."

"You could have killed us," Ryan seethed, unbuckling his seatbelt. "My turn to drive."

Tomio got out from behind the wheel and walked around to the other side. As he was about to slide in, Georjie asked him through the gap between the seat and his door. "Do you want to sit back here?"

Tomio immediately reversed himself. "Yeah, that would be great. Thanks, Georjie."

"No problem."

They switched seats, and Ryan put us back on the road, announcing that we'd need a gas station in another fifty kilometers or so.

No one said anything after that, not until Ryan made the Evoque lurch across the road as he gaped at nothing, out of the driver's side window. With viperlike speed, he hit the panic lights and pulled the vehicle off to the side. Someone's horn blared as they whipped around us. Tires screeched.

Tomio couldn't resist shooting Ryan a self-satisfied look. "You almost killed us."

Ryan bent forward and put his forehead on the steering wheel, ignoring Tomio's barb, hopefully because he knew he deserved it. No one asked him what he saw, and he didn't volunteer it.

Ryan eventually lifted his head. "Georjie?"

"Yeah?"

"How about you drive from now on?"

"I've never driven on the left-hand side of the road bef—"

Our collective expressions could have wilted a palm tree.

She undid her seatbelt. "Absolutely Ryan, I'd be happy to."

Forty minutes later, and without further incident, Georjie steered the Land Rover into a gas station.

When I emerged from the bathroom, Georjie was at the edge of the parking lot, her cell phone glued to her ear. Ryan leaned against the Rover, cheek bulging with food. Tomio deposited the squeegee into its holder, grabbed something from the front seat, and tossed it to me. It was an egg salad sandwich in a triangular plastic box.

"Thanks." My stomach gurgled. I hadn't eaten since yesterday's pizza, but had been too distracted to notice how hungry I was. I'd also had no sleep since the fight with Nero. None of us had. My eyes felt dry.

Georjie finished her call and joined us. She didn't look interested in the sandwich Ryan offered, but peeled back the lid and ate it without complaint. I wondered what the food was like in Stavarjak. Better than gas station sandwiches, I'd wager.

"Who was that?" I asked as she chewed. "Lachlan?"

She nodded.

"Did you tell him what's going on."

She see-sawed a hand.

I left her to eat and joined the boys who were talking quietly in front of the vehicle. They saw me coming and clammed up.

"Don't stop on my account, lads." I tossed my sandwich wrapper in the nearest bin. "What's on your mind?"

Tomio said, "We're wondering if it was a mistake to leave the academy. At least there we could face Nero on familiar territory."

"Running isn't going to get us anywhere but lost," Ryan added.

Irritated, I offered Ryan my best glare. "We knew that when we left. We ran because you told us that the best way to keep the orbs away from him is to keep them moving."

Ryan nodded and looked away.

"This is what it looks like to have no plan," Tomio said with a shrug. "But we can't run forever."

No, he was definitely right about that. "So, what do you want to do, then? Go back?"

It doesn't matter where you go.

I froze as the words blossomed in my mind like an

unwelcome weed in a bed of flowers. It lifted the fuzz on the back of my neck.

Ryan was about to say something when Tomio put a hand out to stop him, his gaze narrowed on my face. "Saxony?"

I can chase you all day, without moving an inch.

Ryan caught on that I was experiencing something. "What are you seeing?"

"Not seeing." I had an involuntary shiver. "Hearing."

It's better to toss the orbs overboard and carry on your merry way. I won't pursue you. Just leave them sitting in the grass near the road. No one has to get hurt.

Tomio and Ryan waited, on edge. Georjie came over, catching on faster than the boys had that I was now the focus of Nero's psychic attentions.

"Saxony?" she whispered, and took me by the shoulders.

I squeezed my eyes closed to block out my friends' faces, narrowing in on the voice.

What will it mean if you absorb the Source Fire? I asked, wondering if I could send thoughts back.

There was nothing at first, but his answer finally came. *What do you think? All the life that sprang from it will be mine. This, you cannot stop. It's useless to try. You know this. You're only dragging out the inevitable.*

My eyes flew open. What did *that* mean? All the life that sprang from it will be mine?

"Let's drive," I told my friends. "I'll tell you in the car."

We scrambled into the vehicle like we were being pursued by a pack of zombies. Georjie hit the brakes at the highway. "Which way?"

We had driven too far to be back at the academy by nightfall, we still had no plan, and I wasn't prepared to dump the orbs just because Nero said fighting was useless. Not yet.

"We passed a campground, maybe two hours ago. Let's go there," I suggested. It was the first thing that popped into my head, and gave us a destination.

It was good enough for Georjie, and the boys didn't protest—they were probably feeling even more shaken than I was, given that I hadn't relayed Nero's message to them yet.

Georjie hit the gas and the Evoque began to eat up miles again, as I told them what Nero had whispered into my brain.

16

TRAIL OF TRILLIUMS

The campground was quaint and inviting, exceeding my expectations for what a rustic getaway might offer the weary traveler. We were fortunate that it was mid-week and had plenty of vacancies. I would have been happy with a tent, as long as we got out of the Evoque, which was getting smaller by the minute, and eventually got a decent meal.

It was sleep that terrified us the most, the magi anyway. Georjie could sleep all she wanted.

With the unknown hanging over us, and with furtive and watchful glances—we must have looked like fugitives to the proprietor—we checked in. We acquired two keys and followed the hand painted signs leading to our respective cabins.

Georjie and I took a little hut with a thatched roof, which had been christened Periwinkle Cottage, and painted the color of its namesake save for the trim, which was forest-green. Ryan and Tomio would bunk in a large, remodeled horse trailer a few meters away. Some clever carpenter had installed windows, flower boxes, a kitchenette and a set of bunkbeds. They weren't glamorous, but I suspected Georjie preferred unglamorous, and the rest of us were too tired to care.

These humble shelters shared a firepit and a yard, which was partially enclosed by a forest of saplings. The sea was close enough to be a whisper on the breeze, but there were plenty of seagulls willing to let the world know that the shoreline was near.

Georjie and Ryan went to buy firewood, and to see what could be scrounged up in the way of dinner in the nearby village. Tomio and I searched out the sawed-off logs someone had helpfully rolled into the bushes, collecting them so we could sit and eat.

I tumbled one of the logs upright and settled it near the pit, noticing something as I did: a trail of white trilliums leading along the path to the parking lot. They were perfect and dainty, with tender white petals. They were lined up like the seven dwarves on their way to work, only there were a lot more than seven. Utterly charmed, I pointed them out to Tomio.

"Yeah." He came to stand on the trail beside me, eyes crinkling at the little flowers. "Georjie did that as we were walking. She was at the back, so I guess you didn't notice. What a sweet talent that lady has."

I stared at him in open astonishment. "Georjie put these here? Why?"

Tomio shrugged and picked his way through some brambles toward another wayward stump. "Why not? Because she can, I guess. I wouldn't mind being able to make flowers pop up wherever I went, leaving a trail of happiness for other people to find. Ouch! Maybe she can do something about these thorns. This place needs a gardener."

Bemused and a little amazed that Georjie had had both the presence of mind and the desire to foster new and fetching life just for the fun of it, I went to help Tomio wrestle with the less friendly aspects of nature and forgot about the trilliums.

After we'd made the firepit suitable to eat around, we wandered through the campground admiring the other quaint buildings. A few families had pitched tents and one had parked a modern trailer, but the place was mostly empty. At the rear of the small forest, an open area of sloping hills and random, crumbling cairns opened to the sea. The wind picked up as we emerged from the trees. I could taste the salt in the air.

"These fields seem familiar," I said.

"All the fields along the coastline look alike. Arcturus could be just down the road," Tomio replied, "even though it's still hours away."

"True."

After a moment, Tomio wrapped his arms around me from behind as we took in the fields of green against a backdrop of evening sky. He murmured contemplatively into my neck: "What are we going to do?"

I had thought of little else all day, yet at the same time trying to guard my thoughts in case Nero went digging. We couldn't stay awake indefinitely. It was not only *difficult* to develop an idea while trying to protect that idea from my own overt consciousness where it might be plucked like a peach, it was *impossible*. I let out a long sigh, saying what I couldn't say in Ryan's presence.

"Would it be so bad?" Meaning, to lose our fire.

Tomio rested his chin on my shoulder. "No. It would be an adjustment, but I think I'd be one of the magi who could cope quite well."

"Me too."

This was expected. After all, we knew what it was like to be a natural. But a born mage like Ryan, and especially a power hungry one, he would not likely cope much better than his father. I wondered how Gage was doing. He'd be settled in at home by now, together with his dad, figuring out what was next. If Ryan lost his fire, at least he could go home to them. He wouldn't be alone.

"All life that sprang from it will be mine." I rubbed Tomio's forearm absently as I repeated Nero's words. "Is he just talking about fire? Or is he talking about every mage who was born, like, they'd become his slaves, or something?"

"I don't want to find out, which is why we can't just give up." Tomio buried his nose in my hair. "Right?"

"Right. So, we can't give up, but we can't formulate a plan."

A call from the forest edge behind us made us turn. Georjie was there, waving and miming lifting a fork to her lips.

Dinner turned out to be a precooked lasagna that Georjie reheated in the kitchenette. There were also butter rolls, apples, ginger ale, and a lot of cold water. We sat around the fire eating dinner as the last of the evening's light retreated. We began to burn away the occasional mosquito, but after the Arctic mozzies, I barely noticed. Everyone seemed either too lost in thought or too full to complain.

"Is anyone going to try going to sleep?" Ryan cradled the box containing the ghost-steel blade across his lap. He looked over at Georjie. "Obviously there's nothing stopping you from getting rest. Nero can't glamour supernaturals who aren't mages, or he would have done it by now."

"If you guys aren't going to sleep, then I'm not going to either. But, I was wondering if you had any sense of how far away he is. Can you feel that?"

We shook our heads.

Georjie glanced toward the trail briefly, watching perhaps for Nero to come blazing through the trees at us. "I figured not. So, when he shows up... we...?"

Ryan said, "We—by which I mean the mages—fight him with anything and everything we have. And given that you have healing powers and we don't, it's best that you keep your distance. You'll be like our lives in a video game."

Georjie sent him a half-hooded, unimpressed look for that line. "Charming."

Silence descended again and we stared into the fire while alternately watching the bushes for signs of Nero. Ryan cradled the backpack containing the orbs between his feet.

"Waiting's the worst." Tomio kicked a burning log back into the fire when it threatened to roll out. "I hate it."

"Maybe we should invite him to come," I said, because I'd been thinking something similar. "We should go to sleep, and when Nero comes poking into our minds, we should just show him exactly where we are."

Georjie sent me a startled look. "And burn down the campground once the fire starts flying? This place is their livelihood. I can patch up bodies and even whole forests, but I can't do anything to fix burned property."

I hadn't thought of that. *Why* hadn't I thought of that? I suddenly felt quite daft and selfish. From the looks on their faces, Ryan and Tomio hadn't thought of it either.

Tomio raked a hand through his hair. "We should never have checked in here. We should have bought tents and camped in a random field. Far from civilization."

"Let's take our bedding into the field between here and the shoreline, then," I suggested. "We'll hang out under the stars."

Several minutes later found us marching through the narrow path to the open fields, carrying pillows and blankets. Only Georjie really needed the blankets for warmth, but they gave us something soft to lie on.

The grass was thick and long here, making a surprisingly pleasant bed. I was laying down a blanket for Tomio and me to snuggle on when I noticed Georjie picking her way, barefoot, through the grass. Little white trilliums popped up in the undergrowth as she passed. There was a whole line of them again, leading over the rolling hills all the way back into the trees.

"What are you doing?" My question caused Ryan and Tomio to take notice of Georjie's fetching little habit.

"What do you mean?" she asked, innocently.

The moment I'd addressed her, the trilliums stopped popping up, like I'd broken her concentration.

I pointed at the flowers and gave her an expression that said, *Those. Hello!*

"They're pretty, don't you think?" Georjie placed a blanket on the grass and proceeded to arrange her long limbs across the surface, putting her hands behind her head for a cushion and crossing one ankle over the other. She looked quite pleased with herself.

I opened my mouth to demand a better explanation—not that I had a problem with trilliums, but my suspicions were running high—when Tomio said, in a voice more awe-filled than I'd ever heard before, "Who is *that*? Am I hallucinating again?"

A petite and slender woman had emerged from the forest like a sylph. She wore a plain tank top and shorts, revealing skin so pale it gleamed in the starlight. The wind picked up her dark hair and flicked it around her. She was barefoot, but carrying a pair of sneakers, and looked like she'd walked straight out of a dream.

"Targa," I rasped, thinking that if she was a hallucination, then Nero had met her before because he'd captured her features and her way of moving perfectly.

Georjie leapt up at the uttered name with a single word that snapped the scenario together like the final piece in a jigsaw. "Finally!"

She was off and jogging toward the approaching siren.

I was too dumbfounded to move, and watched my friends embrace as they stood beside the row of trilliums Georjie had left so that Targa could find us. But... Targa had come all the way from Poland. When? How?

Actually, the how part was easily solved. Targa had access to private aircraft, her company's aircraft. She could go wherever she wished, whenever she wished it. She had vast financial resources available to her, and since she was the boss, she didn't have to answer to anyone or explain herself. Within reason, of course. She did have a board to answer to.

Georjie hadn't been on the phone to Lachlan earlier, she'd been talking to Targa, explaining what was going on, and asking her to come.

Crushing the joy at seeing my siren friend here so unexpectedly, was a cold and heavy dread. It increased in weight with every moment that she closed the distance between us. I knew why these fields had seemed familiar now that Targa was in them, barefoot and wearing shorts. The cliff she'd leapt from in the dream that had me waking up choking not that long ago, was a mere couple of hundred meters from here.

I couldn't move to meet her. My legs and arms felt too heavy, my heart a stone. My stomach seemed to have decided it didn't much care for the lasagna after all.

Targa walked straight up to me, her face inscrutable as her eyes devoured me. "Hello. Georjie mentioned you were in a spot of trouble?"

I lifted leaden limbs and she stepped into my hug.

The realization that I was not hugging one person, but three, rushed through me like a hot wind. I whispered, "Why did you come?"

She pulled back, her bright blue eyes appearing dark in the starlight. "Don't freak out. I'm pregnant, not ill or injured, and a siren pregnancy is not nearly so fragile as—"

"Excuse me?" Georjayna shrieked and came between us, her shock so intense that I heard distant trees creak. "You're *pregnant*?"

"Yes. When you called earlier today, I planned to tell you, but then you explained the trouble they're in"—Targa knocked a head toward the boys and me—"and I knew that if I told you, you would forbid me to come, and you'd also feel guilty for asking in the first place. And we can't have that."

Georjie made a choking sound that could have been anger, could have been indignation, could have even been excitement, and was probably all three.

"Oh boy. Just what we needed, a pregnant chick." Ryan's words were quiet, but they were loud enough that none of us missed them.

Georjie and I whirled on him.

"*Pregnant chick*?" I raged. "Let me tell you a thing or two about this pregnant chick—"

My words were lost amidst Georjie's rant, which I only

caught the tail end of. "—ask your father how *his* confrontation with a siren turned out."

Ryan stumbled back, his hands up in defense. "Sorry,
geez. My bad."

Meanwhile, Targa and Tomio exchanged a handshake
and some pleasantries; I thought I heard him politely thank
her for coming, the way you would a neighbor who brought
you a casserole. Targa responded in kind, having had more
practice at pleasantries than her mother, who was famous
for her abrupt manner.

After Ryan had been appropriately humbled, we stood
around for an awkward moment, until Targa spoke as she
settled onto a blanket.

"So, why are we hanging out in a field that smells like
sheep? And who's going to fill me in about this Nolan
fellow?"

WE SAT IN THE GRASS, bringing Targa fully up to speed. The
moon hauled itself across the sky, the sea whispered, and
the gulls grew quiet.

We resisted the urge to sleep until Ryan pointed out that
if he were Nero, he'd wait until we were well and truly
exhausted before springing on us at an unexpected and
vulnerable moment.

There was no sign of the mage, no one saw anything
strange or heard any voices.

Sometime after two when our jaws simultaneously
creaked with yawns, and our eyes were leaking tears, Ryan
lay in the grass on his side. "You take first watch, Nakano.
Wake me in an hour."

And with that, it was decided. We would execute the age-old tradition of trading the night watch.

Targa and Georjie curled up under a blanket, and I heard Georjie whisper, "How did you convince Antoni to let you come?"

"I called him from the runway," she whispered back.

I lay with my head on Tomio's lap and he must have felt me suppress a laugh at Targa's response. Poor Antoni. What a thing to do to the father of her children.

Tomio bent over me. "What is it?"

I rubbed his hand. "Nothing."

I was too tired to talk anymore, and what could I say? Targa was at times more like her mother than she liked to admit. When she'd come into the full extent of her siren abilities, I'd been daunted by how much like Mira she seemed. But in time she'd softened again, although not entirely. I could only hope that Antoni knew Targa well enough not to be too upset with her for taking off without warning. That's what you get for falling in love with a siren.

My thoughts became muzzy, and the crickets lured me into slumber. It seemed like I'd been asleep for about six minutes when Tomio kissed me awake and told me it was my turn. I sat up, rubbed my eyes and took some invigorating breaths.

Georjie and Targa were a lump under their blanket. Ryan lay sprawled on the grass, his head resting on the backpack containing one orb and the blade, snoring lightly. Tomio stretched out beside me, propping the sack containing the other orb under his head.

I walked wide laps around my circle of sleeping friends, wondering if we'd been silly not to sleep in our cabins. I had thought Nero would have come for us by now, but there was no indication he was even thinking about us, let alone was anywhere near us. But my friends seemed to be sleeping peacefully enough, and it was nice out here. The air was warm and smelled like the sea. Even the insects had gone quiet, and the long grasses made a comfortable bed. So, I passed my hour walking laps and waiting for some tingle that Nero was approaching.

No tingle came.

Then I woke Georjie, and lay down beside Tomio, spooning him.

NERO CAME TO ME GENTLY.

I found myself dreaming that my eyes had opened. He was sitting cross-legged in the grass, watching me. I had no shock or panic because I understood he was not really there. For one thing, my friends were nowhere in sight, and beyond us there was no field or sea, just a vast nothingness that was not important.

"I haven't yet learned your name," Nero said, his voice completely different from the one he'd used in the fire-gym. The tone was the same, the timbre was his, but there was no threat or malice in it. It was warm, conversational, inquisitive.

Some tiny, inner voice hissed to wake up, but I easily ignored it. This was only a dream, not a true confrontation. The curiosity to hear what he had to say was stronger that my desire to flee, Why this charade of civility? I was helpless to prevent this interaction, anyway. I recognized that by the way my fire—for the first time since I'd inherited it—was demure in Nero's presence. It was not merely resting the way it did when it wasn't in use, it was cowed. This was not a good feeling, but I understood that emotion had taken a back seat. Nero wanted to talk, and he preferred for the conversation to be as cool and rational as possible. He brought the full weight of his psychic ability as my superior to that effect.

I brought myself up to mimic Nero's cross-legged position, as calm as afternoon tea, compelled to answer. "Saxony."

"I will permit you," he said, with an expression of contrived grace, "to ask me one question before I take what I want. Consider it a consolation prize. I'm feeling sorry for you, truth be told."

So, he couldn't read my thoughts, otherwise he would have seen the single word blinking in the foreground of my mind like it was a sign for a seedy, underground snooker club. If I understood one thing—his motivation—then perhaps he could be talked out of this relentless pursuit, and the ownership of all life that sprang from the source— as he had put it.

"Why are you doing this?"

He didn't react in any particular way, other than to take a minute to think about my question, evidently wanting to do it justice. "I lived the first six years of my life in an orphanage, you know. In Naples."

I gave no reaction to this strange and seemingly irrelevant statement.

"Don't pity me," he added, as though I'd replied with a sympathetic noise.

"I don't," I said, flatly.

He went on as though I hadn't spoken. "I was fed, and even loved. I had nice friends and an education. The start of one, at any rate. Monks ran this particular orphanage, ones who had been interviewed to the point of interrogation, and watched to the point of surveilled. The head monk had been told by the proprietor in no uncertain terms that there was to be no abuse of any kind at this orphanage and school, as it was funded by a wealthy man who abhorred and condemned the ill-treatment of children."

"How nice for you," I replied, with not a hint of audible sarcasm. I couldn't have let it leak into my tone had I wanted to, and I did want to. I was as much a captive as if I had been chained down with links forged of the same stuff that made up that freezing cold blade.

Nero languished in his storytelling, knowing full-well the spell he had me under. This was nothing like the seduction of his demands when he'd come to me in my sleep the first time, wanting to know what had happened to the crate. His quest for information had not been easy to resist, but I had found will and strength and resisted.

This? I couldn't.

"I was eventually adopted at the age of six, by the wealthy man who funded the orphanage, no less, after I impressed him with my hunger for knowledge. I excelled in my lessons, you see. Unlike the other children, who were normal, uninteresting, unremarkable children. There was nothing wrong with them, but there was something wrong with me. I wished for more discipline, longer lessons, and to be punished when I could not recall facts accurately, which rarely happened. I excelled at everything from mathematics, to language."

"Why did you need to kidnap Janet then, if you were so smart?"

"I said one question, imp," Nero said, but not without an expression that looked something like delight at what he probably perceived as my impudence, though I'd meant the question honestly.

"He took me home, hired tutors, taught me philosophy

and science, and indulged every desire I had for learning. I read books penned for adults at the age of nine. I wrote scientific papers that were published in journals at the age of fourteen. I was good at everything. The best in the city, perhaps in all of Italy. I was invited to learn from eminent minds in a wide range of fields. Some of these men, and they were almost always men, were wealthy, but I noticed that they did not flex their wealth in ways that changed things. At least, not the way I would have changed them. Those I wanted to interview the most had no interest in indulging a young man, even a highly intelligent one. They were too busy politicizing for that."

I was growing dizzy in my attempt to follow this story well enough to ferret out its point, and hoped he'd get there soon.

"After falling into brief and fiery love with your headmaster's sister—she never accidentally revealed what she was to me, in case you're wondering, the woman was a vault. Had she not chosen to trust me with the reality of their, your, existence, my life would have taken a much different turn. But she did. And this, I understood much later—many of the most important things that happen to us in life cannot be understood until much later—was why I met her in the first place. It was not to marry her. It was to learn of the magi. This was a world I had heard nothing of, not in all of my years of study on an extensive range of subjects. As you might well imagine, my thirst for knowledge took a short and violent leap into a thirst for power."

At his mention of Babs, Bellamy sprang to mind. No amount of articulate storytelling would ever change the reality of what the man sitting before me, occupying real estate within my own slumbering consciousness, was: a murderer.

Giving no hint that he'd sensed my accusation, he went on with his philosophizing.

"Power is not unlike money, those with the most have opportunities to influence the world in ways other don't, and not having it, or not taking it when you can, is foolish and weak. Not only are you dishonoring the talents and abilities you were born with, you are crippling your future self, denying the being you are destined to become of resources you'll come to wish you had preserved. So, I found a way to take what I wanted. I had been adopted by a philosopher and into a highly educated family. They taught me that out of misfortune comes fortune, along with opportunity. My adopted father's great-grandfather worked for a powerful company that traded in furs, that's where their fortune began; in Canada, your country, I believe, based on the limited amount of words I've heard you speak."

He waited for agreement, and after I felt my head nod, he continued.

"When reproached and criticized by future generations about how this fortune had been acquired, my father answered that the harvesting of furs would have happened whether his ancestor had been involved in it or not, and that some of that fortune had gone into building the very orphanage I had begun my life in. The funding for those orphanages had come out of the fur-trade, but perhaps another wealthy fur-trader would not have opted to contribute in such a way."

"What are you saying? That you will do good with the power you've taken? That more good might come from you hoarding our idles than the magi you stole from might ever have done?"

Nero shrugged, allowing me to utter not another additional question but three. "I'll have the right to decide, and that's what I want. I take the power for myself because I can, no one can stop me. It will leave others destitute, yes, but they will continue to live out their existence, coping with what fate has dealt them. It wasn't *them* who did all the hard work to find the idles. It wasn't *them* who sacrificed all suggestion of a normal life to inherit this power. They could have, but they didn't. It's those who can reach the moon first who can claim the right to mine it, simply because no one can prevent them. Should a magus choose to end their own life, that has nothing to do with me, and I would argue that they didn't deserve to wield what they were born with in the first place." He leaned forward, blazing eyes flickering through a mesmerizing rainbow of colors. "And you? Will you end your life when your fire goes out?"

"Of course not. I came into this world without it, I can go on without it." I managed to speak blithely, but I knew it would not be so simple. While I would never remove myself from the world because it would hurt my family too much, how could I possibly predict the ways in which returning to the world of naturals would affect me?

His expression softened with a sick species of generosity. "I could have taken them by now."

Meaning the orbs, of course.

"Why haven't you, then?"

"I was curious about your company. They are not magi. Who are they?"

Ah. So that's why he was here, so distastefully invading my mind. Unfortunately, I couldn't produce even a hint of resistance against answering him. He was in control, and I was overwhelmed.

"Friends I've known since I was practically in diapers."

Nero chuckled and rubbed his forehead in a gesture of

self-reproach. "Silly me. I should have been more specific. *What* are they?"

My throat felt bee stung in an increased effort not to respond. It was the first physical discomfort I'd felt since this whole thing had begun. There wasn't much I wanted less than to tell Nero what my friends were capable of, to expose them, and arm him. But I could not have held back my words any more than I could force myself to wake from this illusion. "One is a siren."

"The dark-haired one," Nero murmured. "I should have guessed. I've never seen one with my own eyes, but I've read about them. Dangerous voice, she has. A problem I can easily remedy. And the other?"

My subconscious writhed against his interrogation, begging for me to wake before I divulged further secrets. Already I had endangered Targa to a point of eye-rolling panic. Losing the advantage that his ignorance would have given us was a blow so heavy I wondered if it showed through on my dream-face. But my dream-voice came through unencumbered by the worries that would plague me when I woke. I felt as though I was sitting in the front row of a drama, watching my own performance on center stage with helpless dread.

"A Wise," I said, hating myself.

Nero's brow crinkled beneath his widow's peak as his eyes flashed green, then indigo, then orange. "I don't know this term. What is a Wise?"

"Half-fae, half-human," I mumbled.

He brightened. "How delightful. Well she does not present a problem either, then."

I damned my inability to read his true emotions behind all that colorful light. Was he intentionally misleading me in order to shake my confidence? Did I have any actual confidence left anyway? "So, you want us to hand over the orbs without putting up a fight. That's what you're driving at?"

Nero flexed his fingers and fisted both hands at the same time, then lay them purposefully on his thighs. "The world belongs to those who are powerful enough to take it. Why risk the life ahead of you only to fail to prove me wrong?"

This struck a chord that I had forgotten ran through me, a chord strung by religious parents. I didn't pay much attention to their discussions of intangible, or spiritual, things while I was young. It was a rare young person who did pay attention to such things, but there was an old scripture that had managed to stamp itself into my memory. It came back to me now. "There are those who say the meek shall inherit, not the powerful."

He laughed dismissively. "I have never once seen that happen. Have you?"

I certainly hadn't, and was compelled to shake my head in answer.

"No," he agreed, silently getting to his feet. "And it's not about to start happening now."

And then he was gone, like the flame of a candle puffed out.

17

FIRE-FIGHT

Something blunt nudged against my shoulder, drawing me into wakefulness. Droplets of liquid sprayed across my face and spattered my clothing, bringing me the rest of the way awake with an electrified start. Gasping, I first looked to where Nero had been sitting across from me, where Ryan had been.

Nero was not there.

Neither was Ryan, or his backpack.

Scrambling to my feet, disoriented and wondering if this was another elaborate hallucination, I spun, looking for someone, anyone. Georjie and Targa's blankets lay across the grass, discarded.

I became aware that something—aside from missing friends—was very wrong, something more difficult to define. For one thing, the sound of the sea had changed. Instead of a distant hush of repetitive sighs as waves licked the base of the cliff, it sounded more like a trickling brook. There was something wrong with the horizon, too. It wasn't there.

My heart ratcheted up a notch. Why had no one woken me sooner? Where was everyone, and now that the sleep had been torn from my eyes, why was the light so weird? I wanted to yell for my friends but instinct told me not to. Something was afoot. Was this the beginnings of a plan that was not a plan? Who was in charge?

A gentle touch on my shoulder made me spin, gasping.

"It's just me," Tomio whispered, his features misted with a palette of soft blues and grays. He cradled the boxes containing the orbs against his chest, his fingers splayed and hooked across them like a stretched-out spider. He gave one of them to me, urging me to take it by pressing it against my stomach.

The moment I took its weight in my hand, I understood there was no orb inside. My gaze dropped to his box, wondering if both orbs would fit within one, but the way Tomio shifted the other made it apparent there was nothing inside his, either.

More water droplets landed on the top of my head, making me look up. I held out a hand, palm up, wondering if it was raining. A few more droplets fell, and I licked one off my wrist and tasted salt. It took a moment for my eyes to adjust because there were no sharp details to focus on, no moon, no treetops. A wave of vertigo overtook me as I fought for depth perception. Then my heart gave a little leap as I discovered why the lighting was so weird.

The moon was there, but it was a pale blur, a smudge of white against dark, wet paint. It glimmered down through a thickness of running water, which explained the trickling sounds. We were surrounded by it. Water. A wall of indiscernible thickness. The wall was curved, and moving, slowly and gently, but still moving. It shot high then curved gracefully overhead, like a dome. It met the earth and its currents swept along the grass before sweeping overhead again.

It was a huge bubble, with only me and Tomio inside it.

We were enclosed entirely within a cocoon of Targa's making, though there was no sign of the water elemental herself. My mind staggered at the powers she possessed. Though I'd seen them in action before, I had not observed her magic since the storm in Saltford. This display renewed my respect.

"This is Targa," I whispered to Tomio, though I wasn't sure why I felt the need to whisper. Maybe from respect.

"So I gathered. I'm appropriately astounded," he replied, not whispering,

"How long have you been awake? Do you know what's happening?"

"I heard Georjayna and Targa talking at some point. I figured they were trading watches and went back to sleep. When I woke up again, I saw this"—he pointed at the bubble—"and found these"—he gestured to the boxes —"beside me. Empty. Then I woke you."

I thought, but didn't say aloud in case there were unfriendly ears nearby, that the boxes were to be used as decoys, although if that were part of the plan, it would have to have been communicated to Tomio, and it was apparent that nothing had been communicated to Tomio. Still, decoys they could be.

A glimmer of something appeared through the wall of water, streaks and smudges of a vaguely human shape. It grew in size as it approached, distinctly male in form. It stopped on the other side of the water. The figure raised an arm, and slowly fingertips appeared through the wall, followed by the rest of the hand, though the hand was not entirely corporeal. It flickered with colorless flame. It reached into the space beyond, discovering the thickness of the wall of water was no more than a man's arm, and neither did the water pose any threat to him, or extinguish his blackfire.

Tomio nudged me away, indicating we needed to separate our decoys. He went to one side of the bubble and I went to the other, unable to tear my eyes away from the figure. The distance between us grew as Nero slowly passed through the water, perhaps hoping to make no noise, or thinking it was a trap. By the time Tomio and I reached opposite sides of the bubble—near enough to run a finger against it—we were a soccer field apart.

Nero emerged fully as a figure made entirely of blackfire. The water allowed him through and closed up after his passage, leaving no evidence of a breach. He stood just inside, head turning to take in first me, then Tomio. His face was impossible to read because it wasn't really there, only a mere suggestion of features flickered within the colorless fire. Eyes, nose, and mouth were just shadows inside shadows.

My stomach and throat clenched as this specter observed us, neither fully man, nor fully fire. He radiated something that could not be classified as heat. Perhaps if I'd been closer. But there was something, entirely different from temperature, that marked his blackfire, something that made my eyes smart and my skin tingle. It had to be the supernatural effluent we'd been chasing as a team these last weeks, leaking from Nero like radioactive waste. But the sensation he gave off was not entirely unpleasant, it was irritating to my skin and eyes and acrid in my nose, like ammonia, but I felt my fire fatten in its presence. I felt a flush of energy as my mage's body responded to Nero's presence.

He neither spoke nor made sound as he stepped

forward, flicking his gaze between me and Tomio. He saw the boxes. We made no attempt to conceal them, though perhaps we should have, to make it appear more likely that they held the treasure Nero was after.

One instant he was there, observing us, and the next he was a streak of transparent flames, heading straight for Tomio.

I'd been tense and ready for Nero to charge at me, maybe because we'd so recently exchanged views, but I hadn't been ready for him to attack Tomio. I flinched and cried out on reflex.

But Tomio was ready. He was born ready.

The moment Nero arrived where Tomio had been, Tomio was no longer there. He moved at near the speed of electricity, jumping and darting, ducking and dodging. Never attacking, only evading. He used his fire without wasting energy to conceal it. Flashes of light filled my vision with starbursts. They couldn't be *watched*, they could only be seen in snapshots captured in brief flashes. A flash of Tomio rolling over the ground, then in the air in an athletic vault, then into an impossibly low crouch, head lifted and eyes wide, taking in his pursuer, then rolling beneath. Nero by contrast was a negative silhouette against the world, blocking out whatever was behind him as he reached for and pursued Tomio.

I crouched there in a half-squat, gaze darting and eyes watering as they strained to keep on the magi. I coiled, ready to spring when Nero headed my way. I rejected the idea of leaving the bubble, because it meant leaving Tomio. Why Targa had made it wasn't entirely clear, perhaps it was to protect us, perhaps it was just a spectacular distraction that gave them a chance to get the orbs away. Perhaps Targa didn't know herself, it was just something she was able to do. It also never occurred to me that the bubble would not stay there all night, like a watery womb separating us from the rest of the world.

When the whole thing came crashing down in a torrent of rain, it shocked me. It drummed against my head, taking my breath and sight away as I bent my neck and presented my back to the waterfall with a series of gasps and shudders. The barrage lasted only seconds, stopping abruptly. The moonlight made everything suddenly stark, the audio of the world came to my ears, and the sound of the sea swept close. The air moved again, fresh and cool.

Water dripped from my hair, my clothes, my eyelashes, I blinked and wiped at my eyes with my free hand, desperate to lay my sight on Tomio and Nero again. Across the lake of water and wet grass, they were not difficult to spot.

Tomio was always ready for combat, you couldn't sneak up on him or jump him, but nothing had prepared him for the Niagara that had struck when the water came down. Nero, the opportunist, had not wasted the surprise. Tomio lay at Nero's feet, frighteningly still, his face half buried in wet grass. Nero stood over him, a figure outlined in blackfire, holding the box open in his hands.

My heart leapt into my throat and my hearing narrowed to exclude everything but the sound of my own breathing. I tore my eyes from Tomio's prone form in time to see Nero's head twist toward me. A suggestion of a grimace in the black cave of his face was all the expression he gave before he was a blur again, coming straight for me.

WITH NO PREMEDITATION about how I should deal with the mage of god-like proportions streaking across the soggy field, my fire, which had been crouched and snarling like an angry canine, ignited with so much heat that my eardrums popped and my eyes felt like twin blast-furnaces. My form swept with fire and I let its fury and power propel me. I didn't care where.

The box vanished in an instant, reduced to ash. I didn't bother preserving it, the way Tomio had done. I'd become a meteor, leaving showers of sparks and blackened foliage in my wake, making the puddles I skimmed hiss and steam. I felt uncatchable, unstoppable, like a raging locomotive.

Until I was struck from behind with alchemy. If I couldn't see it, I couldn't brace for it, and if I couldn't prepare, it raked over my nerve endings like razor-sharp claws. My fire now recognized and absorbed alchemical-fire, though not without mistakes. Redheat and boron-laced flames singed and burned. I changed directions, trying to stay far enough ahead to come up with a plan, and looking around so I wasn't taken off guard.

Tomio. Was he alive?

Thoughts of him kept me from abandoning the area. I strained for a glimpse of him, but my vision had become evanescent. A glance over my shoulder revealed Nero as a mere outline of black filled with swirls of color and gashes of light, barely recognizable as human in shape. He spread both arms out as he flew after me, as though floating on a wave of fire, spewing up sparks behind him like a rooster's tail. A looming nightmare, he halted abruptly and fell away.

I stopped. My fire cooled and dwindled. My heart and lungs labored inside my volcanized insides. Trickles of heat washed through my body as I scanned the fields, assuming Nero had let off his pursuit because he realized I did not have an orb in my possession. Between searching glances for Nero, I scanned the area where Tomio had fallen. But he no longer lay where I'd last seen him.

A lance of pain shot through my lower back, like some monster with wide jaws and jagged teeth had clamped into me. I cried out and twisted to see what devilry this was, coming down to one knee and straining to see my wound.

The skin across the back of my waist and my right hip appeared to be made of coal and ash, not black, in the manner of the shells, but a deep plum color, threaded through with seams the bloody hue of a freshly sliced beet. It felt like I'd been splashed with chemicals—which spread as I watched—eating into my spine and pelvis with an acid agony that drew pained whimpers from my throat.

"Where are the orbs?" hissed a bodiless voice, chains scraping over gravel.

I beheld the world through prisms of welling tears. Every nerve channeled lightning and my pulse was jagged. I wondered if I might pass out. The ground came up to meet me and I landed on my elbows, feeling no pain other than that spreading across my back, more caustic than lye, moving like a living thing trying to claw its way through me. I curled forward in on myself, writhing in an effort to get away from the pain.

"Here, you cock-eyed, finger-pricked loser!" A taunting voice yelled from somewhere beyond my blurry sight.

I kept myself balanced on my elbows and knees, because I was scared that if my back touched even a blade of grass I would break apart and drift away on the wind. This was how I would die. The poison—now above my waist too— felt like scalpels carving through muscle and tendon as it journeyed up toward my shoulder blades and down toward the backs of my legs. It would break apart my entire being, render me to dust.

Struggling up to my hands, I lifted my head to look around. As though seen through warped glass, I recognized Ryan's form. He stood at some distance in the knee-length grass. He hefted an orb, tossing it up and down like it was a tennis ball he intended to serve. His other hand was hidden behind his back. Even in my brain-numbing pain, I knew what he held hidden. I felt the edges of a smile flicker at the corners of my mouth, even as my cheeks were wet from my watering eyes.

Come on, Ryan. If he could get close enough, be fast enough, he could use the dagger.

And then I saw something truly remarkable, something that made me forget for an instant that my body was being eaten away. It played out in glorious slow-motion.

Nero's form ignited and shot forward, heading straight for Ryan, who cocked back an arm and threw the orb as hard as he could—really hurled it. The orb arched through the sky, flickering with reflected moonlight.

Either unable to stop his momentum or intent on killing Ryan for his insolence, Nero did not change course. The two of them became blurs of firelight. Twisting and writhing and spitting like a nest of brightly colored, pissed-off snakes.

A beautiful illumination of an entirely different brand emerged from the earth like a fountain. Hair flying, skin glowing, her form moving like liquid mercury, Georjayna emerged from the ground, arms outstretched. Wrapping lit fingers neatly around the orb, she arced in a graceful breach, like a dolphin, and disappeared underground again, along with the artifact.

In the next moment I felt hands clutch at my shoulder. A panicked curse word hissed past my ear. Tomio had his hands on me now, inspecting my back.

I tried to look over my shoulder and focus on his face,

filled as I was with relief and pride and wonder. "You're alive! Did you see her? Georjie?"

"What did he do to you?" His voice was pained and full of cold rage.

I tried to explain that some blend of chemicals—so artfully concocted that I could not determine the ingredients or ratios—was eating its way through me, an inch at a time, but the words came out slurred and jumbled. My neck was aching from trying to see what was happening.

Somewhere beyond us, a fire-fight of obscene proportions was taking place. Rainbow flashes of light reflecting everywhere, like maniacal, super-charged fireworks. Against the backdrop of these beautiful bursts, the head and neck of my beautiful fae friend appeared. She was soothing to my vision, like a cool cloth against a fevered forehead.

Hardly conscious now, I felt them lower me to my side so I lay along the ground. I heard Georjie exchange words with Tomio and felt her magic seep into me, spreading cool, questing relief where it touched. It soaked into my side from the ground, up through my thighs and into the back of my legs. It curled over my waist, and around my back and shoulders like a hug. It swept up my pelvis, into my spine and across my back. Where it met Nero's alchemy, it slowed, prowling forward like a cautious cat, nosing its way up to a mystery. Then it touched, and pulled back a few times, as if unsure how to proceed. It felt just like the way a feline bumps their nose against food before deciding whether or not to eat it. This seemed wonderful and deeply charming to me for some reason.

"It's like a cat," I said. I sounded like a frog. A sick one. And that made me laugh, which hurt my entire torso, which then made me moan.

Tomio said something about it affecting my mind, and I

heard Georjie say something about searching the area for what she needed.

An altogether different sensation followed the first. Blazing the same trail through my body, came an entirely different compound. Where the first was soothing and slick, like aloe juice over a sunburn, the second moved through me like it was made of cactus. A prickling sensation, not entirely unpleasant, but not pleasant either, clawed its way to the site of injury, where a battle of ineffable proportions raged. It rendered me utterly speechless and senseless for what seemed like time immemorial. I drifted in and out of awareness on a current of sensation that was both agonizing and reconstructive, but always intense. There was no escaping it.

I wondered where Targa was, briefly, before my mind was fully distracted by physical sensation. As fibers were knit back together and chemical compounds resisted neutralization, I lay there, as impotent and helpless as an infant. I thought it would never end.

But it did end.

When I came to my senses, Georjie was nowhere to be seen. Tomio held me like I was a baby, peering intently into my face for signs of wakefulness. I couldn't remember being rolled onto my back, but now I could see the sky.

"You're going to be alright," he said. "It's nearly all gone."

My back tingled but no longer pained me; I flexed my spine and felt my joints respond and lubricate. I felt stiff and tender, but the feeling of crawling acid was gone.

The light show was still going on as Tomio helped me to my feet, so I couldn't have been out of it for long. I became aware that I was almost naked. Only ruined fireproof underwear clung to my body in ragged, frayed scraps. Someone had draped a blanket over me, so I clutched it.

"Where's Targa?" Surely, I'd asked this a thousand times already. Or had I only thought it? I struggled to separate what was real from the twilight of pain.

"I don't know. She's got the other orb." Tomio wrapped an arm protectively around me. His eyes were on Ryan and Nero, continuing to blast fire—Ryan with intent to kill, Nero easily defending himself. Ryan had yet to get the blade in contact with Nero, the mage was simply too fast. One could hardly make out human outlines within all that blazing light.

I imagined I could hear Tomio's thoughts. He was torn between leaving my side and leaping into the fray.

"Do you hear that?" I asked, turning an ear to the sea.

Tomio cocked his head.

It was a familiar sound, though at first I couldn't place where I'd heard it. It was the sound of a great volume of water moving very fast in this direction. Yet we still had yet to lay our eyes on our siren.

Tomio stiffened, then pointed. "There."

She was a small pale figure in the distance, in a gap between us and the ocean, standing on a gentle swell of ground. She appeared to be in meditation, with her head down and her hands held open, palms forward, at her sides. Her back was to the ocean, and the ocean was coming to her. The sound of menacing, rushing water grew until even Nero and Ryan heard it and stopped to listen, panting and staring, crouched to spring.

A tidal wave, that's why the sound was familiar. Targa had once prevented a tidal wave from destroying Saltford, now she was making one.

By the time the water she'd drawn was visible, it was so loud it shook the earth beneath our feet. And it was not just a tidal wave, it was a battering ram. It rose up behind Targa, like the head of a mythical sea creature emerging from a primordial sea. It shot up and up into the sky, frothing and boiling and roaring like a dragon. It arced high and seemed almost to pause and tip its nose down to look at us mere ants.

Eyes stretched wide, I looked to Ryan and Nero, heads craned back to see what was coming, faces aghast. I screamed for Ryan to get out of the way. In the same instant I noticed something that turned my blood cold: the ghost-steel blade had somehow made the switch from Ryan's possession to Nero's.

Targa's hands were high now, like a conductor's, then she dropped them like someone starting a race. The creature she'd conjured from seawater, dove straight for the two magi, icicles of huge proportions visible at its furious leading edge, gnashing and snarling.

My fire burst to life and I streaked straight for Ryan, screaming from a throat filled with enough heat to melt iron. Nero's form flickered from solid to blackfire. The knife seemed to hover of its own accord, then streaked to make a white laceration across a backdrop of fantastic color, like a slash in the universe.

I struck Ryan as his body ignited. We tumbled like tar-soaked flaming projectiles shot from a medieval catapult. The world behind us exploded with an impact of ice and water that blasted us further afield like half-drowned rodents. Our flames extinguished with a loud hiss, we tumbled and rolled, limbs flailing to grip at something—anything—stable. We came to a sodden, bruised stop in a dip filled with brambles and long, fibrous grasses. I rolled onto my back, sucking in air and looking up at the peaceful night sky. All went quiet for several long breaths as we recovered ourselves.

Ryan coughed and gave a groan, but it sounded amused. "She's more of a blunt instrument than I was expecting, that friend of yours." He followed that with more coughs.

I found my feet and rose unsteadily, clawing wet hair from my face and looking for Ryan. We'd slid to a stop in a pool of shadows.

He moaned somewhere off to my left.

"I'm not sure why she hasn't called him off with her siren voice." I swung around looking for him in the disorienting darkness, moving toward the sound of his voice.

"She tried," he said, giving another groan of pain. "As long as he's blackfire, her voice has no effect. The bugger must have figured out what she is, clever bastard. He's never once fully taken his flesh form. That's why she dumped the ocean on him. She's trying to put him out. But how did he figure out what she is so quickly? That's what I don't understand."

His words were a wet glove slapped across my face. No one knew about the conversation Nero and I had had, what he'd wrung from my mind.

Ryan's groan, more pained this time, brought me back. I found him, a sodden lump with hot, bare skin. I felt his back and shoulder. My eyes had begun to adjust to the darkness. "Are you okay?"

I was desperate to get back. Had Targa's trick managed to hurt Nero, or quench his blackfire? We couldn't see them from our dip in the earth, and no sounds were coming to my ears.

"I think I'm finished, Cagney," Ryan said, with a gurgle in his voice that hadn't been there a second ago. "The steel... the ghost—"

Shaking water off my hand, I lit and lifted a hand-torch, holding it up so I could look him over. It wasn't difficult to find his wound. All that remained of his clothing was a pair of fireproof boxer shorts, which was more than what I had left to cover myself. Had there been time, sunlight, and less distractions, I would have felt embarrassed. The gash along Ryan's ribs was bleeding profusely. His blood was stark against his pale skin and staining the grass around us. It looked black in the firelight.

I made a snap decision not to pick Ryan up and carry him. Not only would it have hurt immensely, I couldn't bear to see more blood gush from the wound, which looked deep and angry. I helped Ryan place his hand against his side in a way that minimized the bleeding, since he couldn't see the wound very well for himself, and told him to try cauterizing it while I went to get Georjie.

"Already tried that," he said through gritted teeth. "It won't cauterize. It's the steel. It feels like someone shoved a shard of ice into my ribs."

I ran then. Using fire to speed me along, but finding the ground slippery and treacherous, I crested the shallow hill. Chunks of ice lay in the grass. It looked like there'd been a collision of glaciers. Movement pulled my gaze toward the sea.

Targa's small pale figure sprinted toward the cliff edge, one fist clenched around what could only be an orb. The way her ghostly soles flashed white yanked me straight back to the dream I'd had weeks ago at the academy. She flew over the dark landscape, heading for the even darker sea, her stride as sure as a thoroughbred's and as smooth as a jungle cat's. Her hair flew out behind her, a magnificent mane of ink and starlight.

But closing fast was a line of caustic fire, surging and writhing malevolently in shades of acid green and neon orange. Nero's figure was not moving, he didn't need to, his fire was doing the chasing for him. He stood facing the running siren, arms straight out and flickering with black-fire, like a flaming cross.

It was apparent watching the siren run and the chemical fire closing the gap that she might not make it to the cliff edge before the flames overtook her, and I was too far away to do much of anything to help.

A thin white shape in the grass caught my eye, a brighter white than the icicles melting in the grass.

The blade.

Thoughts of Ryan dissolved as distant as an echo now, I shot like a cannon ball loosed, blazing across the landscape. Scooping up the blade by its handle, I flipped it and caught it by the blade. Icy pain stabbed into the flesh of my fingers, and I clenched my teeth against it, knowing I couldn't throw a blade by its handle. Firing along my arm and back, my fingers scorching, I threw the blade as hard as I could manage, wishing but hardly daring to hope it would find its mark.

In near disbelief, I watched as the blade struck Nero's shadowy side, just underneath his left arm. His form briefly indented and his spine seemed to curve sideways in reflex. A gap opened in his blackfire where flesh was visible, like his fire magic had been chased back by the presence of the blade, leaving a vulnerable opening.

There was a sound like a scream echoing through a canyon.

Then the screech of metal being torn in two.

A car alarm blared from the distant parking lot.

Startled and confused, I looked toward the campground when I heard a tree branch snap, then another, and another. Something was charging through the bush. I whipped my focus back to Targa in time to see her leap.

She jumped from the cliff edge, propelled by powerful siren legs, then hovered in the air for a moment, a delicate form against the backdrop of an endless black sky and blanket of stars. I sucked in a breath, unable to tear away, even as I heard nearer trees snapping and breaking to my right.

She stopped falling, hung suspended and then flew in the other direction; straight up, and going fast.

It appeared as though some giant had snagged her by the hand and yanked her several meters upward. Then she stopped dead, dangling by the hand clenched around the orb. She looked up. I was too far away to see her face, but could read in her body language that she was trying to figure out why the orb was hanging in mid-air, dangling her like a doll from a hook. Her legs swung as she tugged on the orb, her long hair flying in the wind. She craned her neck and bounced in an effort to dislodge the orb.

Finally, she released the orb and fell, plummeting out of sight.

Like it had been waiting for her to let go, the orb flew through the air parallel to the ground, toward Nero. But it didn't just fly... it *shot*.

I was close enough to Nero to make out his profile. He still had his arms out to the side, but his torso had a weird bent shape. He faced the oncoming projectile and put his arms out for it, as though to catch it. I could only watch as the orb—moving so fast now that it was almost impossible to see—came straight for him. He looked like he'd called it, but it was moving far too quickly now to stop in his hand.

With a sound like a melon striking pavement and splitting open, it shot straight through his chest and out his back.

My jaw dropped and my mind staggered to understand.

Nero made no sound. Every flame he had ignited along the landscape and along his body instantly snuffed. Slowly, he fell to his knees, hitting the ground with an exhalation of breath. I was close enough to see splatters of what looked like black blood and coal dust along his olive skin. He looked like any ordinary man—with a hole in his chest, and the handle of a blade protruding from just beneath his armpit.

He toppled forward into the grass and didn't move.

I froze in shock. I don't know how long I stood there, weak and staring mutely at Nero's body, half expecting him to leap up. My heart still skittered like a frightened animal, but I had seen what I had seen. The fingers of my right hand throbbed from contact with the ghost steel, but I barely noticed.

Recovering the power of my legs, I closed the distance between us and knelt at his side. He smelled of ash and cinders, blackened flesh, creosote and charcoal. I didn't have to touch him to know that he was dead.

Colored light drew my attention to my right, where seven orbs hung still and silent in the air over the field. They formed a perfect circle, hovering out of reach, even for a mage. Not that I wanted to touch them, not after having seen what one of them did to Nero.

I drew as close as I dared, picking my way through chunks of ice with my bare feet. A soft wind blew in from the sea. The car alarm had stopped at some point and everything was quiet. Quiet enough to make out soft voices coming from where I'd left Ryan: Georjie's soft tone and Tomio's deeper one.

I was alone with the orbs. It was just me and them. All of them. All seven.

They hung in the air, still and silent.

Then they ignited, all at once and in perfect unison, with colored flames so vivid that for a moment I couldn't draw breath. Seven floating orbs had become seven floating torches. Emerald green, deep indigo, candy-apple red, juicy orange, sun yellow, vibrant violet and rose pink. They flickered and danced, licking at the night, the shape of each orb visible at the base of each flame. They were tall, taller than me, these tongues of colored fire, and so beautiful I found myself unable look away.

Then, like some giant invisible birthday cake set atop a turntable, the seven novel torches began to spin in a circle. Slowly at first, then picking up speed. They made arches of searing spectral light against the sky. The sound of fire whipping through the air was at first gentle, then increased to a soft roar. I was reluctant to blink, loath to miss a moment of the spectacle.

As they spun, the space between them narrowed, and the spinning slowed again. The orbs approached one another. They were siblings who had been separated at birth and who had spent lifetimes apart, coming together for the first time in millennia. They drew close enough to touch. Sparks flew where they shared borders. They closed the gap further, and the protruding lines laced over each orb inserted themselves into the recessed lines of the others, locking all seven of them together. Like the drawing but far more spectacular. Then the individual orbs began to turn, slowly, smoothly, guided by the interlocking lines, they twisted and rolled, each rotating in its own unique way yet all at once, in a display that defied physics.

The flames intensified, paling in color, as though bleached, until there was no color left, only a single spectacular white flame with a level of brightness and purity I should not have been able to look upon without going blind.

But I wasn't blind. I could see and watch it all. I watched as the white fire grew and grew. I watched until it blanked out everything and swallowed me entirely.

18

______

THE WHITE GOD

A pale vacancy filled my vision and I was immediately transported into a familiar sensation, that of the bodiless skating and sliding that had carried me through the orb's journey, what felt like a thousand years ago. I had no ability to look down or up or behind, such things were impossible without a head sitting atop a neck. I was without sensation of skin or muscle, fire or bodily aches. I was of no more substance than a thought, yet I occupied a broad and expansive world. There was no field, no sounds of the sea, none of my friends were present.

Yet, something was present. Or someone. A sentient consciousness.

This something or someone exuded no threat, and felt nothing like Nero. It had a cool yet curious detachment about me, that much I understood. In fact, I understood a great many things that I'd not understood before, and almost all at once.

We had been right about some things, and wrong about others.

This was the Source Fire. That was not debatable. The

other thing that was not debatable was that never in his wildest dreams could Nero hope to absorb or claim this power for himself. This power dwarfed Nero as the sun dwarfed the Earth, as the Euphrates dwarfed a trickling brook.

As God dwarfs man.

How foolish he was to think he could rule the Source, and how foolish we'd been to believe him.

Silhouettes formed in the blazing white vacancy, moving like characters against powerful backlighting floodlights in a play. Seven of them, of course. Faceless and without detail, more like stylized animation of humans than actual humans. I understood more, comprehension soaked into me like bread soaks up milk. The Source Fire pressed knowledge gently into my consciousness, rather than communicating in words, just as the fire had pressed a fraction of itself gently into its visitors all those millennia ago.

When they had stepped into the white fire, the fire had communed with them, much the same way it was communing with me. They were to carry these tiny subdivisions of the white god within themselves for all their lives, pass it on, and use the power it gave them as they would. A stranger to our world, the white flame had arrived with a near insatiable curiosity, from a far-off place with dimensions, language, beings and wisdom that humans did not have the capacity to grasp.

I understood that our world appeared to the white god to be a marvel of ingenuity and miracles, and the humans who occupied this world were beautiful too, beautiful, and deeply flawed. There was depth here, there were things to be understood, things to learn. Each tiny tongue of fire the white god sent into the world would collect experiences through its host, while lending them a heightened ability so potent it killed the weaker ones before the power could fully quicken within them.

The progenitors understood this, that they were to be the fountainheads of the Source. They emerged from the belly of the white flame wholly changed, each carrying an orb in their palm, a symbol of the gift they now carried within them. No human craftsman had formed them, they'd been forged in the same moment the alliance was agreed.

None of the original magi had refused the covenant, it had not occured to even one of them.

When the time was right, these orbs would make their way back to each other. As surely as raindrops and sunlight conjured a rainbow, the orbs would conjure the white fire, the eighth fire. This segment of a pan-millennial data gathering process would come to an end, though it was a mere step in miles of timeline.

The Source Fire would depart in much the same way it had come. It had been attracted by the radiant, restless grid of mysterious energy wrapping itself through and around our Earth. It was resourceful, patient, and clever, sending tiny bits of itself, not only out into the world wedged inside the hearts of this world's most intelligent beings, but also into and through these mysterious lines. It learned not just of human nature, but of the nature of the Earth itself.

Had I been in full possession of my emotions, I might have collapsed under the vast expanse of my new understanding. The power within me had never been mine, nor had it been Isaia's. It had never belonged fully to any mage, even the ones who were born with it, as much as they liked to believe it did. When the white god left, as it was preparing to do, my fire would go with it. Its time here was done. This was always its plan.

I knew also that it had heard everything that had ever

been said or thought by a mage, and everything said by those standing within hearing distance of a mage. It knew my conversation with Nero, knew of his threats and his bottomless greed.

I wanted to ask, perhaps even to beg, that it leave something of itself behind. As untethered as my mind was to my own life in this moment, there was a place in the background for beloved faces. Basil, Gage, Isaia, Tomio, Dr. Price, Christy, and so many more.

In the same instant, a new understanding was pressed into my mind, staggering me afresh.

Above all, the white god had wanted to learn about love and hate, the way we experienced and manifested these extremes. Isaia had approached me with love, without any desire to hurt me but with a deep need to be rescued. I had loved Isaia in return, and my heart had been full of longing to help him, to put an end to his suffering. The love we shared played a part in the passing of his fire to me, and its firm rooting within me and me within it.

By contrast, Dante had lusted after fire for power and supremacy. He'd taken Gage's fire by force, heedless of how it would leave the former host, what it would do to him, or whether he would even survive the plundering. But it was Dante who did not survive. The fire did not quicken in him. He did not thrive.

The Source Fire knew all of this, it had been there, observing, the whole time. It did not intervene or play a part, just watched. Learned. It was nothing if not patient. Knowing the rules of nature and super-nature would remain constant, and events would play out how they were meant to.

Would every magus who relentlessly pursued the fire for personal gain suffer or die from that pursuit? No. This was also the way of things. It was no different in the natural world. Some who do not "deserve" to dominate, do, while others who are good and deserve better, do not thrive. It was the way of things everywhere. We viewed it as tragic, but by standing beside or within the Source Fire's detached wisdom, I understood that both opportunity and blessing sprang from crisis. Bad things happened, and good things come from it anyway. Good things happened, and bad things come from it anyway.

It was the way of things. Here, and beyond here.

And then there was the matter of the adopted. We, Tomio and I, were not among the Source Fire's offspring. For all the secrets it had shown me in this moment, I could not anticipate how it felt, if it even had feelings, or whether it might leave behind something of itself in the wake of the knowledge it had gathered. But without any doubt, as certain as life follows death and death follows life, it would depart.

I became aware of a distant sound, like wind, swirling somewhere remote from here, but approaching, and fast. An intense pressure and suction closed in around me, pressing in on all sides, stealing all sense of air and breath and space. It was like I had been swallowed and was now working my way through the gullet of some large creature.

Then it released and the world spun, loud and full of color.

Blindly, I fell to my hands and knees, jarred, shocked, feeling overpacked full of perspective, the way a scarecrow's head is stuffed haphazardly with straw. My jaw ached and my eyes blinked. All light and color vanished and the present darkness seemed fathomless. I wondered absently if the white god had taken my eyesight along with my fire.

White sparks burst in my periphery and I collapsed,

rolling onto my back. The fragrance of wet grass and mud filled my nostrils. Staring upward, a thin trail of white formed in my vision, flying through pinpricks of light.

A shooting star. A huge one, beautiful and bright and streaking across our galaxy. Time stopped as I watched that streak of light carve a path through the firmament.

Then it was gone.

The sound of the sea shushing against my eardrums drew me back to myself. When the world formed a coherent picture of the field and sky at very early morning, and I knew that I was alive, I thought of Targa and the others, and rolled over. Lurching to my feet, I paused and swayed there, looking around.

Every tree and shrub within view was bowed towards me. All of them lay completely flat against the earth, as though crushed by some monstrous steamroller, as far as I could see. Looking down revealed the same mystery repeated in the grass. Every blade was pressed toward a central point, like a massive crop circle made with a huge blunt instrument.

And I stood at the focal point of it all.

I looked up at the sky, almost falling over as I did so, straining for another glimpse of the white god. There was no sign. The sky hinted of sun to come with peaches and soft pinks.

I called my friends' names as I gaped around at the land-scape, searching for anything that was not a flattened tree. Had my friends been flattened too?

A groan made me spin and find my stride. Movement in a shallow divot drew me to a human shape. My heart stopped then jumped as I recognized Tomio. I helped him get to his feet as he stretched his jaw and rubbed the muscles there.

"What happened? I feel like... I don't even know. I was with Georjie and Ryan in one moment, then I was sucked across the grass. It felt like I got licked by a giant dog with a big dry tongue and then swallowed down a really tight throat, or maybe squeezed through an icing tube. I lost consciousness, but I don't know for how long." Tomio looked at our surroundings and amazement filled his features. His dark eyes fell on me and swept me from head to foot, touching my shoulders, my face, then pulling me into a hug. "We're alive."

"Yes, and we need to find everyone else." I squeezed him back then released him. Until I'd seen Georjie, Targa, and Ryan in the flesh, breathing and with a pulse, nothing else mattered.

It didn't take long. We followed the sound of voices.

I stumbled over Ryan's backpack as we headed in their direction. Rooting through it, I found the box for the ghost-steel blade— crushed—a pair of running shoes, a t-shirt and boxers. I pulled on the clothes and slung the pack over my shoulder.

All three of the others were together in the divot; Georjie had her hands on Ryan's side, checking him over as he stood patiently. He looked unharmed now. Targa looked up as we approached.

"You're here," She ran her hands through her wet hair, twisting it into a rope. "We were about to come find you. What happened? All I saw was colored reflections against the clouds and a crazy explosion of light so bright I could hardly look at it. I climbed the cliff and then followed Georjie's voice. Where's Nero?"

"He's dead. The ghost steel hurt him, but it was an orb that killed him. It went straight through him, right in front of me." I told them what I'd done, what I'd seen, then took a closer look at Ryan's side. "Georjie fixed you, I see."

Ryan nodded, but his expression was flat and his complexion waxy. He didn't say anything. In the very early morning light, with only a hint of light on the eastern horizon, his pupils appeared flat black. It was a subtle change, and yet nothing could have made him look less like Ryan than the absence of firelight in his eyes.

Georjie looked me over, checking my back again, and healing my fingertips where the ghost steel had blistered me "I couldn't heal him at first. It was the strangest thing. The cut refused to mend. It was so totally foreign to me, and it seemed to be getting worse, as if the blade was still there, cutting into his flesh." She shot a look of compassion at Ryan and put a hand on his shoulder. "I really thought you were going to die in front of me. Then the world was full of color and you healed." She snapped her fingers. "Just like that. Easy as buttoning up a shirt."

"That was the moment I went from mage to natural." Ryan's gaze swept to me and Tomio. "But you didn't go natural. I can see it in your eyes. You still have fire."

It was true. We did, and Georjie shouldn't have been able to heal my fingertips either, but she had. Whatever power the ghost-steel had had over magi had vanished along with the Source Fire.

Ryan rubbed a hand hard over the top of his head, then gave a bitter laugh. "Well, I suppose I would have lost it anyway, even if I hadn't been carrying an idle. It's the adopted who inherit. Whoever or whatever the Source Fire was, it has a sense of humor."

I wanted to share everything I'd learned, but a bigger desire to keep it to myself for a while won. It was too big for me to put into words, and I didn't feel ready to share it. I was tired.

"What about you?" I looked at Targa. "Everything okay?"

"You mean am I still pregnant? Yes." The siren grinned. "I told you, a bit of running and jumping isn't enough to shake them loose. But, as fun as its been, you will want to get back to your kind. You'll have fallout to deal with. And, I need to get back to Antoni, I have some explaining to do."

"And you'll be wanting to get back to Lachlan." I smiled at Georjie, watching as she inspected Targa. She nodded as she moved to Tomio, checking him over with the attention of a master artist. Any little scratch or bruise eased away under her deft hands, any invisible ache or pain we pointed out was quickly dealt with.

We climbed out of the divot and crossed the field, looking at the flattened foliage. It was a bit like Basil's photographs of Tunguska, only in reverse.

"I could fix all this," Georjie said, looking at the broken trees between us and the campground. "It would take some time, but I could have it back to normal in a matter of hours."

"I think we should leave it," I ventured, when no one responded. "People will have noticed the comet, but that it was going instead of coming. They'll want to figure out what happened. They never will, but if we leave the evidence, it'll give them something to document."

"They'll think it's a crop circle," said Tomio. "It'll become a tourist attraction until it grows up again."

Georjie let out a breath. "I wouldn't mind leaving it, to be honest, if only for selfish reasons. I'm exhausted."

"And what about him?" Targa pointed to Nero's body where it lay in the grass, looking from a distance like someone taking a nap.

"If we leave him, naturals will find him and study him," Tomio said.

"I can accelerate his decomposition," Georjie suggested. "Give me ten minutes and there'll be nothing left."

We agreed to let Georjie get rid of the body, and gathered the wet bedding and our things as she did so. I didn't watch. I didn't think accelerated decomposition was something I would enjoy seeing. When she was finished, she returned to us and handed me a black object.

"Do you want this?"

It took me a moment to realize it was the ghost steel knife, but the blade itself was gone. I took it. "What happened to the blade?"

"It decomposed along with Nero. Melted away like snow."

I mused about this, and decided to keep the handle for now. Maybe Basil would want it.

We wandered through the flattened landscape on our way to the cabins. The buildings had not been flattened the way the landscape had been; it seemed the departure of the Source Fire had affected only nature, not manmade things. But the cabins were nevertheless damaged from trees crashing down upon them. I thought that not straightening the trees and shrubs was the right call after I saw the flattened trailer and crushed cabin. At least the owner would know how their property had been damaged.

There was the sound of a child crying, and a mother trying to soothe him. The sky had begun to brighten, revealing a few campers picking their way around the bent and broken forest. I hoped no one had been injured.

We left the bedding outside the damaged cabin and returned the keys to the lobby, which was open but unmanned. The radius of flattened foliage ended just before the parking lot. But it was in the parking lot where we discovered another remarkable thing.

Basil's Land Rover had been parked in the open lot, too far from trees to have been damaged. But a few parking spaces over sat a Volkswagen Jetta with a hole blown through the side of its trunk. The metal was peeled back like the tip of an exploding joke-cigar.

"What happened there?" asked Targa, as Tomio got behind the wheel of the Land Rover and we were tossing our bags into the back.

The sight of the damaged Jetta pulled things together for me. "That has to be how Nero arrived," I said. "He must have had the five orbs in the trunk when he was coming to get ours. I heard them come through the trunk and the alarm go off. I didn't know what all the noise was about at the time, but now it makes sense. It was the orbs breaking out of his car and crashing through the trees."

Ryan said, "Let's get out of here before the police arrive."

"Where should we take you, Targa?" Tomio pulled on his seatbelt as we closed ourselves in the car.

"Ivan is waiting at a hospital just ten miles inland." She rifled through her bag and produced a cell. "I'll let him know I'm coming."

Georjie turned in the front seat to look at Targa where she was squished between me and Ryan. "Why a hospital?"

"Helipad," she replied, opening up her messaging app.

"How did you get to the campground?" I asked.

Targa tapped out a text. "Uber, of course."

Georjie and I exchanged a look. This was so Targa. Simple, direct answers explaining simple, direct actions. She'd utilized the resources she had to get from point A to point B as quickly as possible. I wondered what the Uber driver had thought of her when she got into his vehicle.

I was fairly certain she would have asked Ivan to park his chopper on the field behind the campground if the pilot had been willing to do it, but even Ivan had limits, and Targa had told me in the past that she would never use her voice on anyone unless there was absolutely no choice.

"What about you, Georjie?" I asked as Targa's phone zipped with messages sent off to her pilot, and probably to Antoni, or maybe she was saving that for a phone call.

"There are trains to Edinburgh multiple times a day from Dover," she said. "I have all my stuff already. Just drop me off at the station. Unless you think you might need me for something else?"

Ryan, who was staring out the window, muttered a question he already knew the answer to: "Can you return fire to a snuffed mage?"

Georjie's brow pinched and she gave Ryan a pained look. "I'm afraid not."

I was half of a mind to reach across Targa and smack Ryan. I wanted to tell him to thank Georjie for everything she'd done for us, and Targa too. Neither of them had to get involved. But Ryan was in shock and bereft. There was a tension in the car, an uncertainty we all felt concerning his mental state, so I didn't reproach him. But Ryan surprised me several long moments later when he looked at Georjie again of his own accord.

"Thanks for saving my life. Our lives," he said, simply.

"You're welcome," she replied, and found the courage to ask what I'd been wondering, maybe all of us had been wondering. "What will you do now?"

He looked out the window again. "Go home. My family needs me."

...and you need them. I conjured the words to follow these

in the silence of the Evoque, as the tires drew us close to our destination.

We exchanged hugs and a tearful goodbye to Targa at the hospital, then Georjie at the train station. Ryan didn't get out of the back seat of the Evoque, but he did wave to the girls from the window.

We were quiet as we pulled into the Academy's driveway. Birds chirped and sunlight illuminated the bricks and made the windows glitter, almost like we were being welcomed home.

I unlocked the door and we walked into the lobby, bedraggled and tired and dazed. I checked my phone to send Basil a message and saw that its battery was dead.

Ryan tossed his backpack beside the nearest sofa and tumbled onto the cushions. He pulled a throw pillow under his head and stretched out, yawning.

"You okay?" I asked him quietly.

His eyes drifted closed. "Of course not, Cagney. Now go away and let me sleep."

Tomio took my hand and I followed him up the stairs. We beelined for his bedroom. I plugged my phone in to charge and joined Tomio on top of the blankets. With his arm curled over me, I was unconscious a moment after my cheek struck the pillow.

EPILOGUE

Dead leaves blew across the road as Tomio and I got out in front of the Wendigs' house on Shaker Street. It hadn't yet snowed in Saltford, but there was a bite in the air. Most of the leaves had fallen, leaving the trees largely bare. Seagulls screamed their lonely cries. Somewhere in the distance a dog barked.

I had borrowed my mom's van, which she'd been happy to lend me when she heard we wanted to go visit the Wendigs.

"That Mr. Wendig looked awful when I saw him last," she'd said, and added that had been back in late summer, "shuffling after that pretty wife of his in the grocery store, like a poor lost child."

I had explained that if he'd been out in public and doing errands, he'd actually improved.

Tomio folded my hand in his as we took the paved walkway up to the Wendigs' front porch. A windchime jangled in the blustery fall air. The cushions had been removed from the wicker furniture for the winter. There'd be no more breakfasts outdoors this year.

At the sound of our feet on the wooden steps, the front door opened and Angelica stood there, beaming. She pulled me into a hug, told me how beautiful I looked, then hugged Tomio.

"Come in, come in. We're dying to see you both."

The Wendig home smelled like vanilla and wood polish. They lived in a heritage home. It had been built in the early twenties and still had old-fashioned light switches, the kind you expected to see on an antique switchboard. Speaking of antiques, they were everywhere, naturally. Antique furniture, antique books, antique paintings, antique clocks. The hardwood floors squeaked, too.

Gage appeared in the hall as we were kicking off our shoes. He came into the entryway wearing a thick, cotton hoody with the hood pulled up over his head, a pair of black jeans, and thick woolen work socks. I'd never seen him so bundled up.

He greeted Tomio first, with a hug, then turned to me. I hesitated, but he pulled me into his arms. My cheek touched his, skin to skin. No fire rushed beneath my skin. It was just plain human contact. It relaxed me to feel that he was relaxed.

"You met Saxony's family?" Gage asked Tomio as we followed him and Angelica into the kitchen. "RJ is a cool guy. I see him at the gym sometimes."

He said nothing of my younger brother, Jack. Probably because the first and only time they'd met, Jack had insulted me. He hadn't meant it, but maybe Gage hadn't forgotten.

Gage took us through the kitchen into the back yard where we stood on their rear deck in our socks. Ryan and Chad were raking and cleaning up random gardening tools and backyard detritus. Ryan held up a gloved hand in greeting but didn't stop what he was doing. Chad, coiling a length of thin yellow rope, came over to say hello. He looked like a guy who'd been working in a back yard all his life. He was thinner than when I'd last seen him, but other than that, if he was still emotionally fragile, he didn't show it. He even took off a work glove to shake our hands. His eyes were clear, his pupils soft and opaque, his brow relaxed.

"How is Basil?" he asked.

"We spoke to him yesterday. He seems well," I told him.

"About those kids?" Gage squinted, blinking in the late afternoon sun. "The ones who got their fire back?"

"How did you know about them?" Tomio asked.

"He calls Gage once a week," Angelica said. "He's the twin's godfather. I'll be right back." She disappeared inside the house.

Gage continued: "He said that he was thinking about putting Chaplin Manor up for sale, if you can believe it, after the memorial of course. But then he got a series of phone calls. Young mages whose fires were snuffed, but they'd ignited again. Out of nowhere."

Tomio nodded. "And all at the same time. Pretty strange."

In fact, they'd ignited on the same morning—or night depending on time zone—the Source Fire had left our world, like little random parting gifts. It was strange, but then again, in another way and possibly only to me, it wasn't strange at all.

"So, it's true?" Chad let the rope hang at his side. "There are some natural-born magi again? Not just adopted folks like you two?"

It was true. There weren't many. The magi population was still a tiny fraction of what it had once been, consisting only of those who'd received fire by plenary endowment, and a handful of young people. After those phone calls,

Basil had sent feelers out, and learned that this small group of individuals had something in common, none of them were over the age of fifteen, and all of them were known as quiet, even shy.

The headmaster had asked me for my thoughts about it when we'd spoken yesterday. Why had their fires ignited? Why so few, and why them? Why only young, shy kids?

I didn't know. The only answer I could give him was that it had happened because I had, in a way, asked for the Source Fire to leave something of itself behind. I'd been asking for the people I had cared about, but the white god had decided that the people I cared about were not the people it would return fire to. Maybe it liked what I'd said to Nero about the meek inheriting. We'd never know the reason.

"Is it true he's not going to sell the academy because of these kids?" Angelica had returned to the porch with a tray of steaming mugs of hot chocolate.

I took the drink she offered and thanked her. "There's only fourteen of them, that we know of. All natural-born magi whose fires were snuffed. Seven girls, and seven boys."

"Where are they from?"

"All over. Quite literally. There are two from each continent." I didn't need to specify that there were also two magi for each idle color. It was one of the first things Basil deduced upon meeting them when he'd arranged for the group to come to the academy in October, to meet him and each other. Idles were now something the headmaster paid a lot more attention to. These young magi were the future of the species, given that those who were not natural-born magi couldn't pass on supernatural genes.

Gage took a cup from his mother and hugged it between his palms. "It's not like Basil can teach them anything anymore. I mean, he's no longer a mage. None of the academy's staff or former students got their fires back."

"He can teach them theory, and that's why he wants me and Tomio to go back to Dover. To talk about the future of the school."

Basil was hosting a memorial at the academy to commemorate the memories of the magi who'd suffered or died. We'd get to see some of the academy's staff and students, but I'd been surprised at the number of acquaintances who weren't coming. Basil had told me he wasn't surprised. Life went on. Some didn't like to dwell on the past, and that was perfectly fine.

"What future?" Ryan asked from where he was leaning on his rake. He didn't appear to be interested in the hot chocolate.

"He's wondering if he should open the school up to other elemental kids, not just fire magi. See if he can get staff from other species," I explained. "He's got all that space, after all. So why not?"

"That'll never work." Ryan went back to his raking.

"Probably not," Chad said, "but when Chaplin gets an idea in his head, he doesn't give up. If anyone can make something like that work, it'll be him. Mage or not." He squinted at me and Tomio. "You going to help him then?"

We didn't know. We'd only committed to going to Dover. I was actually dying to see Basil in the flesh, but I hadn't thought any further than a visit. After Dover, we'd go on to Japan so I could meet Tomio's relatives. While we were there, I wanted to visit where Akiko had been born, have my own private memorial, and also see as much of Japan as I could.

"He told us where the ghost steel came from," I said.

This caught Ryan's attention. He stopped raking, but didn't come over.

I told them what the headmaster had said. "It was found laced through volcanic rock in Northern Turkey. Only a few hundred kilometers from where they found the green idle. It's unique to the area. No one mines it or anything, it's not worth much as a rock. Basil thinks it was where the Source Fire first landed."

Ryan listened, nodded and went back to raking without comment.

"How about that," Angelica said politely.

It was clear the Wendigs weren't much interested in mage-lore anymore.

"Can we go inside? I'm freezing," said Gage.

"Nice to see you," Chad said. "Ryan and I have an appointment at the harbor, so we'll leave you to visit with Gage and Angelica."

We said goodbye and went inside the house, carrying our mugs of hot chocolate. We sat around their dining room table.

"I won't lie to you," said Angelica. "It's been hell for Chad and Ryan." She leaned over the table and squeezed Gage's forearm. "And Gage, too."

"I'm alright." Gage dimpled and dismissed his mother's sympathy good-naturedly. "I'm learning a lot. I have ideas." Gage told us that while the antique business had always bored Ryan to tears, he himself had always felt an affection for old things.

Angelica smiled. "You get that from me, sweetie. You have your grandfather's radar for treasures."

"I just got why your company is called Radar," I said with a laugh.

"Yeah, you should see some of the stuff we have in those

old seacans out on his property." Gage shook his head. "I still have trouble going into those cans though. I think we should move everything into a warehouse here in town. It'd be easier to access."

"Gage was once locked in a seacan for several hours when he was a kid. He's never liked them since. Understandably," Angelica said.

"How did you manage that?" Tomio asked as he took the last swig from his mug.

Gage rolled his eyes. "How do you think?"

"Ryan," I guessed. "Wait, is that why you're afraid of the dark?"

"Took you long enough," Gage replied, with a touch of sarcasm.

It struck me that while Gage hadn't asked me much about my life, family or history, I hadn't been that curious about his either. I sent him an apologetic look and he waved it away with a grin.

"How are those lovely girlfriends of yours?" Angelica asked as she got up to put the empty mugs into the dishwasher. "Tell us how it all went down."

So, we relayed the story to Gage and Angelica. It was a spectacular story, with water, earth and fire magic, but I got the sense they were listening mostly out of good manners. They were no longer part of the supernatural world, not that Angelica had ever been supernatural, but she'd been married to one and had given birth to two. Now her family consisted of naturals, and I suspected that she was secretly thrilled with the outcome. I didn't share anything about my experience inside the white fire, it felt too intimate to divulge, especially with those who seemed only marginally interested. But I did plan to tell Tomio everything, when I was ready.

"It's the end of an era," Gage said when we'd finished, pulling up his hood and shifting in his chair. He checked his watch.

I'd never seen him wear a watch. It looked expensive. Magi didn't wear cheap watches, let alone expensive ones. Now that I was looking, I also noticed that he'd had an ear pierced. This discovery shocked me so much that I hardly said anything for the next several minutes. Gage, with an earring? How weird.

We carried on chatting until Gage had checked his shiny new watch two more times, then we said goodbye, and headed back to the van. We sat in the vehicle for a minute in silence.

"He's changed," I said. "Not for the worse or anything. He's just different."

"Maybe he is just who he always would have been if he hadn't been born a mage," said Tomio, his eyes focused up the street.

"Yeah. Maybe." Nero's question came into my memory. *Who are you without your fire?* I guessed Gage was figuring that out.

I was reaching for the key when Tomio said, "Check this."

A girl was walking down the sidewalk toward us. She carried a small basket with a tea towel draped over it. She wore a red coat cinched in at her tiny waist, and tall black boots with a high heel. Her hood was up, hiding much of her face in shadow. She approached the Wendigs' walkway and turned toward their house. She hadn't noticed Tomio and me sitting in the vehicle, watching like a pair of nosy neighbors. The wind kicked up and her hood fell back revealing a long brunette ponytail, curled and waving in the wind. She had a slender neck, and even from the back I could tell this girl was beautiful.

She took the steps up and rang the doorbell. A moment later she was greeted by Gage, who took in her appearance with the kind of grin he used to save for me. He took her into his arms and gave her a good thorough kissing, right there on the threshold of his parent's house.

My heart felt suddenly lighter.

"He's met somebody," Tomio said, turning to me, smiling.

"Seems so." I started the van.

"Come here." Tomio reached over and wrapped his fingers around the back of my skull. He pulled me to him and kissed me over the console, deeply and sweetly. My chest expanded with happiness, so much I wondered if I might pop.

When we parted, he smiled with his eyes, our noses so close they were almost touching.

A green glow appeared beneath our faces. We looked down at my hand where it rested on the parking brake.

Three of my knuckles were alight, each with a small flame the color of emeralds.

I made a soft gasp and shared a look of delight with Tomio. He kissed me again and held my forehead to his for a long moment. I closed my eyes and sent a silent thought of gratitude into the universe that I had him.

He let me go and settled into his seat. "Come on, show me the beach and the harbor. I want to see where you played as a kid."

So that's what we did.

THE END

AFTERWORD

Gosh, I can hardly believe its the end of another series. For an author, this is an exciting (and nerve-wracking) time. For one thing, a final book in the series is the culmination of a ton of hard work and planning, and the one where readers have the highest expectations. For another, as a book is prepared for launch an author's brain (or mine, anyway) is already leaping ahead to the next series. At a certain point, you just have to shove the baby bird out of the nest and have faith that they'll fly.

I hope you enjoyed Saxony's story. I have to admit, it went to a more extreme place than I thought it would when I first began it. But stories have a way of telling themselves, and I try not to fight that, but let the muse have its head.

If you've read much of my work you'll know that I love to have my characters travel internationally, because this is something I love to do myself. This story includes two locations I have experienced in person: Turkey, and the Arctic (specifically Great Bear Lake and Kugluktuk). I loved both for different reasons, but I wasn't exaggerating about the mosquitoes on the tundra. If you ever go, be prepared for amazingly fresh air, a lot of empty tundra, and a ton of hungry mozzies. As for Turkey, I've now seen quite a bit of it, and it truly is an amazing place. I visited central Turkey (and Cappadocia) shortly before starting to write *Source Fire* and I knew I had to include it. It's a place more rich with history than any other I've seen (and that's saying something, because I've also lived in Italy). I think you could spend a lifetime in Turkey and never see all it had to offer.

Since I've had a reader ask, I should clarify that the cave drawing in Turkey that Basil mentions of the *Source Fire* is fictional. Tunguska was a real event, and is still unexplained. Most think it was a meteor, yet there was no impact site, so that doesn't quite explain it. The subterranean beneath Naples really is full of tunnels and artifacts and antiques, and there really are abandoned mines around Dover. Setting inspiration is everywhere!

If you're wondering why our darling Tomio isn't on the *Source Fire* cover, its because I ordered the artwork before I actually knew he and Saxony would end up together. I would like to add him to the art at some point, but this is an expensive venture. Maybe I can afford to down the road.

What's next? As I write these notes my mind is alive with fairy magic and I'm cooking up an exciting and lush series that will return the reader to the fae dimension we dipped into with the *Earth Magic Rises* series.

This series will be full of earth magic, flora and fauna fae, animals and insects, and a new cast of characters I think you'll fall in love with (I'm already in love with half of them).

Will there be any *Elemental Origins* characters in this series, you ask? While I'm still doing the plotting for the series and its too early to say exactly, I can tell you that you'll see at least two characters from *Earth Magic Rises*. Probably more, but that's all I can share for now.

Thank you to my group of VIP readers, my ARC team, my editor Nicola Aquino, and my proofreader Victoria Knorr for all their assistance in helping me wrap up the Arcturus Academy series with a pretty, shiny bow.

I'm consistently amazed at the support I get from readers, and so grateful. Without you, I wouldn't have this dreamy career. While its a lot of work and sometimes lonely, I wouldn't switch to anything else for all the croissants in Paris. Thank you. And if you loved this story, I would appreciate it if you took a moment to post a review for it, on Amazon or wherever you like to post reviews. They help authors and other readers immensely.

Until next time!

Abby

Antalya, June 2021.

BOOKS BY A.L. KNORR

ELEMENTAL ORIGINS SERIES

BORN OF WATER

BORN OF FIRE

BORN OF EARTH

BORN OF ÆTHER

BORN OF AIR

THE ELEMENTALS

THE SIREN'S CURSE

SALT & STONE

SALT & THE SOVEREIGN

SALT & THE SISTERS

EARTH MAGIC RISES

BONES OF THE WITCH

ASHES OF THE WISE

HEART OF THE FAE

ARCTURUS ACADEMY

FIRECRACKER

FIRE TRAP

FIRE GAMES

LEGENDS OF FIRE

SOURCE FIRE

RINGS OF THE INCONQUO

BORN OF METAL

METAL GUARDIAN

METAL ANGEL

MERMAID'S RETURN

RETURNING

FALLING

SURFACING

ELEMENTAL NOVELLAS

PYRO, A FIRE NOVELLA

HEAT, A FIRE NOVELLA

THE KACY CHRONICLES

DESCENDANT

ASCENDANT

COMBATANT

TRANSCENDENT

Visit www.alknorrbooks.com to sign up for A.L. Knorr's newsletter.
Get notifications for new releases and free stories.

COME A LITTLE CLOSER, MY DEAR...

Want to be kept updated on new releases, be the first to know about sneak peeks and 'read by yours truly' audio snippets? I'm no Judi Dench but I do try not to make too many swallowing sounds. I host the occasional sale and sometimes join themed multi-author promotions that are good fun. Join my newsletter at www.alknorrbooks.com or request access to my private VIP Reader Lounge on Facebook (don't forget to answer the three questions to get in). I also have Instagram for those who are curious about the life of a traveling fantasy novelist. I tend to visit a lot of ancient places, there's inspiration to be found there, doncha know. See you in them virtual hills!

Love, Abby